HOME TRUTHS

HOME TRUTHS

*The Compelling
Sequel to Safe Place*

B. DELAMERE

EPIGRAPH

<u>From Lochálainnin to Mealláiáthn</u>

-

 Away the Hooker along the road to Lochálainnin twisting,
turning, dipping as it wanders through the rocks past
thatched and white-washed homes.
Snipe and black-backed gulls swoop, climb and dive
above the water, which gently moving, mirrors the
ever-changing Cullenmara sky.
Over bridges and causeways, westward stepping stones
through rocks that scatter towards the hills and pile up to
check the sea, like multi-coloured, multi-sculpted dials, the
sun's gentle traps, and kaleidoscopes of westward-moving
light.
Chapels of winter warmth stand at gates along the road,
rich and dark, as sods of turf are carried, the thuribles
of which glow and fill the air with earthy incense.
Still stands the cow, lightly treads the island donkey,
and out runs the dog, and a man stands staring out across
the grey and turquoise sea toward the Inish Isles.
A land like a lichen magnified a thousand times, its colours
splashed with orange flowers of the sea, and carrageen
moss spread on the grass to dry.
Dark lakes keep the glimmering light from yesterday,
rocks merge and loom around to point their edges east
again, and wait quietly for the dawn.

Erick Harper 1966

DEDICATION

To my late uncle, who was always such an inspiration to me.

FORWARD

My first book, **Safe Place** is an intriguing, thought-provoking, sometimes harrowing, yet uplifting tale of love, strength, and belonging stemming from the chance meeting of three quite different people:

Rhona had led a very sheltered life until she fled her abusive husband in Devon, after having a brief affair.

Erick, an unconventional artist who lived off-grid on the remote West coast of Ireland; and Irishman Rory who, trying to escape his tragic past, had recently begun a new life in Cornwall.

Their paths become entwined and following several strange coincidences and twists of fate, Rory discovers an astonishing family secret that alters their lives forever.

PREFACE

Home Truths, the second book in the trilogy, continues the compelling, sometimes harrowing, controversial, and yet inspiring family saga about love in difficult times and courage in the face of adversity. Despite tackling complicated family dynamics and forbidden relationships head-on, the book is richly interspersed with humour, intrigue, and romance.

The book opens with an unexpected funeral and surprising outbursts; an intriguing but confusing deathbed confession; a dramatic turn of events for Rhona and Erick; and Zena, who had disappeared overseas, reappears with shocking news.

Sister Shauna, a character only briefly mentioned in the first book, plays an important role as more gradually comes to light about her traumatic past and the terrible secrets she and those around her have been keeping are revealed.

As with the first book, this is a work of fiction loosely based on events that happened but to completely different people at different times. Any character similarities to anyone still living or dead are purely incidental, and as before, some place names have been changed to preserve the anonymity of family members still living.

The third book in the Trilogy should be available by the end of 2024.

B. Delamere

ACKNOWLEDGMENT

I must start by thanking my late mother, as without hearing numerous stories of her past in Devon, I would not have been able to write this Trilogy.

I am indebted to my late uncle for providing me with plenty of first-hand experience of what living in the remote West of Ireland was like, many years ago.

I also want to thank everyone who bought my first book Safe Place, and enjoyed it enough to want to discover what happened next......

PART ONE

Chapters 1 - 50

CHAPTER 1

Rory and Family September 2014

It was raining as the funeral procession wound its way around the narrow lanes and through Trevaunce, and local residents stopped at the side of the road and stared as it silently passed. It eventually turned onto Beacon Lane and pulled outside Sunny Corner a few minutes later.

Hobbling with a stick, Rory, Padraig, and Orla got into the third car. Meanwhile, their other sister Belinda, already waiting in her car, silently watched them through the passenger-side window.

"I just don`t understand her sometimes," said Orla, quietly.

"I smiled, but she just glared back at me."

"She's hurting, that's all, don`t take it personally," said Padraig.

"I don't think she`s angry at you," Rory interjected.

They went quiet, each absorbed in their thoughts. The accident had been so sudden that it still had not sunk in. But after catching the first glimpse of their father's coffin, it was becoming more real.

Orla started sobbing loudly, and Rory put his arm around her to comfort her. He hated seeing her crying, and while fighting back his tears, he smoothed her mousy blonde fringe and kissed the top of her head.

"It's all right, just let it all come out," he said.

He exchanged glances with Padraig, who looked back at him blankly. Although they hardly knew each other, Rory felt like part of the family, and the three weeks they had all spent together at the cottage had been lovely. His new brother and sister had accepted him without hesitation, and he had been relieved. Not every day do you discover a half-brother you did not know about.

The journey up to Treyrow took about half an hour, the cars and hearse drove slowly up the Crematorium`s winding drive and finally halted at the small chapel. Although it was blustery and there was rain in the wind, people were milling around outside.

Seeing the funeral procession arrive, everyone disappeared inside, leaving only the immediate family members waiting, while the funeral directors got organised and ready to go in.

"I hate funerals," Orla said suddenly.

She stopped crying and pulled away from Rory to look out the window.

A passenger door opened in front of them, and they watched Belinda climb out, smooth her black clingy dress down, and hold on to her hat in the wind. Rory stared at her. She looked like a film star and very much the sad bereaved daughter, and her partner Toby was also dressed completely in black.

They waited as the pallbearers positioned themselves and followed them slowly into the chapel, and Belinda and Toby joined them in the front pew.

Being only a very recent addition to the family, Rory could sense the rest of the congregation watching him as he walked down to the front of the church, and having ended up sitting at the aisle end, he felt very self-conscious. He grabbed a copy of the order of service and began reading Erick's poem about Cullenmara printed on the inside cover. Doing this immediately brought tears to his eyes, which he hurriedly wiped away.

The act of sitting in front of a coffin compels the bereaved to stare at it and imagine its contents, prompting them to think about what they have lost, and sniffles and cries resonate throughout the congregation.

Now standing at the pulpit, the Vicar began speaking when suddenly there was a loud bang, and the chapel door flew open, and in stepped two women. The younger of the two was wearing a white uniform, and the elder was in blue, and between them stood Rhona.

He paused and waited as Rhona walked gingerly down the aisle with two sticks, a nurse on either side.

Seeing her, Rory could not prevent a loud sob from emerging from the depths of his gut. Although he had visited her in the hospital many times since the accident, he had not seen her quite as much since she moved to the Care Home, and he returned to his job at the Centre. Her additional weight loss was apparent, and she looked like a mere shadow of her former self. He noticed that although now a month on from the accident, through her sheer tights he could see her legs and her arms still covered with fading bruises, and her grey hair was now almost white.

Studying her as she passed and stood in the middle of the aisle, and having shrugged off her nurses, gazed at the coffin in front of her, Rory watched her wobble towards it, and could hear her exclaim loudly,

"Where's Erick? Where is my husband? I`m sure he said he would meet me here. I hope he is all right, it is not like him to be late."

The nurse wearing the white uniform tried to whisper to her that she was now at Erick's funeral and that he had died. Hearing that, Rhona dramatically broke down and began sobbing uncontrollably. Unable to stop her, both nurses and everyone else watched in horror and disbelief, as when with her arms outstretched, she prostrated herself over the coffin. The nurse in blue tried to pull her off it, but she clutched on defiantly, and, witnessing this, the congregation went completely silent.

After getting slowly to his feet again, Rory limped awkwardly over to Rhona, and, having placed a hand on the middle of her back, suggested,

"Rhona, why don`t you sit next to me now, will you?"

Hearing Rory's familiar soothing Irish lilt, and recognising his mop of dark hair immediately, Rhona did as he asked, and with his arm now fully around her, and still wobbling himself, he guided her over to the front pew and the others shuffled along to make extra room.

"Do not believe a word they are saying. They are making

it all up. Erick would never leave me," she whispered,

loud enough for the congregation to hear.

Aware of Rhona's dementia diagnosis since the accident, Rory whispered,

"Yes, I know he would not intentionally leave you,

Rhona."

He grabbed a handkerchief from his pocket to mop his eyes as they filled with tears and clouded his vision. When the vicar encouraged everyone to get to their feet and sing the first hymn, he had no other option but to mime, not only because he had never been good at singing but also because he could no longer see the words.

He held the hymn book so Rhona could see it, and she sang with such gusto that the atmosphere in the chapel completely changed. Next to him, Orla and Padraig were singing their hearts out to Jerusalem, their father's favourite hymn.

CHAPTER 2

Rory and Family September 2014

Everyone sat down after the hymn ended, and the vicar gave a short and funny sermon. Knowing Erick and Rhona for many years, he had even visited them at their cottage in Cullenmara, and like Rory's late vicar grandfather Tomoltach, possessed the same clever knack of making a congregation smile, even in the depths of their grief, as he recounted heart-warming tales of Erick's escapades.

A relief to have a break from all the sombreness himself, Rory knew Erick would not have wanted people to be too sad. He had always had a sense of fun and enjoyed life. He remembered Erick's seventy-second birthday back in early July, and when they were all in Cullenmara together and could picture him and Rhona giggling over something they found funny.

Gazing at Rhona's bedraggled appearance now, he felt sad for her.

Looking around, he could see Belinda scowling at him from under her wide-brimmed hat, further down the row. Feeling his face burn, he turned away and back towards the vicar again. He had never felt comfortable around her and presumed she must be upset to have not celebrated her father's birthday in Cullenmara with the rest of the family, especially now, after what had happened.

Aware it had been Erick's wish to have only a brief service, the vicar then led the congregation in prayer, and standing beside the coffin, gave his final solemn blessing. After he had done that, curtains drew around it to the sound of Yehudi Menuhin and Stephan Grappelli. The vicar reminded the congregation that this was one of Erick`s favourite pieces of music, and Rhona smiled and began tapping her feet along to it.

Soon those sitting in the front pew got up to leave, and the rest of the congregation followed.

Rory waited and let Rhona and the nurses walk slowly out in front of him, and then he and the rest of the family filed out behind.

Outside, although still windy, the clouds had parted enough to allow the warm sun to shine through.

"Isn`t that supposed to be a good sign?" asked Orla.

"A good sign, a good sign of what exactly?" asked Belinda who was in her immediate earshot.

Ora looked flustered and replied,

"Well, like he is now in a good place and is smiling down on us?" she said.

She shrugged her shoulders uncomfortably; aware Belinda always saw things in black and white, a trait that had made her an ideal lawyer.

"What absolute rubbish," said Belinda.

"No, Dad is gone forever and will not be looking down and smiling, especially knowing what Rory's done."

Orla was stunned by what she had just heard and relieved no one else was in earshot, particularly Rory, she watched him and Padraig milling around and chatting to mourners.

Gazing across at Rhona, she saw her swaying on her sticks, looking frail enough for a gust of wind to blow her over any minute. The nurse in blue had hold of her hand and although much more composed, was still wobbly on her feet and looked very confused.

Unusually her long grey hair was in a neat bun, and tidier than normal, which made her face look much thinner, and her eyes looked hollow and sunk into her face. Seeing Orla looking over at her, she smiled and waved and as she did so, the lines on her face relaxed, and she looked much more like the step-mother she knew and loved.

Belinda and Toby had walked to the chapel entrance and stood silently watching everyone around them.

Particularly aware Belinda kept staring at him and wanting to find out why, Rory walked over and joined them, and it was then she shouted at the top of her voice hysterically,

"Get him away from me. It is all his fault Dad is dead.

I will never accept him as my brother."

Hearing the sudden loud outburst, the crowd went quiet, and everyone stared, apart from Rhona, who could heard loudly telling the nurses,

"Belinda's always had a quick temper."

She reprimanded her daughter,

"Be quiet Belinda, everyone's looking at you."

Not knowing what to do, Rory withdrew awkwardly from Belinda's side, shocked by what she had just said, and looked at the ground in embarrassment.

But she had not finished.

"Look at him everyone, can't you see he has guilt written all over his face? he is a liar, a fraud, and a murderer and I`m going to prove it! It should have been him that died that day, not my dad."

Flying at Rory in a rage, she slapped him squarely on the jaw, and he nearly fell backwards but managed to steady him-self. Not wanting to retaliate, he stood and watched Padraig trying to pull Belinda away from him.

Toby had retreated from the scene and beckoned her to join him and walk back to their car, but she remained where she was, lashed out at Rory again, and scratched Padraig's face by accident, drawing blood.

Orla ran over to her brother and gently patted his cheek with a tissue, while without apologising, Belinda continued her tirade of abuse.

"I`m going to prove it, you know. You`re not my brother. Why couldn`t you have died instead? It is so unfair!"

After saying that, she completely broke down in tears again and was escorted to Toby's waiting car by Padraig.

Toby wanted a quick getaway and started the engine, and was sitting, waiting, looking awkward.

He made eye contact with Rory and mouthed,

"Sorry."

Rory nodded, aware Belinda's emotions about her father were running high.

After going over and giving Rhona a big hug and kiss good-bye, he hurried down to his and Padraig`s car and climbed in. He had not wanted to make any more of a scene but wished he had answered Belinda back, but that chance had gone now.

Does she think that I am enjoying all of this? he wondered. That I allowed the accident to happen on purpose and had somehow sacrificed Erick to save myself? He had been worried about how Belinda would react when she heard the news after returning from her holiday in Italy but had not been expecting that.

He sat silently, his mind racing over what she had said, and decided Belinda had been right about one thing, it should have been him that died, instead of Erick. It had all been so wrong and, despite the hospital staff`s assurances Erick was un-conscious and would not have known anything, lying trapped under his beloved campervan on the M5 tarmac, had been such a horrible way for him to die.

Rory clutched his throbbing leg; he had forgotten to bring painkillers, and the pain was becoming unbearable, but he was far more tormented by what Belinda had said.

The extreme sadness he had felt to lose his lovely father after only knowing him for a short while, was difficult enough to deal with on its own, without her snidey accusations, too.

Feeling suddenly overwhelmingly tired and fighting back tears again, he bowed his head and pretended to be asleep. But there was a knock on the window, and worried Belinda had come to have another go at him, he cautiously looked up.

To his relief, it was Orla, and when he opened the window, she smiled, bent down, and peered in.

"Are you alright bro?" she asked.

"Not really no," he said.

CHAPTER 3

Rory and Family September 2014

Padraig remained the most composed on the drive back and fixed his gaze on the road and scenery around him. The lane down to the Trevaunce cottage always reminded him of Cullenmara, as it had his father when he bought it with Rhona years earlier.

He had not cried since hearing the news of his passing but had often pondered why he had to go so soon. Why did he have to die now? Why, even before he had met his partner and soon-to-be fiancée Lou?

Although a part of him had never forgiven him for abandoning him and Orla for so long when they were young, he loved his dad and, in those moments, they had spent together since, had witnessed how happy he was with Rhona and how pleased he was to have found his long-lost son, Rory.

As he drove, memories kept popping into his mind, and he fondly recalled the lovely holiday they had just the two of them, back in 1987, and when they had climbed Ben Cullen. It had taken quite some time to ascend the mixture of soggy peat bog, loose stony ground, and thick tufty heathland, but it was exhilarating, gazing down at the view and battling the intense winds at the summit. Their adventure had continued after a dense fog engulfed them, less than halfway down. But as usual, his father had remained calm and confident they would get down safely.

Reflecting again on their most recent visit to Cullenmara, for his father`s seventy-second birthday, he thought how lovely it had been to be back there again. They went on walks, went fishing in the lake, and had beach picnics as a family. With Erick navigating and Rory driving, they had also headed back into the mountains and ended up in the picturesque town of Cullycliff, where they had supped Guinness outside a particularly colourful pub their father had always liked.

However, their most enjoyable day trip had been to Snáithe-coiréil. Rory`s childhood friend, Diarmuid, had joined them at the local pub for lunch, and afterwards, they had all gone skinny-dipping in the lovely nearby coral beach, even Rhona and Erick. It had been hilarious watching them running into the sea together, Erick completely naked, and Rhona protecting her modesty with a pair of what turned out to be very see-through-when-wet knickers.

She had not noticed until she started to wade back out of the water, and Erick had run up to fetch a towel to cover her up as quickly as possible. He had been worried about him when he started coughing from all the exertion but had put that down to his pipe smoking, which he knew he would never give up.

Although they had all had a wonderful time, Padraig had been sad to witness the decline in traditional wayside white-washed cottages, which had instead been replaced by stark-looking square modern buildings, with wrap-around tarmac drives, as they drove around. He preferred remembering what it had been like there as a child before his parents separated and the tourists properly descended on the area. Although there had been a lot of poverty back then, due to unemployment, it had been such a wonderful place to spend every summer.

But it had been a lovely family holiday, and one he would never forget, but his only regret was that his partner Lou had not been there too. He had missed her terribly, and when he had talked about her so fondly, they had all been eager to meet her, especially Erick.

He had returned to Somerset feeling invigorated, excitedly told her all that happened and promised to take her to meet him the next time he went, unaware of how things would pan out.

Pulling up outside the five-bar gate at Sunny Corner, he gazed at Orla and Rory in the rear-view mirror. It was heartbreaking to see them looking so sad, and wanting to be the stronger responsible brother, would save his tears until he returned to his Somerset home.

CHAPTER 4

Rory and Family September 2014

Rory had thought about nothing else but the accident since it happened, and already blaming himself, his nights remained plagued by nightmares, and he often wondered if he could have done more, somehow protected Erick, or reacted quicker.

That day, the weather had been warm and sunny, and after a calm crossing from Dublin Bay to Swansea, their journey back had been good, until the tyre burst. He had got out of the van and Erick had joined him on the hard shoulder to have a few draws of his pipe. He recalled him standing to his right, watching and explaining how to unlock the spare wheel from the front of the blue VW campervan when the lorry hit.

The force of the impact sent Rory toppling backwards and although grappling to get away, his right leg became trapped. Shuddering, he recalled what it had been like lying there with everything happening around him in slow motion.

Remembering that he called Erick just before the lorry hit, he still could not recall seeing what happened to him. Still, he could not forget the loud bang when the lorry hit the side of the van, and being deafened by the scraping sound of metal on metal as it spun the van around, and then propelled itself onwards, until finally hitting the motorway bridge with such force, it partially collapsed.

There had been a moment of silence after the lorry hit and he remembered watching it beginning to smoulder, filling the air with noxious fumes. Lying with his leg partially trapped and unable to move, Rory was frightened the lorry would explode right beside him.

He was lying like that with the side of his face resting on the hard gritty tarmac, for some time, and from this level, all he could see was a constant blur of swiftly moving rubber tyres, passing so close, that he could feel the ground rumbling underneath him.

To his horror, the lorry did catch fire, which being only feet away, was truly terrifying and he lay there, almost resigned to his fate. But, with the help of the adrenaline flowing fast through his body, after taking a big deep breath, he suddenly found the strength to pull his leg free, but in the process, the lower part of it went limp and numb.

Trying his best to avoid the broken glass and twisted metal debris on the ground all around him, and unable to stand up, he managed to roll himself down into a drainage gully, just before a ball of fire completely engulfed the lorry and it exploded. Luckily, being down in the gully, most of the flying debris showered over the top of him, apart from a few bits found embedded in his arms and legs later.

It was a huge relief to hear sirens approaching, and blinking through the maze of flashing lights, he recalled seeing the blurred outlines of people in high-vis jackets, hearing an electric saw being used, and the hiss of the high-pressure water hoses being aimed at the lorry by the fire brigade.

An ambulance crew were over by the van and he prayed hard that Erick and Rhona were all right. Rhona had been inside the campervan and happily listening to The Archers on the radio when it all happened.

Seeing a female paramedic nearby, Rory tried to call out, but his voice came out hoarse and more like a whisper. After managing to call louder, he was relieved when she heard him above the traffic noise and seeing him, immediately summoned another ambulance over.

He remembered being lifted from the gully and into the awaiting ambulance, but everything went blurry. The main thing that stuck with him since was the extreme pain in his leg and a horrible icy feeling that seemed to have penetrated his bones. It was a scene he had played out in his mind numerous times since, and the horror of witnessing just how easily the van turned and toppled on its side, the lorry hitting the bridge, and then exploding in front of him, leaving no chance anyone inside would still be alive, still haunted him.

Padraig pulled up at the cottage, and they both exchanged glances through his rear-view mirror. Although not having known each other long, Rory was aware his half-brother tended to keep things inside and did not like to show his feelings. But he could tell by the dark circles under his brown eyes, his greasy brown hair, and his fixed frown that he, just like him, was also struggling to keep himself together.

CHAPTER 5

Rhona August 2014

It had been an absolute miracle that Rhona survived the crash, let alone had been able to walk free, with only a small head injury and bruising. She had been sitting happily listening to the radio and gazing out of the van window, when the next thing she knew, she was waking up in a strange dormitory-type place, feeling very confused. What was most disconcerting, was she had no recollection of what had happened, nor did she recognise anyone around her.

Thinking it must be past five in the afternoon, she attempted to get out of bed. Erick would be waiting at home and wanting his supper. But something was not right, and there were bars on the bed, and she rattled them defiantly, and started shouting at the top of her voice,

"Whoever you are, you cannot keep me prisoner here like this."

Almost immediately, a healthcare assistant in a white uniform appeared at the foot of her bed, and through Rhona's blurry eyesight, she thought she was an angel.

"Oh, have I died?" she asked.

The healthcare assistant came round to face her, put the side down, and took hold of one of her hands caringly. Rhona blinked back at her and, having briefly come to her senses, asked,

"Oh, am I in hospital?"

The healthcare assistant nodded and began explaining about the accident. Rhona appeared to understand, and smiled, but then asked suddenly,

"Can I see my baby? Where is my baby, you cannot keep her from me, my Bryony, not this again. I must see her."

It was obvious the small bump on Rhona's head, sustained during the accident, needed further investigation, and the care assistant left her for a few moments to report this to the senior nurse.

Meanwhile, Rhona burst into floods of tears, and to distract her, she quickly asked,

"Rhona, would you like a nice cup of tea?"

Rhona stopped crying, looked at her, and smiled and said,

"Yes please, that would be lovely," and promptly drifted off to sleep again.

Consultant Geriatrician Thomas Lee and his team of white-coated medical students were around her bed when she awoke again.

"Mrs. Harper, I just need to examine you a bit more, if that's all right," he said.

After sitting herself up, she picked up the now luke-warm cup of tea from the bedside table, and sipped it politely before replying,

"Ok Doctor, do whatever you need to do."

Dr Lee gave her a thorough examination and told her,

"You've been through a lot, Mrs Harper, it is advisable that you undergo a brain scan and some other scans. You did sustain quite a nasty head injury."

Rhona looked perturbed.

"What exactly have I been through, Doctor?" she asked.

He explained how she had been in the back of the van when the lorry hit, and although wearing her seatbelt, hit her head when the van overturned. She had also sustained some bruising where the seat belt dug in, and some on her legs and arms, and had been unconscious for some time, and this had caused her confusion.

Rhona looked at him, trying to get it all straight in her mind.

"Where did the accident happen?" she asked.

"On the M5 just past the services. The lorry also had a tyre blowout and the driver lost control," he said.

"So where am I now, please?"

It was frightening not knowing where she was and not being able to remember much.

"You are in Tanton Hospital."

"Oh," she said,

"I've never been to Tanton before."

The Consultant and his team left and afterwards; a porter came to take her for her scan.

CHAPTER 6

Rhona, August 2014

Rhona thought it was funny being pushed, still lying in her bed, along to the CT Suite in full view of everyone, and smiled and gave regal waves to strangers passing along the way. Finally, after it seemed, she had been pushed to the absolute far end of the hospital, she arrived at a large, brightly lit room with a massive grey metal machine in the middle. It made a loud whirring noise as she approached, and a narrow bed seemed to slide out of the middle of it.

Two radiographers helped her onto its thin, firm mattress, and she immediately felt extremely uncomfortable. There was an incredibly low hard pillow placed under her head, and another, under her knees, and after being told she must not move her head at all during the scan, they had strapped her in. Rhona felt claustrophobic and vulnerable almost immediately, especially after large headphones were placed over her ears from which there appeared to be weird music playing. The radiographers disappeared into another room and shut the door, and she could see them sitting behind glass, watching her.

Suddenly, the bed she was lying on moved slowly forward, and she found herself entombed in grey machinery. A bit of grey metal came down close to her face, so close that her vision was just a blur of grey. This was horrible, and she wanted the ordeal over soon.

Through the headphones, she heard a faint voice emphasising that she must not move, for the duration of the scan, and then the machine started to whirr even louder. At its loudest, it sounded like someone was digging up the roads beside her and, despite the headphones, was deafening. It was unnerving left alone in a sealed room and trapped in a noisy scanner.

In an attempt not to dwell on it, Rhona tried desperately to focus on what had happened during the accident but was still unable to remember anything. At some point, she must have dropped off to sleep and awoke suddenly, and seeing nothing but blurry grey metal, and thinking she was in a coffin, she screamed.

Luckily, the scan was virtually over, and almost immediately, the lid of her grey tomb whirred slowly back, and a radiographer came swiftly to her rescue. Whether it had been the shock of thinking that she was in a coffin, a delayed reaction from the accident, or her head injury, she could not help but burst into tears.

"I`m so sorry, what must you think of me? I`m a silly old woman," she said.

The radiographer fetched a tissue and sat with her until she had completely calmed down, and she was grateful for that. But in contrast to earlier in her bed on the way back, she no longer wanted to make eye contact with anyone and after pulling the covers over her head, did not peep out again until she was safely back in the ward.

CHAPTER 7

Rhona August 2014

Rhona had been back in the ward about ten minutes when a bit of her memory suddenly returned. She could recall seeing Erick standing outside the van smoking his pipe and talking to Rory, while she remained inside, listening to the Archers. She pressed her wall buzzer to summon assistance but got no answer, and after climbing over the bedsides, began pacing up and down impatiently beside her bed.

A different healthcare assistant to the one she had met earlier eventually appeared.

"Where's my husband, Erick? Did he come in with me, only I need to know he`s all right," she said.

The healthcare assistant went to get more information and Rhona looked extremely worried.

"I`m sorry," the assistant said,

"But no, he did not come in with you."

Rhona was upset,

"What do you mean? He must have. We were all together in the van..."

Her voice trailed off and, having wobbled and nearly fallen over, the assistant helped her back into bed. When she turned to leave, Rhona grabbed her arm and gripping it tightly, pleaded,

"You will find him for me, won`t you?"

Over the next few days, nightmares, and strange visions like excerpts from videotapes were playing over and over in her head. These snippets were often so vivid that she woke up convinced she had just heard a loud bang, the screech of metal on metal, and felt sure she could distinctly smell burning oil.

One morning, when a male nurse she had not met before, approached, pulled the curtains around the bed, and sat in the chair beside her. Before any words left his lips, sensing he was the bearer of bad news, she broke down in tears and cried out,

"No, noo, no!"

The nurse let her cry, and when she had calmed down a little, he explained,

"Erick`s body was found when a paramedic found his broken glasses on the ground beside the upturned van. The fire crew spent over six hours cutting him out of the wreckage, and I am sorry, but he died at the scene."

Rhona was inconsolable for days; she did not eat anything and barely drank, and soon lost lots of weight, and the ward staff who were closely monitoring her, became increasingly concerned. Gradually, she withdrew deeper into her little world, a world where everyone she had cared for had died. She thought of her mother, little Bryony, Bryn, Billie, and now her beloved Erick, and it was all too much.

"What have I done to deserve this?" she often asked herself, but the answer never came.

Her first trip to the main bathroom was strange and seeing herself in its large mirror for the first time since the accident had been a huge shock. Blinking, she stared at her reflection, her eye sockets seemed to have sunk into her now thin, gaunt face, and she had lost so much weight, that the skin around her neck and arms was sagging more than she remembered; her limbs were also covered in a tapestry of dark bruises; and her hair also was a lot whiter now. Instead of the young, fit healthy woman she thought she was, an old woman she did not recognise, was staring back at her.

Panicked, she pulled the emergency cord, and when the assistant came to her rescue, temporarily forgetting all about the accident, she immediately burst into floods of tears again, and shrieked loudly,

"What on earth have you done to me?"

The ward staff grew used to her outbursts and would try to calm her as best they could, but feeling continually confused, she did not trust any of them and remained on her guard.

From then on, it was as if all the days seemed to merge into one, and with her confusion worsening, she often did not know what time of day or night it was. She hardly slept, because whenever she shut her eyes, all she could think of was Erick lying trapped under the van. It was all so overwhelmingly sad and painful, that very soon she wished she had died and not Erick, at least that would have meant an end to her pain.

But something unexpected happened that did relieve her despair a little.

CHAPTER 8

Immediately after the paramedics found him at the site of the accident, Rory was transported to the Emergency Department at the main hospital in Bristol, and taken straight to the Resuscitation Unit, where he began losing a lot of blood. After undergoing two different operations, he was told he had recovered well, considering the severity of his injuries, but disliking hospitals, he hated being in the busy orthopaedic ward. Despite doing everything the surgeons requested following his operations, he still needed further intensive physiotherapy on his leg and had to wait until that was finished.

It was horrible not knowing what happened to Erick and Rhona, and no one at the busy hospital seemed to be able to tell him anything. Relieved when moved to a quieter ward, he was surprised to receive a visit from a paramedic, returning his mobile phone, which had been found in the ambulance. Having assumed it must have been lost in the accident, he was relieved and thankful to have it again. At least now, he could try to establish what had happened to Erick and Rhona, but to his dismay, the phone battery was completely dead, and he had no means of charging it. But one of the ward nurses came to his rescue and lent him their charger, and he could finally use it.

Scrolling through all the numerous photos taken in Cullenmara, of Erick, Rhona, Padraig, and Orla, many of which were taken on their last day at the beach, although making him briefly smile, was also very upsetting. When he searched for any online information about recent accidents, hoping to discover what had happened to Erick and Rhona, finding a Tanton local newspaper's coverage, his heart sank when he read the headlines.

"Two people injured and two dead, in a horrific motorway crash."

Fearing the worst, he rang Tanton Hospital, wanting more information. After explaining who he was and asking the Admissions Department receptionist if Erick Harper had been admitted anytime over the past few weeks, he was concerned to hear that no one with that name had been. However, when he mentioned Rhona's name, he was extremely relieved to hear the receptionist say,

"Yes, she was brought in that day and is currently in Ward Seven."

It was great to discover she was still alive, but he remained gravely concerned about Erick's whereabouts. The following day, he received a visit from a traffic police officer called Philippa, who broke the news of Erick's death.

"There will, of course, be a post-mortem, but I can`t say when that will be yet."

Rory's voice went hoarse and he was filled with emotion at the thought of Erick's body cut open, but he was able to ask,

"Can you tell me where he is now, please?"

She told him that for the time being, he was in Tanton Hospital mortuary and would be released to the funeral directors immediately after the post-mortem. If he wanted, he could visit him before then. Rory tried his best to remain composed while she explained what had happened to Erick and thanked her for coming to tell him the news. But the minute she left, he quickly pulled the curtains around his bed, the bedcovers over his head, and cried.

He was touched when, despite being extremely busy, the Ward Clerk, who had heard what had happened, brought him a cup of sweet tea.

"This will help you with the shock," she said.

With his face wet with tears, Rory managed to smile and say semi-jokingly,

"You couldn`t put a whisky in it for me, could you?"

CHAPTER 9

Rory, September 2014

After completing six weeks of gruelling intensive physiotherapy, Rory was discharged from the hospital, caught a coach
down to Tanton, and booked into a bed and breakfast nearby,
to easily visit Rhona. But there was something he strongly felt
he needed to do beforehand, and he booked an appointment.

Arriving at the hospital mortuary early, he sat in a chair in
the corridor and waited. It was a surprisingly busy part of the
hospital and he watched numerous porters burst in through
the double doors, pushing lidded, rattling, metal trollies past
him at considerable speed.

Seeing how many there were brought home just how lucky
he and Rhona had been to survive, and it was also strangely
comforting to realise that at precisely the same time as him,
hundreds, maybe thousands of other people, were mourning
their loved ones too, he was not alone in his grief.

A man wearing a white coat over blue theatre scrubs eventually wandered down the corridor to meet him, and immediately
apologised,

"I`m sorry, you should not have had to wait out here,
but there's a leak in the roof above the waiting room and
we cannot use it right now."

Trying to distract himself from what he was about to see,
Rory chattered away nervously,

"Three bodies have passed in the last ten minutes. How

many do you normally contend with in a typical day?"
The mortician explained,
"Well, it can vary. On a quiet day, I guess around twenty, our maximum capacity, but we can handle more should the need arise, as we have portable refrigerated trolleys, too."

They turned off the corridor and walked through a restricted area. To the left, there was a small bare room in which he could see the outline of a person lying on a trolley, covered in a white sheet. It could have been anyone under there and it was hard to believe that it was Erick, and he felt a lump rise in his throat.

"When you are ready, I'll uncover him for you," said the mortician.

Rory nodded, dreading what he was about to see, but after the sheet was pulled back, he was pleasantly surprised. It was certainly Erick lying there, no doubt about that, and considering what had happened to him, he looked remarkably peaceful. Someone had glued his glasses back together and positioned them, minus the lenses, back on the crook of his nose. He stared at his father`s exposed torso and marvelled at how normal it looked. The rest of him remained covered and, although tempted, decided against trying to get a better look at him.

Instead, he pulled up a chair, picked up one of Erick's hands, and held it against his face. It was icy cold, which was a bit of a shock. Staring at him and studying his features for the last time, Rory felt an overpowering love for the father he had only recently discovered. The previous two years had passed quickly, and he regretted not asking him more questions, and unable to stop himself, began to chat to him, just as he had done so easily when he was alive.

"Well Erick, you are certainly not alone in here, they are arriving like buses, three in a row passed me earlier. I`m glad to see they found your glasses, so I am. Sure enough,

you would not be you without those, would you now?"
He sighed and continued,
"Jeez Erick, why did you have to get out of the van?
Perhaps if you had stayed inside, you may have survived.
I`m so sorry I could not save you, Erick, and could not
help you, and I will always feel guilty about that. Please
forgive me, Erick. I am so sorry."
He placed Erick's hand back under the sheet, got unsteadily
to his feet, leaned over, and kissed him on the forehead.
"Don`t you go worrying about Rhona, I`m looking out for her
and will visit her as much as I can. But bless her, I have no
clue how injured she is, but the main thing is that she
survived, and I will always be there for her. I don`t know
whether you are aware I`m here. I know you don`t believe
in all that stuff, but please if you somehow know I`m here,
I want to tell you I was so pleased to discover you were my
father, and I loved you very much, and whatever else I do
with my life, I will always want to make you proud."
It had all felt surreal up to that point, but gulping back
a large sob, he sat back down in the chair again, sighed and
put his head in his hands. It was all still so raw, and although
pleased to have seen Erick looking so peaceful, it was unbearable to contemplate never seeing him again.
Feeling like he was about to go to pieces, he was relieved
when the mortician returned to escort him out of the room. It
was hard to leave Erick, but Rory knew he could not stay any
longer.

CHAPTER 10

Rhona, September 2014

One morning when another care assistant tried to help her out of bed, Rhona made it obvious she did not want to get up and clutched the bedclothes defiantly. But when told she needed to get up and dressed, because she had a visitor coming to see her, she did as instructed.

She was sitting in her chair with her head buried in a copy of The Guardian, after having just finished breakfast, when she heard a remarkably familiar voice.

"Need any help with the crossword, Rhona?"

The gentle Irish tones were unmistakable, and she put her paper down and looked up excitedly.

Rory was wobbling on crutches in front of her.

"Rory!" she shrieked excitedly.

She jumped to her feet and hugged him tightly.

"Careful Rhona, you'll burst my stitches," he said.

"Please sit down," she said smiling, and pointed to her chair, "I`ll get back on the bed. You must tell me all that happened to you."

Rory explained that he had been at the front of the van, having just removed the spare wheel when the lorry approached at speed. Although he remembered shouting at Erick to get out of the way, that had been the last time he had seen him. He stared at the floor for a few moments, trying not to get emotional, before saying,

"I`m so sorry Rhona, I could not do anything. I ended
up with my leg pinned under the van and after yanking
it free, rolled down into a gully. The emergency services
did not see me at first, but I`d badly broken my leg and
suffered internal bleeding, hence, the stitches. I was
taken to the Bristol Royal Infirmary and had no idea
whether you had survived, or where you were, until now.
When I found out I had to come and find you, I know how
much you hate hospitals."
Rhona was so relieved to see him, but admitted,
"I`m so sorry Rory, I've been so upset about Erick that I`d
forgotten you were there too."
She looked at him sheepishly.

Rory had already had a long chat with the Ward Sister
and was aware the results of Rhona's scan had shown she was
suffering from trauma-induced dementia.

Also, he was aware the last time she had been in a hospital,
had been after Erick fell from the cottage roof, back in 2010,
and, he remembered her telling him about when she had lost
her baby, Bryony, and how awful that had been, so had been
concerned what state he would find her in.

"It`s all right Rhona, don`t you fret about that. I`m here
now, that`s all that matters, and I`m so relieved you`re ok,"
he said.

He leaned forward and hugged her, and they both cried
silent tears.

CHAPTER 11

Rory September 2014

Rory became a regular visitor to Rhona's ward and, pushing for her to be transferred somewhere nearer to home as soon as possible, was told she needed to be more fully medically assessed before that could happen. It was difficult not knowing how she would be on each visit. Some days she was very lucid and attentive, or in her own little world.

Regardless, she always seemed to recognise him, which he was very relieved about, but he had lost track of the number of times he had to explain what had happened all over again and witness her grieving afresh for Erick. Constantly re-living it all was very painful, and not having been able to do anything to save Erick, still played on his mind.

One day he arrived with a bunch of Rhona's favourite freesias but, having been told flowers were not allowed on the ward, had handed them to a healthcare assistant for disposal.

Rhona watched the healthcare assistant take her flowers and after angrily getting out of bed, accosted the girl, and tried to grab them, saying,

"They are my flowers, not yours!"

He watched in dismay as a struggle ensued during which Rhona dug her nails into the girl's arm and made it bleed. Although she apologised immediately, and genuinely seemed concerned for the girl, this was so out of character and left Rory feeling shocked.

When he visited a few days later, the Ward Sister explained she had arranged a place for Rhona at Treavy View Care Home, and Rory was relieved, hoping that being somewhere more homely, would help Rhona relax.

The Home was situated on the coast road near Treavy lighthouse, about fifteen miles from the cottage in Trevaunce, had a good reputation locally and could take patients with dementia. Rhona would not only get the correct dementia care there but there were also dieticians and physiotherapists working on-site who could also help her with her mobility.

Rory had been getting increasingly concerned because although having been referred for intensive physiotherapy immediately after the accident, due to there being a long waiting list, she had only ended up walking a little while in hospital.

He and the hospital transport driver arrived at the ward early, on the day of her move, to find Rhona still in her nightie after another unsettled night. Appearing not to mind, the driver went for a coffee, while Rory helped Rhona dress behind the curtains.

She was in a very buoyant mood and giggled as he helped her pull her knickers up.

"It's been a very long time since a man pulled those up
for me, my dear, but many more have pulled them down,"
she said, winking.

Aware of how close the other patients were, on all sides of them, Rory felt a bit embarrassed by her comment. But knowing her sudden disinhibition was down to her dementia, he had giggled back and quickly changed the subject, and soon had her ready for her trip.

Rhona remained in high spirits for the whole journey down to Cornwall and, much to Rory's amusement, chatted happily with the driver most of the way. After they arrived safely at the home, she leaned forward and gave the driver a peck on the cheek.

"Well, you know where I live..." she said, winking at him,
and Rory could not help but smile.

After he helped her out of the car, Rhona stood, looking around her for a few seconds, and then shrieked loudly,

"No, there must be some mistake. This is not my home!"

Having attempted to calm her down, his efforts were in vain, but luckily, having seen the commotion outside, Erica the Matron came out to join them. Rory reckoned she was in her mid-fifties, and had a pretty, kind face, and he immediately warmed to her.

She had been expecting Rhona and already knew all about her.

"She's a bit confused," Rory told her quietly.

The Matron walked forward, took hold of one of Rhona's hands, and said politely,

"Hello, Rhona, my name's Erica, I've heard lots about you
and am pleased to meet you."

Erica was relieved when Rhona blushed, smiled once again, and said,

"I`m pleased to meet you too Erica."

Recalling having met her before, she added, much to Rory`s surprise,

"I think I may have met you years ago but cannot remember
where."

Rhona was slightly familiar, and Erica smiled, trying to recall when that was. She had dealt with so many people over the years, but at that moment did not recognise the woman who had worked in her shop, before she had done her return to nursing course, over thirty years earlier.

"You must be tired after your trip. Shall we go inside
and make a nice cup of tea?" she suggested.

To Rory's surprise, Rhona continued smiling and replied,
"That would be lovely, thank you."

CHAPTER 12

Rhona, September 2014

About a month into her stay at the Care Home, the local vicar whom Rhona knew very well but now did not recognise, visited to discuss her plans for Erick's funeral.

He found it very sad to see her looking and behaving so differently, and unlike the good friend he had known and loved over the years. It had been bad enough to have lost Erick, someone he already missed terribly, but to see her like that, brought a lump to his throat, which he cleared loudly, whilst entering her room.

Hearing him, Rhona appeared to jump.

"Hello Rhona," he said

"Sorry, I didn`t mean to startle you, my dear."

She stared at him blankly, but when he spoke, his voice instantly brought back memories of Bryony the baby she lost, and her funeral at the Woodland Burial Site, and she started to cry.

Waiting quietly until she stopped, he asked if he could sit on her bed, and sat down when she nodded.

After taking hold of both her hands, he asked,

"Shall we pray together, Rhona?"

This was exactly like he had done under similar circumstances, previously. She nodded and, as before, appeared initially appeared calmed by his soothing words. Quickly realising that seeing him, reminded Rhona of her late daughter,

Bryony`s funeral, a service he had taken over thirty years earlier, he decided to make it only a short visit, and asked,

"Would you like me to come back and see you again, sometime?"

To which she had said extraordinarily lucidly,

"Oh, I don`t think that will be necessary, do you, after all, I don`t even know who you are."

Upset, by what she had said, he smiled at her sympathetically before leaving, and once outside in his car, had a little weep.

After he had gone, Rhona felt even more muddled. It had been nice to hear such a comforting voice from her past, but she wondered why he had come. Remembering who he was much later when feeling more lucid again, she cried herself to sleep, upset to not have recognised such a good friend.

The monotony of life at the care home meant that time seemed to pass slowly and missing and wanting to be in her own home, she soon became very depressed and withdrawn. She could not understand what she was doing there and why she could not leave. Most days, the care staff would find her waiting by the door immediately after tea, with her bags packed and convinced that Erick would pull up outside in the camper-van any minute, to take her home, but he never came. Sometimes she would refuse to budge in case she missed him, but the care staff usually won her around with the promise of a nice cup of tea and a piece of cake.

It was a lovely surprise to see Orla and Padraig when they visited early on the day of Erick`s funeral, unable to stay, they left, telling her they would see her later, after dropping off her favourite black dress and accessories, and she was a bit confused. Although unsure why she needed them, she was glad to put on some of her nicer clothes again. Since her move, she had only had scruffy old, oversized clothes that the Home found for her.

Helena, her favourite care assistant, carefully helped her into her tights, and dress and zipped it up. When she had got her smart-heeled shoes on, Rhona practised teetering around beside her bed for a while, but seeing how wobbly she still was, to her disappointment, Helena suggested she needed to take her sticks.

When the car transporting her, Helena, and the Home's matron Erica, had pulled up outside the Crematorium, Rhona immediately recognised where she was, turned to Helena, and asked,

"Oh, has somebody died?"

CHAPTER 13

William June 2014

A tall, thin man with glasses and hazel eyes cautiously descended the steps of the American Airlines plane. It was his first time back on Irish soil for over forty years, and as he made his way across the tarmac at Dublin Airport and toward the connecting bus, he remembered his childhood. Picturing the row of two up-two-down terraced houses where he had spent his early years, clearly in his mind, he recalled how it had felt when they had first driven off to start their new life. It had been a while since Evelyn, who had always thought of as his mother, had passed and although it had not been a surprise, he had been ill-prepared for the barrage of different emotions returning to Ireland would bring.

Clinging tightly to the overhead strap as the bus jolted several times before pulling up outside the terminal building, he felt a nervous anticipation rising. After climbing down from the bus, he swiftly passed dawdling groups of tourists, wayward children, and a couple walking with sticks, and soon arrived at Passport Control. Once through, after collecting his luggage, he sped out of the "Nothing to Declare" exit and into the Arrivals Hall.

Finding the correct booth did not take long, but wading through endless paperwork took longer. Finally receiving the hire car keys, he went outside, hoping he would be happy with his choice. It was more impressive than he thought it would be and relieved it had satellite navigation, after tapping in the postcode, he set off when the route suddenly appeared on the screen. Soon reaching the outskirts of Dublin, when the roads around him became familiar, he switched off the navigation system for the last few miles.

Having eventually pulled over outside number twenty-two, he sat with the engine still running, thinking. He did not need to be here and could easily turn the car around and return to normal life. But Shauna had sounded so insistent in her message, and he could not let her down, he needed to know what she wanted to tell him so urgently and face to face.

Eventually, after he summoned the courage to get out and wander up the front path of Shauna's house, William saw the door was left ajar, which he thought was strange. He tentatively pushed it open and walked in. Greeting him was the smell of musty dampness, and wandering into the front parlour, he saw the dark wooden furniture it contained was covered in a thick layer of dust.

Hearing a faint cry from a room above, he immediately came out and hurtled up the stairs, taking two steps at a time. What he saw through the open bedroom door from the top of the stairs was disturbing and he stood and stared, hesitant to go in.

Shauna was lying in the bed and only the very top of her head was visible from under a thick eiderdown. He went a little closer, and when he moved the bedclothes to get a better look, she seemed to be in a deep sleep. Her breathing sounded laboured, and a rasping noise accompanied her every out-breath, which was disconcerting.

The last time he had seen her, she had appeared to be a picture of health, and he could not believe the contrast now. She looked as pale as white porcelain, had lost weight, and had a bluish tinge to her fingers and lips. This was alarming, he had never seen anyone looking this ill before.

Unsure what to do and afraid to wake her, he sat in the armchair beside the bed. But it was becoming increasingly obvious she was struggling to breathe, and when she began gasping for air, he tried gently shaking her awake.

Shauna suddenly loudly cleared her throat in her sleep, opened her bloodshot eyes a fraction, and looked directly at him.,

"William is that you?" she asked.

Her voice sounded weak and husky.

He took hold of one of her hands and it felt cold and clammy, and he noticed her fingertips were blue.

Still looking at him, she sighed,

"I`m so glad you`re here, there's something particularly important I need to tell you."

When her voice trailed off and she appeared to have drifted back to sleep again, William remained beside her holding her hand, wondering what she had been about to say.

After a while, she stirred again, pulled him close, and whispered,

"Evelyn isn`t your actual mother, I am."

He went to explain that he already knew but decided against it. He had heard the cancer had spread to her brain and that she would be confused.

Gripping his hand tightly, she spoke again,

"I may not have been with you, but I've always loved you, my son."

When she appeared to drift off into an even deeper sleep, he continued stroking her hand caringly. He had never been this close to her before and studied the contours of her face, her high cheekbones, long nose, and mane of thick light grey hair, most of which was pinned up. Some strands had come loose and splayed over the pillow, and unable to resist, he gently touched them, and they felt soft in his fingers. He had never realised how pretty she was before; she had always worn her hair so severely pulled back from her face and had looked cool and standoffish in the past.

After a while Shauna suddenly sat bolt upright, looked directly at him, and with her eyes wide open, mumbled something he did not understand.

It sounded like,

"This is important; you must find the babies in the woods and then get to the root of the problem."

This was very odd, and William wondered what she meant.

Wanting to understand, he asked,

"What do you mean, mum?"

But instead of answering, appearing transfixed by something in the corner of the ceiling, she suddenly pushed his hand away, and he watched in disbelief, as with her arms outstretched and palms facing upwards, she dramatically reached towards it, smiling.

Seconds later, she slumped back into her pillow, let out a little sigh, and was gone.

Shauna's demise was so sudden and dramatic that William remained glued to the chair, unsure what to do, he had never seen anybody die before. The room was eerily quiet, apart from a loud ticking clock on her bedside table. He looked around him and back at his mother again and started crying. This was unusual, as he never usually showed emotion.

It did not take long for him to compose himself and after a while; he pulled the covers back, placed her arms across her chest, and smoothed his hand over her eyes to close them, just like he had seen done in films, and felt calmer.

Although they had never been that close, neither geographically nor emotionally, because of his unconventional upbringing, he mourned the loss of her from his life in those few moments. Aware that before he left America, she had been ill for a while, he had held onto the romantic notion that they would spend quality time together, and get to know each other better, during his visit. But the cancer had taken hold faster than anyone expected.

Still trying to come to terms with how sudden and un-expected her death had been, he was unable to stop further tears streaming down his face and snot dripping from his nose. Feeling suddenly and overwhelmingly tired, he removed his glasses, grabbed a tissue from a box next to the bed and patted his eyes, blew his nose loudly, and soon drifted off to sleep in the chair.

Awaking after it was dark, he scrabbled around in the black-ness trying to find his glasses which had fallen on the floor by his feet, and with them back on, could locate the nearest light switch.

Seeing Shauna again by the light of the dusty dim shadeless light bulb hanging from a frayed cord above the bed, felt even more traumatic, and after quietly closing the door as if she were just still asleep, he hurried downstairs.

CHAPTER 14

William and Shauna June 2014

The darkness was very disorientating and not knowing his way around the house, William panicked, rushed outside and up the path of the house next door, and knocked loudly. A young girl with red hair and freckles slowly opened the front door and peered out at him shyly.

"Are your parents' home?" he asked.

She nodded and then yelled,

"Mammy there's a strange man at the door," in a soft Dublin accent.

Moments later, a tall white-haired woman appeared on the doorstep, looking worried.

"Jesus William, is that you? I remember you, so I do when you lived here with your mammy. You have grown up well, so you have Shauna must be so proud."

She looked him up and down, making him feel uncomfortable while he explained what had happened, and she ushered him quickly inside.

"I will call Doctor Mc Kinley out immediately. Come on with me now. Will you have something to eat?" she asked.

Compared to his mother's, this house seemed very warm and welcoming, and following the woman along a short corridor, he could smell lovely aromas wafting from the direction of the kitchen. He had just polished off his second bowl of potato soup and eaten chunks of soda bread when he saw a man standing in the hallway.

Noticing the surprised expression on William's face, the white-haired lady, as he now remembered her, as his childhood, "Auntie Eithne," explained,

"None of us need to lock our doors in this street. This is Doctor Mc Kinley."

He followed the doctor into the front parlour where he explained,

"I have confirmed that Shauna is now deceased, God bless her soul. Although I knew she did not have long, I`m surprised it was so quick, but I`m happy to sign the death certificate for you, so, I am. She was a fine woman, your mother, and her passing is an enormous loss for all of us."

William nodded and, feeling worried, could not help but ask, "What happens next, I've never had to deal with anything like this before."

Doctor Mc Kinley explained,

"I took the liberty of arranging for the local undertakers to come and collect the body. They should be there any minute. I hope you do not mind. You can visit her, of course, at the funeral home later if you want to."

He also mentioned that William would need to take the death certificate with identification, to the General Register Office to register the death within the next forty-eight hours and, that he could arrange the funeral after the Will has been read.

William thanked Eithne for the lovely food and went back next door, just as the undertakers came to remove Shauna`s body. It seemed strange to think of his mother lying in that black bag as he stepped to one side to allow them to carry her almost vertically down the stairs.

Unable to face being in that house overnight alone, he booked a room in a bed and breakfast for the next few nights on his mobile and was soon snuggled up in a small, warm, cosy room. The jet lag must have caught up with him again because he fell asleep on the bed, still fully dressed.

He awoke to sunlight streaming in on him and blinking in the brightness, lay there for a while, thinking. Although feeling sad and alone, it was comforting that his auntie Eithne remembered him as a small boy. He had not wanted to correct her, but it had been Evelyn, who he had lived there briefly with when he was young, and not his mother. It had been just before they had moved away.

After a traditional Irish breakfast, he returned to the house and wandered around curiously. It was obvious Shauna had been too ill to clean, as everywhere was exceedingly dusty.

Returning to her bedroom, he replayed her last moments over and over in his mind. The entire ordeal had seemed surreal, and feeling a strong need to speak to someone about what he had witnessed, he decided to go to the local catholic church he had passed on his way there. Although never having been particularly religious, he felt he needed answers.

CHAPTER 15

William June 2014

As soon as he had stepped through the door of the very modern, white-painted Catholic church, a jolly-looking rotund man with a bald head approached, and appeared to know who he was, before he had a chance to introduce himself.

"Ah, you must be Shauna's son, William, she's told me all about you over the years."

"All good, I hope," he said, assuming this was Father Pat, the priest.

Being in such a tight-knit community where everyone knows everyone, with his posh hire car and American accent, William realised he must have stuck out like a sore thumb.

Father Pat beckoned him over to a small room accessed through a door from the main hall and pulled out two chairs for them to sit on.

"What can I do for you, my son?" he asked.

After William described how Shauna had behaved just before she died, he told him he had previously seen that sort of thing happen.

"You hear of people who have near-death experiences and say they felt drawn towards a bright light in the corner of the ceiling, so don`t worry about that, it is all perfectly normal. I must say, though, your mother was an amazing woman."

He continued,

"Even up to the last few weeks before she became ill, she

was working on that bit of land she had bought, planting trees, wanting to get it all finished and open to the public as soon as possible. People thought she had gone mad, but she was a woman on a mission, and by Jesus, bless her, she finished it all on her own."

William told Father Pat that he wished he could have spent longer with her, got to know her better and that her passing so quickly had been a massive shock.

Sympathising with him Father Pat explained,

"It's a real privilege to be present for the last few seconds of someone's life, and to have you there with her come the end meant more to her than anything else."

Hearing that, William's eyes welled up with tears again. Father Pat placed a comforting hand on his shoulder and held it there for a few seconds, and he asked him if he would take Shauna's funeral. He agreed to do it but suggested he try to find her Will, in case she had left specific instructions. He also told him to go back and see him anytime he needed to talk and left him to contemplate his mother's passing in silence.

Touched by what Father Pat had said, later, having returned to the house, gazing around at Shauna's things, felt much closer to her again. The house was full of photographs of people he had never met, but who obviously must have meant a lot to her.

Deciding to look for her Will, he opened all the drawers in her desk in the parlour, and eventually found it, along with other documents. As he had assumed, she only wanted a simple service. Amongst the other paperwork, were the house deeds and the piece of land that Father Pat had mentioned, with a map attached.

After studying it thoroughly and curious to see it, he set off on foot as it was only a few streets away.

The beautiful green area, enclosed by a traditional dry-stone wall, was easy to find. As soon as he entered, despite the hustle and bustle surrounding it, it was a little oasis of calm, and he assumed his mother must have gone there to relax. Gazing around at the beautiful flowerbeds interspersing the many fast-growing newly planted trees from a park bench he had sat on, he smiled, and having tried to count them, lost track when he reached number seventy.

The trees had spread their leafy shoots to create a canopy, through which beams of sunlight shone down, and he marvelled at how the sun illuminated every bright green veiny leaf in perfect symmetry above him.

Smiling to himself and sighing contentedly, his tense body relaxed, and he soon fell asleep.

When he awoke, he felt the calmest and most relaxed he had been since his mother's death. What she had done, despite being so ill, was amazing, and he wondered why she had been so keen to get it all finished before she died.

He was about to leave when having looked back at the trees, he suddenly realised that on the front of each one, was a little brass plaque with a number on it, and the trees numbered one to seventy, and he wondered why.

CHAPTER 16

Shauna late 1970

Shauna was born in 1954 in a small Dublin suburb called Dubh Artach. Her father was Conan O`Shea and her mother, was Lucy Flannagan. Both were staunch Catholics, and she had a strict upbringing. On the surface, she was the model child and was always ready to help her mother with her younger twin sisters, do housework, and even go off to bed early, but underneath she was much less innocent than she appeared.

Just after Shauna turned sixteen, her father started working away, and although both managed everything very well, they were getting tired, every month without fail, Shauna found herself engulfed by waves of negativity and despondency. At such times, her mother would comment on how sad she looked, and ask her how she was, and she would always utter the same reply,

"Yes, mammy I`m fine, stop your worrying now, will you?"

Her mother's interventions seldom helped and instead made her feel even more self-conscious. She would often tie her mousy hair back from her face, and stare at herself in the tiny mirror above the sink in the outside toilet, wondering why she looked and felt so terrible. But instead of giving her the answers she sought, what she saw staring back at her only made her feel worse.

"I look so awful," she told herself one day while splashing her face with water.

Staring at her rosy-cheeked reflection and after a brief cry, she patted her sore stinging eyes with a towel despondently and sighed,

"Why do I have to feel this way each month?" she asked aloud.

At such times, she would feel a powerful compulsion to run away from the confines of home and escape for a few hours. Waiting until dusk, she quietly exited the house via her back bedroom window, on the second floor. After carefully manoeuvring herself onto the tiled roof of the pantry below, dressed only in her long white cotton nightgown, she walked, delicately balanced on the sloping tiles until reaching the drainpipe, and clinging to it tightly, slowly and silently lowered herself to the ground. She then sprinted unseen down the long narrow garden, quickly climbed over the back wall, and dropped into the alleyway behind, and once there, she felt free.

Although it was dark, she knew her way, and ran through the maze of old back alleys, until finally reaching the dimly lit main road. Off that, another smaller alleyway led her out to the playing field. The familiar flicker of Micky's cigarette was just about visible in the descending smog, and Shauna was out of breath by the time she joined him.

As usual, he was on his own, and remained still and silent for a few seconds, before pulling her to him and kissing her passionately on the lips. There was always a sense of urgency about his kisses and feeling his tongue on hers, she eagerly kissed him back. They stood embracing each other for several minutes and when they finally separated, she tried to gaze into Micky's eyes in the darkness, but they only looked like dark pools.

As usual, after kissing him, the taste of stale cigarettes lingered in her mouth, but this time she could also detect alcohol, which was strange because Micky rarely drank. An icy shiver went down her spine and she started to back away; suddenly unsure it was him she had kissed in the darkness.

Feeling increasingly scared at the thought, she started to turn to walk back, but sensing he was right behind her, with her heart pounding fast in her chest, she managed to utter,

"For feck's sake Micky, what you are playing at tonight?"

He did not answer and instead, appeared to grab at her hair and pull her backwards. Losing her balance, she fell onto something soft, which seemed to have something hard under it, and when her head began to pound and her vision became blurry, she was even more frightened. Feeling very disorientated she lay motionless, paralysed with fear, and fixing her gaze on the glinting half-moon illuminating the sky between the clouds above her, trying to blot out what was happening, a black shadow soon eclipsed her view.

Straining her eyes in the damp blackness, she saw only the whiteness of her breath and could feel chilly air dampening her nostrils. Her heart was pounding in her chest and echoing in her ears, and for some reason, the pain in her head was worsening.

"Please don't hurt me," she begged the black shadow.

CHAPTER 17

Shauna late 1970

When Shauna came around, the grass under her was stiff and a thicker fog had filled the air. Having made her first attempt at getting up, her head was spinning so much that she had to lie down again. Although shivering violently in the cold, she had no other option but to wait until the dizziness passed. Pulling the cold damp blanket tightly around her, trying to warm up, and having no idea how long she had been there, when eventually able to sit up, in the half-light of the early dawn, she could see dark stains on her white nightgown.

"Holy Mary mother of god, mammy's going to kill me!"
she exclaimed aloud.

Attempting to stand again, she immediately fell backwards, landing heavily on the cold, crunchy frosty grass, which felt like ice splinters pressing into her back.

What has happened to me? she wondered.

The dizziness dissipated after a few minutes, and she sat back up again.

It was then that upon inspection, she saw to her horror, that not only was most of her white nightgown heavily soiled and stuck to her leg, but her white panties, instead of being where they should be, were just above her knees and speckled with blood.

After hurriedly pulling them up and rearranging the rest of her clothing, she managed to stand properly this time, but her legs felt very weak, and she continued to shiver violently in the cold.

The sun was beginning to rise and she worried someone would see her, she staggered as quickly as she could back across the field, along the alleys, and back home again, her teeth chattering loudly with every tentative step. To her relief, she saw no one, except a milkman in a distant milk float that could be heard chugging up the main road.

It took three exhausting attempts before she managed to climb back over the garden wall, and wandered up the back garden, bracing herself for the accent up the drainpipe. This was even trickier than usual, and it felt like the cold had sucked all her strength out of her.

Extremely relieved when she finally slid through the bedroom window and back into the warmth again, she hurriedly removed her nightgown and panties, hid them at the back of the wardrobe, donned a clean gown and got into bed, still shivering. After wrapping the eiderdown around her as tightly as possible, she fell deeply asleep.

She awoke much later to the sound of her mother and Doctor O'Rourke`s voice, who were both peering at her from the side of the bed.

"I was worried; you were shivering so much that I thought you weren`t ever going to stop," her mother said, looking concerned.

Taking hold of her daughter's hand, she stroked it caringly.

Blinking in the bright daylight, and recognising the doctor, Shauna flushed red, worried how thoroughly he had already examined her.

He told her,

"You just need to stay in bed today, my dear, keep warm and drink plenty of fluids. If you do that, my girl, I am confident the fever will soon pass, it will to be sure."

She was relieved he had not checked her over that fully and had assumed she had a severe case of influenza. Neither noticed her matted-up hair and when she attempted to run her fingers through it, the back of her head felt tender. Touching it after they left, she found a raised area the size of an egg, and briefly considered calling the doctor back, but it was too risky, as awkward questions would be asked.

Despite her still pounding headache, desperate for answers, she re-ran the events leading up to the kiss several times in her head. Remembering the smell of alcohol, a smell so unusual on Micky's breath, she immediately felt sick to her stomach. Certain that Micky would never hurt her, realisation dawned, what if it *had* been someone else, someone else, and *not* him, she kissed in the darkness?

There was a stinging soreness between her legs, the likes of which she had never felt before, which was worrying, and re-membering she had found her panties down by her knees, she shuddered. The thought that a stranger may have done some-thing to her, *down there,* was too horrifying to dwell on, and she sunk back into her bed and slept again.

Later, having awoken feeling better, she ventured down-stairs and across the garden to the toilet, with last night's gown and panties concealed under her dressing gown. Staring at herself in the mirror as usual, apart from her matted dark blonde hair, she looked the same as she had always done but felt very different. Now feeling much more vulnerable than usual, she worried what exactly had happened to her.

It took over ten minutes of brushing to get her hair look-ing normal again, and after filling the sink with icy water, she scrubbed her bloodstained nightie and panties until the water turned pink. But realising had she just left them as they were, her mother would have assumed she had the curse, and not been concerned, she worried that unusually trying to wash them, could look suspicious.

Even if her mother did see her stained clothing, she never mentioned it and Shauna's life quickly returned to normal, and the stinging sensation went. But still haunted by what happened, she never saw Micky or returned to the playing field in the night again.

But something else happened that changed the course of her life forever.

CHAPTER 18

Shauna late 1970

It was not long before the early morning nausea started, and assuming it was merely a stomach upset, her mother dosed Shauna up with horrid-tasting pink medicine she had found at the back of a cupboard. But after over a week had passed, and she was still violently sick in the mornings, Doctor O Rourke was called back again.

After having examined her thoroughly and got her to pee into a little pot, he quickly announced that Shauna was pregnant. Her mother fainted and Dr O'Rourke just caught her in time to position her on the nearest chair.

The news was difficult to take in, and all Shauna could do was stare at the floor in shame, and after bursting into tears, tried to explain.

"I`m so sorry, but it wasn`t my fault mammy!" she said.

Shaking with emotion, she looked pleadingly at her mother, wishing her to understand, but it was obvious she did not when she slapped her hard across her face.

Shocked, she immediately burst into tears, it was unusual to see her mother so angry.

"How could you? How could you bring such shame to this family? You little whore!"

Her words and the slap stung and made her cry more.

"Please mammy, it is true, I was unconscious, I was so, jeez I`m telling you the truth, I swear," she whispered.

Her mother went quiet for a few seconds and then said, "I`ve never heard anything so ridiculous, you`re not only a whore, but a liar too! This is too much! I can`t deal with this now."

She stormed out of the room and after placing a comforted hand on Shauna's shoulder and smiling sympathetically, Dr O`Rourke swiftly followed.

CHAPTER 19

Shauna late 1970

Shauna's father's prompt return from overseas heightened local gossip. Seeing his familiar rotund figure ambling up the front path, through the mist and mizzle, her heart sank, and she instinctively ran out the back and locked herself in the outside toilet, afraid of how he would react. Even from that distance away from the house, she could hear him shouting and the sound of doors banging.

Several hours later, when the cold had got to her, she tentatively crept into the back kitchen, where she found her mother standing voraciously stirring something in a pot on the stove. Without acknowledging her, she continued to stir and when the smell of burning filled the air, she calmly switched off the gas, dramatically sank to the floor, and buried her head in her hands.

Shauna ran over and joined her on the hard flagstone floor, and they cried and hugged each other for some time. Finally, her mother announced,

"You know you cannot stay here. Your pappy wants you gone. He cannot handle the shame you have brought to our door. We are a good catholic family, and you have sullied our name."

"I`m so sorry mammy!" Shauna said.

She was unsure what to say next and her mother interjected,

"Your pappy is going to arrange a place for you at the Mother and Baby Home, next to the convent."

"But mammy!" Shauna exclaimed, horrified.

She had often heard rumours about that place and suddenly felt very afraid.

"Shush my girl, you have committed a terrible sin and need punishing. Do you understand? No matter what went on..."

Her mother's voice trailed off, and Shauna started crying again.

"Honest mammy, it wasn`t my fault, I didn`t know what had happened, I`d fallen and hit my head," she said, in a whisper.

Her mother looked shocked, pulled her towards her, hugged her tightly again, and after they separated, she stared into her daughter`s eyes.

"No one would ever believe that my child."

Cupping her hands around Shauna's face, she added,

"You do realise that don`t you?"

Although scared of leaving her home and family, she had disgraced them all and knew she must leave.

But what came next remained etched on her memory forever.

CHAPTER 20

Shauna late 1970

Her mother stood silently watching with tears streaming down her face, as her father removed his leather belt and having made Shauna lie across the old pine table, thrashed her over and over with it. Continuing to thrash, despite her desperate screams each time the leather struck her pale, fragile skin, he eventually stopped, abruptly left the room, and was soon heard snoring in the front parlour, as if nothing out of the ordinary had happened.

After laying for a while wincing in pain, Shauna gingerly stood herself upright and shivered. It felt like her whole body was burning and stinging, but she was too shocked to cry.

After checking the coast was clear, her mother came to her aid.

"I've got calamine somewhere, that should help,"
she said.

"As if that would magically make everything better,
mammy," she replied, sarcastically.

Her mother applied the lotion using cotton wool to the deep sores on Shauna's back, but when she gently embraced her, she just hung limply in her arms.

Pulling away from her mother's clasp, she gazed into her eyes and with an earnest expression on her face, admitted,

"I`m sorry mammy, but it wasn`t my fault, it wasn`t.
On my poor little twin sister's lives, it wasn`t."

Her father awoke when she began crying again and seeing her cowering in a corner when he promptly re-entered the room, he sneered,

"Oh, woe with you! Wasn`t your fault my arse, of course, it was you little slut."

"I'll do whatever you want, but please don't hurt me anymore," she pleaded.

"Well, maybe I have knocked some sense into the girl then," he said, winking at his wife.

She looked away in disgust and continued the washing up in the Belfast sink.

Still shaking with fear, Shauna stared nervously at her father, searching for any slight remorse for what he had done in his eyes, but they were blank, and his face was completely expressionless. To her relief, he returned to the parlour, and after slamming the door, could be heard speaking to someone on the phone, but Shauna could not make out what he was saying.

He returned later,

"Well, that is all sorted, they are collecting you at nine in the morning. You need to pack a small bag to take with you."

Later, Shauna slowly climbed the stairs to her room, climbed into bed with all her clothes on, and cried herself to sleep. Awaking early the following day, she quickly washed, dressed herself in the outside toilet, and not wanting to bump into her father, hurried back to her room to pack.

Unsure what to take with her, she decided on, "Artful Ted," a teddy bear she had cuddled so much, that most of its fur had worn off, but the artful look in his eyes always made her smile. She also added a simple dress, a nightshirt, some panties, and a single little photo of her mother, and twin sisters, to the small bag, and was ready and pacing the room in anticipation, when her father hollered up the stairs.

"Get yourself down here now, girl, they are here."

Brushing past him with her head down, after quickly giving her mother a peck on the cheek and asking her to say goodbye to the twins, who had no idea she was going, Shauna wandered outside.

Everyone in the street would immediately know what the small black van belonging to the Mother and Baby Home meant, and although they had told no one, as she walked outside to the road and the waiting van, curtains twitched all around her and Shauna knew she was the talk of the street.

The van door swiftly opened, and she felt herself being pulled inwards.

CHAPTER 21

Shauna late 1970

Shauna found herself sitting between a nun with a shrew-like face who glared at her with dark blue piercing eyes, and a solemn-looking younger woman with long reddish-brown curly hair, tied in a ponytail, who found it hard to even look up at her. Seeing them, she hugged her bag on her lap, prayed hard in her head, and meant every word. They were soon pulling up outside the Mother and Baby Home.

To anyone passing, the Mother and Baby Home looked very grand. It was a square Georgian building with large white symmetrical windows and stone walls the colour of light sand. Elegant stone steps led up to a large entrance flanked by white stone pillars topped with intricately carved masonry, and slim windows straddled each side of its grand front door framed by abundant green foliage, interspersed with pretty flowers.

Its appearance was, however, misleading, and cleverly concealed the true horrors that awaited any unmarried pregnant girl who dared to enter, many of which were never seen again.

CHAPTER 22

Shauna late 1970

The solemn-looking girl led Shauna from the luxurious grand foyer, into a maze of narrow and sparse windowless corridors, each lit by a solitary dim flickering light. Eventually, they arrived at a small hallway off of which, were two large rooms. She paused and stared in horror. The room to her left was full to the brim with neatly made narrow beds, each with barely any space between them and was a dormitory. The white bedclothes were heavily stained and everywhere was dirty and dusty.

A door opened to another room to her right and a malodourous stench filled the air. This appeared the equivalent of a maternity ward and had more narrow single beds down one side, all filled with pregnant women crying out in agony, already in labour. Opposite them were wooden cots with bars on them, full of screaming babies and young children.

It was seeing them that Shauna found particularly harrowing, especially as they were the same age as her twin sisters. No one was attending to these children apart from one skinny girl, who looked even younger than her. This place looked more like a prison than a place of comfort for these recently bereaved children, and she was horrified and felt sick to her stomach, at what she was seeing.

She continued to stare around her.

"Dump your bags here," said her solemn escort.

Looking like she would cry at any moment, she silently handed Shauna a rather screwed-up stained white apron.

"Put this on, we've got work to do," she whispered.

Shauna did as she was instructed, and suddenly from a side door, an older woman with a large round face and glasses appeared dressed in a white uniform and wearing a nun's coif and veil.

"Bow," the girl whispered loudly.

Shauna bowed her head in the woman's direction.

"And who on earth do we have here, Roisin?" asked the nun.

"I`m Shauna," Shauna told her.

"Did I ask you to speak, girl?" the nun asked.

She shook her head, and Roisin cleared her throat and declared,

"This is Shauna, Sister Mary."

Sister Mary eyed Shauna up and down and tutted.

"Another of our younger pregnant whores," she said,
and Roisin did not reply.

Sister Mary smiled at Shauna and, still maintaining eye contact, unexpectedly brought her knee up and promptly kneed her in the stomach. Having no chance to back away, she doubled up in pain.

"Stand up straight and look at me, girl. I`m in charge here,
and you will do everything I say. Do you understand?"
Shauna mumbled,
"Yes, um Sister Mary."
"Sorry did not hear you girl, have you lost your tongue and
your virginity?"
"Yes, Sister Mary, I understand Sister Mary," she replied.

Blinking back tears and still reeling from what Sister Mary had done, Shauna tried to remain strong, but her stomach hurt, and she feared for her baby. It remained tender for the next couple of days, and there was absolutely nothing she could do to soothe it. Sleeping in a very narrow single bed, covered only by an itchy rough blanket that smelt of pee, did nothing to help either, but resigned to the fact she had sinned in the eyes of God and needed punishing, she put up with it.

As a child, Shauna's mother forced her to attend Mass regularly. Finding herself in such an awful place, she suddenly started praying with all her might. All the other girls in the dormitory did so too, every night without fail.

As the days went by, it became apparent that the neighbourhood expected any unlucky girl who got pregnant, regardless of how far along she was, to work all day, every day without a day off.

CHAPTER 23

Shauna Late 1970

Shauna liked the night's best; the days were so long there. She and the twelve other girls had to be up at five every morning, and most did not see their beds again until midnight. It was an exhausting routine, and she often wondered how the other girls, who were much further on in their pregnancies, managed.

Although short, the nights were an escape from all the horrible things they had to contend with during the day, and their only time apart from Sister Mary, who watched them like a hawk. The girls were not supposed to talk to each other day or night, so they became very adept at eye-rolling and other non-verbal forms of communication. The funniest was their night-time farting competitions, which made them snigger quietly under the bedclothes.

It was cold in that room, with its high ceilings and big draughty sash windows, and during the winter nights, the girls decided it was best to sleep two to a bed, top to toe. This provided some much-welcomed extra warmth, but they had to be careful to be in their normal beds again by five.

Getting up so early was difficult, especially with ice on the inside of the Dormitory windows and the toilets and showers, all of which were in outhouses, and away from the main building, and entailed traipsing over wet grass to get to.

At least the maternity wing had warmth for those able to work there.

None of them knew where they would be allocated each week. Shauna, the most recent in, had to clean the toilets and sluices and don an old pair of ill-fitting and very perished Wellington boots to trudge across the long grass at the back of the building, dressed only in a thin dress, where she spent hours scrubbing bedpan after bedpan in the cold draughty outhouse.

Sister Mary would often appear from nowhere, glare at her and make her clean everything again, until her cold hands were red-raw, as she watched on, nice and warm in her heavy blue wool cloak.

The best thing about being out there was Roisin`s visits. When out of Sister Mary`s view, compared to her silence at their first meeting, she was one of the more cheerful girls and would arrive pushing an old rickety metal trolley piled high with bedpans, the sound of which Shauna could hear well in advance.

Although not supposed to, they would then have a chance to talk. Roisin explained she had grown up in the Home, after her mother left her on the doorstep in a cardboard box, and Sister Mary had taken her under her wing. Shauna was surprised to think she had never lived in the outside world and immediately felt sorry for her. But after putting a comforting arm around her, Roisin swiftly pulled away and told her,

"I've got to be getting back, or Sister Mary will be wondering where I am."

She guessed Sister Mary had never done that, and watched her run back up to the main building and disappear inside. It got her thinking; she had not yet worked on the ward herself but wondered just how many girls had also lost their mothers, and what their stories were.

By the end of her first week at the Home, she felt like she was running on empty. Not only were the days long, but food rations were in short supply. Apart from a large bowl of gloopy porridge, they wolfed down every morning, their only other sustenance was a bowl of lukewarm soup and a piece of stale bread, at five o'clock every evening. Having always had an enormous appetite, she often thought of the piled-high platefuls she always ate of her mother's cooking back home.

Although managing to appear composed on the outside, on the inside, she was struggling to deal with the fact that her family had completely abandoned her. Missing them all badly, she thought of them often and prayed hard she would get to see them again one day.

CHAPTER 24

Shauna Late 1970

The following week, Shauna came in from the cold to work in the ward and washrooms in the main building. This was shockingly arduous work, although her upbringing had been strict, she had never imagined living like this. From when the bell rang at five o'clock every morning, in the main ward, they had to yank everyone out of their filthy beds and give them a bowl and flannel to wash themselves. This was particularly harrowing and the noise of the screaming children, some of whom tried in vain to defiantly hold onto their cot rails and refuse to move, was deafening. She wanted to hug them all, just as she had always done to her twin sisters back home, but that sort of behaviour amongst the girls was forbidden.

There was no privacy in the ward and fully pregnant women and young girls had to strip-wash themselves in full view of everyone. There was also no soap, which Shauna thought strange. Already dreading being in their shoes herself, for now, she was pleased that her early morning nausea had ceased, and she was feeling a little better generally.

She and another girl had to strip all the beds and cots, handwash the cotton sheets in large vats full of boiling water and run them through massive mangles that required two girls to manage. This was particularly dangerous, and she was horrified to see a girl getting her hand mangled. There was blood everywhere, but when Sister Mary arrived, all she was concerned about was the sheets and not the girl.

Often wondering what happened to that girl, especially when she had not seen her for some time, Shauna was shocked to see when she eventually returned that her face was black and blue and that she no longer appeared pregnant.

Attempting to talk to the girl when sister Mary was looking the other way, she had been concerned when she refused to make eye contact, kept her head bowed, and with her hand resting on the little silver cross around her neck, appeared to be chanting "Hail Mary's incessantly," under her breath.

Each group of girls had a senior girl in charge, and in Shauna's case, it was Evelyn. She supervised them, reprimanded them if there were any creased sheets, and scolded them with boiling water if she found any stains. She reckoned she was only a few years her senior, but her grim expression and furrowed forehead made her appear older.

She did have a pretty, kind, freckled face, framed by a mass of curly reddish-brown hair, which despite being severely pulled into a ponytail, always came loose and dangled by her ears. Compared to the other senior girls, she appeared very shy, and spoke much more quietly and only when necessary, and Shauna liked her the most.

Gastroenteritis had been spreading through the girls like wildfire, and unusually as Shauna had contracted it, she was allowed to spend a morning in bed but needed to wander outside to the toilet block several times. On one such occasion, hearing crying emanating from an end toilet, having made her way down to it, she gently knocked on the door.

"Are you all right in there?" she asked quietly, in case Sister Mary was within earshot.

She could hear shuffling from behind the locked door, followed by the sound of someone vomiting. Then, without warning, the door burst open, and Evelyn flew out, grabbed her tightly by her arms, and said,

"You have not seen me, you understand?"

Evelyn looked even paler than usual and appeared petrified. Shauna nodded, concerned, and after she let go of her arms, watched Evelyn quickly scuttling back inside the main building. Shauna was even more curious when she appeared to be avoiding her when she returned to the ward later and wondered what could be so terrible that no one else must know about.

After spending a month solely in the washrooms, the warmest place in the building, Shauna was put to look after the younger children. She hated seeing their wide-eyed, sad expressions as she approached, and how they cowered beneath her when she reached up to let their bedsides down.

Often left all night in soiled bedding, when trying to help them wash, she noticed not only red-raw areas on their skin where excrement had been, and had left scars, but there was also evidence of recent and older beatings, all over their faces and bodies. Some of the young children appeared very scared, but she always smiled, and when neither Evelyn nor Sister Mary was looking, she put her arms around them to comfort them. But after about a month, the little ones started to get very clingy, which made it difficult for her to leave at the end of each day.

It was a relief to be allocated to the Delivery Room, somewhere she had not been before.

CHAPTER 25

Rory Late August 2014

It was a long time since Rory had last been at the cottage in Trevaunce, and he was apprehensive about going there alone. But, after checking that Rhona had gone inside the Care Home, the hospital transport driver offered to drop him wherever he wished.

The short drive to the cottage was uneventful, and after thanking the driver, he got out of the car, opened the five-bar gate, and gazed around him. Everything looked the same, apart from the abundance of weeds now gathering in every spare corner of the grassy track up to the cottage, and the grass itself was considerably longer.

The traditional old, thatched Cornish cottage that had been his home for over two years looked just as it always had, apart from a few extra cobwebs hanging precariously from its thatch, that were gently undulating in the cool breeze.

He wandered slowly up the grassy track to the front door with some trepidation, and after rummaging around for his keys, which luckily had not been lost in the accident, let himself in through the thick wooden door, which creaked as he opened it. There was a loud bark, and an overly excited Dougal, the West Highland white terrier, immediately greeted him, wagging his tail so furiously, that he knocked off the post that Rhona`s close friend, Heidi, had kindly left on the shelf just inside the door.

Aware of how fond both Erick and Rhona had been of this dog, seeing him again, Rory burst into floods of tears and sat down on the hard flagstones to give him a big cuddle. Somehow sensing Rory`s sadness, Dougal snuggled up close and let him hug him tightly.

After he began whining and running over to his bowl and back a few times, he got up to feed him. By the time he had located the dry dog food and poured it into Dougal's bowl, his tears had subsided, but he was left with a feeling of unease, unsure whether he had done the right thing going back when it all still felt so raw.

Still appearing concerned about him, Dougal quickly gobbled down his food, returned to his side, and nuzzled up to him, wanting more cuddles and tummy tickles.

"I know, it is not the same. Everything is changed, yes
 everything has gone belly-up, not just for you, mate,"
he told him as if Dougal understood every word.

He was pleased that Heidi had dropped Dougal off, it was nice to have him there, it would have been horrible coming home to an empty house.

The cottage felt cold and damp because the Aga had gone out, and Heidi had shut all the room doors during one of her visits while he was in hospital. Relieved to see she had already brought some wood in, and he just needed to light it and stoke it up a bit, to take the chill off the place. Despite being early August, it was cold, and he could hear raindrops hitting the windows, the deep howling of the wind down the chimney, and through the cottage's many cracks and crevices, a sound that had become so familiar when he lived there with Rhona and Erick. But that seemed an age ago now.

Shivering a little, he pulled up a chair and sat down at the old, stripped wood dining table, waiting for the house to warm up, and remembered Rhona telling him,

"Thatched cottages are great in the winter once they are

warm, but cool in the summer."

It had been quite soon after he first met her, and it was so strange being there, alone now.

He pictured Erick sitting at the head of the table smoking his pipe contentedly, and Rhona standing at the Aga stirring something, and sighed. The cottage was certainly full of wonderful memories.

At that moment Tigger, Rhona, and Erick's originally stray ginger cat, shot in through the cat flap, deposited a mouse at his feet, and sat looking at it and at him as if to say,

"Well, I kept my side of the bargain, where's the proper food now then?"

He waited expectantly while Rory retrieved the dried cat food from the end cupboard and put some in his bowl.

"Not sure I`m going up the ladder today though," he said aloud.

He remembered when he had first asked Rhona what the large wooden stand with the ladder up the side of it was for, it had been when he had first sat in her garden not long after they had met. Recalling just how quickly she had scaled the ladder, despite being in her late sixties, and how they had both stood marvelling at the buzzard she had called "Stanley", as he majestically swept down, with his wings completely outstretched, grabbed the mouse in his talons and carried it back up into the sky with him. He remembered Rhona laughing, watching him witnessing the spectacle, his mouth open in complete awe and surprise.

It was too wet to climb up the ladder today, so instead, he donned a pair of Erick's Wellington boots, trekked across the garden and tried throwing the mouse onto the stand. After three failed attempts, with Dougal watching on with his tail wagging, he eventually managed to get it on the flat stand at the top and stood back under the shelter of the overhanging thatch, to see what would happen.

But unlike previously, there was no sign of Stanley after ten minutes, and feeling a bit perturbed, he went back inside. Thinking Stanley had gone and that he might never see him again was horrible and made him feel very sad, and he made himself a pot of tea, which had always been Rhona's go-to answer to all of life's ills. After drinking some, he immediately started to feel warmer, removed his coat, and took the rest down to Erick's studio room at the far end of the cottage.

It was strange being there without him and he looked around aimlessly. Wandering to the far end, he surveyed the view through the large full-height gable-end window. The room smelt quite musty, and when he opened the window to let in some fresh air, he saw remnants of Erick's old tobacco, strewn around the rose bushes growing below. Erick had often stood there smoking his pipe and cogitating, and he remembered Rhona jokingly telling him off for contaminating the roses.

Now it had stopped raining and the sea mist had gone, across the fields, he could see the sea, bright blue and mirroring the sky above it, standing with tea in hand, was mesmerised by the large, white-topped waves crashing against the cliffs in the near distance and could hear its gentle roar being carried towards him on the breeze. He had forgotten how atmospheric, living at the cottage had been.

Shutting the window when another black shower cloud loomed, eclipsing the sun, he went over to sit on the sofa and gazed around at the numerous pictures his father had painted, adorning the walls.

Although sad, it was comforting to see them again. Having finished his tea, he stretched himself out, and closed his eyes, intending to have only a quick nap.

CHAPTER 26

Rory September 2014

Rory awoke again after it was dark, and after removing a grumpy Dougal from his stomach, got to his feet and climbed the steep wooden stairs up to the bedrooms. Doing this reminded him of how determined Erick had been to get up to his bed after his fall, over three years earlier, and how he struggled until he finally and triumphantly made it to the top with his help.

Wandering into his room, he saw the picture on the wall of his mother, whom Erick had painted years earlier and before he knew him. He had forgotten how beautiful it was and what a lovely reminder of what she had looked like when he was a young boy, it was. Remembering how it had always felt like she and his grandma had been watching over him since they passed, gently guiding him toward the truth, he smiled.

The whole situation had been very unusual. It had been such a coincidence that out of all people, he had struck up a friendship with Rhona and that only happened when his delivery van broke down outside her house. It was unbelievable that she turned out to be his actual biological mother! Then, also discovering that her husband Erick, was his biological father, was surreal. But being in their cottage without them now, the reality of his situation was hitting home fast.

Feeling suddenly very emotional again, he could not help but replay the last few moments before the lorry hit, in his mind. It had been the last time he had seen Erick alive before he was so cruelly snubbed out of his life.

The accident took not only Erick but most of the Rhona he had come to know so well, leaving a mere shell, containing only some sparse remnants of the real her. But he still loved her despite the worsening dementia and was so thankful she had survived. As he had told Erick in the mortuary, he was determined to stick by her, no matter how badly things panned out.

After a few days hauled up on his own at the cottage, not wanting to talk to or see anyone, he returned to work at the Centre and began visiting Rhona at the Care Home, usually in the early evening.

Just like when she was in hospital, he never knew what state he would find her in from one day to the next. Sometimes she was perfectly lucid, and they would complete a crossword together, and on other occasions, she would be sitting, staring into space, looking worried and uncommunicative, which was the hardest to deal with. The staff explained that most days they would find her staring out of the window and across the bay towards Seachapel, looking incredibly sad.

During one of his evening visits Erica the Matron, called him into her office and asked,

"Who 's Bryn, Rhona keeps mentioning him?"

He explained all about Bryn and their life together in their flat on the Wharf in Seachapel, and how after Rhona became pregnant, he died in a climbing accident.

"She lost the baby, and I do not think she ever got over that. She met Brynn when she moved to Cornwall from Cullenmara, after she had given birth to me. Both of my parents were married, but to other people, and back then due to the stigma of their situation, they felt they had no other option but to put me up for adoption. It was the 1970s."

Erica looked surprised.
"I did know Rhona back then, but had no idea what she had been through."
Rory looked at her.
"Really? I wondered what she meant when she said she knew you."
"I had a shop, well a Clothing Agency, to be exact, in Treyrow, and she worked for me for a few years, after she rekindled her relationship with Erick and until getting pregnant with who must have been your sister."
She continued,
"Wow, how awful that must have been for Rhona, to have not only lost you, but her other child Bryony, and Bryn. Working somewhere like this, you realise people have such complex and interesting pasts, most of which we never get to hear about because, by the time they arrive, they have full-blown dementia."
Rory nodded and Erica continued,
"I know it is hard for you to have to deal with, but I do have a theory; I wonder if dementia acts as a protection mechanism. We would all like to go back and forget the horrible stuff we went through and rewrite a new history. It is common for dementia sufferers to think they are back in a time when they had no worries, their heyday I suppose, or a time when they were in love, and when everything was rosy.
Rory found what she said, interesting.
"I get what you mean, but Rhona seems to flit around. One minute she is talking about getting Erick's tea, and the next time I visit, she will tell me she saw her mother and is back in her teenage years again. It would be fascinating if it was not so sad," he said.
Erica nodded in agreement, before explaining further,
"The best way to handle her confusion is to go along with it. A person with dementia finds it all difficult because they

get lucid moments, and often realise what state they are in. Being in a Home can feel like all their choices have been taken away, and what they say or think doesn`t matter anymore. Dementia does not mean stupid. It is important to resist the urge to correct them when they spout nonsense. As to them, it all makes perfect sense."

A buzzer rang and Erica apologised because she had to leave.

Mulling over what she had said, it certainly made sense, and from then on, Rory looked at his mother through fresh eyes and felt he understood her much better.

Erica had finally put two and two together, after hearing Rhona's husband Erick was an artist, and realised Rory's father was her best friend Zena's partner, for several years back in the 1980s, she had met him on several occasions. Realising this, she understood why Zena lost touch with Erick; he had moved on and begun a new life with Rhona. She remembered how upset Zena was when unable to find him, during her only recent fleeting visit to Treyrow from Australia. She had wondered why she wanted to see him so desperately. Although she never disclosed the real reason it was obvious she regretted leaving him and still loved him very much.

CHAPTER 27

Zena 1985

Zena and Erick had been in a relationship for around four years when she suddenly left with no explanation, and he had no idea where she had gone and why. The truth was, she had panicked after realising she might be pregnant. Although hating leaving him and their life behind, she needed time to think and to decide what to do next.

After catching the earliest train from Trezance and finding a vacant window seat, she had apprehensively settled back and tried to relax. She had always liked trains and usually found their gentle rocking motion, calming, but this time, with her head so full of so many different thoughts, she felt fidgety, rather than calm.

It was hot on the train and after peering out of her window, mesmerised by the fast blur of the rocky greenery of the Cornish coast, and the welcoming rolling hills of Devon, she fell asleep and only just awoke in time to see the "Dawmester" sign.

It was a rush to get off the train quick enough, but luckily the guard saw her and waited while she disembarked. Flustered, once on the platform, she anxiously checked the time-table for her connecting train to Riverton and was relieved to see she had enough time to pop into the station bar for a quick drink before it was due.

It had been a long time since her last visit, and as they had argued the last time, unbeknown to her, her mother had been getting increasingly worried, not seeing her for so long. But knowing she could be unpredictable, her father had always maintained that she would turn up, and it was just a matter of when.

"She always returns when she needs something. You mark my words, she will be back soon," he had said, trying to placate his wife, over a month earlier.

Zena knocked on the old ornate wooden door of her parents' house loudly and waited for someone to answer. After a few minutes, her mother opened the door and peered out curiously. Seeing her looking so bedraggled, she gasped in surprise and quickly ushered her inside before any of the neighbours saw the state she was in.

Zena stepped over the threshold leaving a puddle of water on their new parquet floor, and before she could utter a "Hello," her mother disappeared into the kitchen to get a cloth to wipe it up.

Studying her daughter briefly on her return, she tutted. Although wearing a Mac, she looked soaked to the skin, her hair was sopping wet, smudged mascara was running down her cheeks, and water was dripping off her nose. Seeing her physically shivering, she fetched a fluffy towel from the downstairs toilet cupboard and put it around her shoulders, before asking,

"So, you are back then? Any idea how long this time?"

Before Zena could answer, while still patting her hair dry with the towel, she was ushered into the large farmhouse kitchen, where a fire was burning in the grate took off her wet Mac, which her mother took, and hung above the Aga to dry.

Sitting in one of the nearest comfortable chairs, "Grandma's chair," as she remembered, under the weight of her mother's disapproving looks, she started to cry. But instead of comforting her, her mother continued staring and having retrieved a

bottle of finest malt whisky from one of the kitchen cupboards, Zena watched her pour a single shot into a glass and
drink it down in one.

After clearing her throat loudly, she asked abruptly,

"What have you done now, then?"

Hearing voices, Zena's father appeared, and she leapt up
from her chair and hugged him tightly. They held each other
tightly for a few moments before separating.

She exclaimed,

"You're looking very well, daddy."

Sitting back down in Grandma's chair, she asked politely if
she could have a whisky, and having taken quite a large gulp,
began explaining more calmly,

"I met someone, and he was lovely and well, we were happy,
only..."

Her voice trailed off, and she took another loud slurp of her
drink, before saying,

"I think I might be pregnant!"

The words came out of her mouth in a rush. Her parents
appeared stunned and continued silently staring at her in disbelief.

Suddenly her mother promptly got up, walked over **and
wrenched** the half-full whisky glass from her hand.

"Well, if that's true, you've got to stop this for a start."

She went quiet and looking intently at Zena, then asked,

"What exactly do you expect us to do about it?"

The abruptness of her mother's tone made Zena cry again,
and her father went over to her, put his arm around her, and
told her,

"My darling girl, I`m sure we'll be able to help you, just
like we always do."

He glanced over at his wife, and she rolled her eyes upwards,
shrugged her shoulders, and left the room.

Zena and her father sat up talking way into the night and, polishing off all the rest of the whisky, both stumbled upstairs to bed.

CHAPTER 28

Waking up the next morning was very strange and as Zena came to, she stared around her, astonished. All her original childhood toys were arranged on shelves, a photo collage she had made of all her school friends was still on the wall, and even her old, well-loved cuddly bears were still lying around her on the bed, just as they had when she was a child. It felt like time had stood still, which was disconcerting, especially when it must have been well over ten years since she had last stayed in that room.

Needing the toilet urgently, she got out of bed and wandered into the en-suite. The relief she felt after emptying her bladder was immense, and she sat on the toilet for a while, thinking. She remembered when she was last there and thought fondly of the good times she and Erica had together, which usually involved copious amounts of alcohol, live music, and dancing. Neither of them had any responsibilities back then and were free to do what they liked when they liked. How she wished that were the case now.

She had always been aware her parents disapproved of her lifestyle and assumed it was a phase she was going through, which it was, up to a point, but a very long phase, which had taken until meeting and settling down with Erick, for her to break. But although she had tried, she had never managed to give up drinking completely.

Grabbing a new toilet roll from under the grotesque pale blue knitted woman`s skirt, a very fashionable item to put over a toilet roll in the early 1980s, finishing what she was doing, she washed her hands in the basin and looked at herself in the mirror.

Staring back at her was not a very pleasant sight. Not only was her smudged mascara still all over her face, but her eyes were also extremely puffy, her hair matted, and some strands were stuck to her face. Seeing herself, she desperately needed a drink but remembered she had left her bag containing a small bottle of vodka, outside in the rain on the doorstep the previous evening.

Feeling better after showering, she hurriedly dressed and crept down the stairs, intending to dash to the front door unnoticed. She was poised to open it when she heard her mother say,

"Is this what you are looking for, Zena?"

She held up her bag for her to see.

"I brought it in last night and have dried it by the fire
for you."

Zena nodded sheepishly and her mother gave it to her, and said,

"I have put the bottle of vodka that it contained in the
cupboard for safekeeping. You should not drink it in your
condition."

"Please Mum, I need it, and anyway, I may not be pregnant,"
Zena pleaded.

She was annoyed and upset that her mother had taken it, and glared back at her, shaking her head. Her mother did not respond and instead, turned the radio up to listen to the To-day Programme, and proceeded to cook bacon, eggs, sausages, and baked beans for them both, which she brought over to the table where Zena had sat down, feeling hungry.

"Has daddy gone to work?" Zena asked

She began gulping her food down ravenously.

Her mother nodded and explained,

"Yes, he`s got a new staff member and needs to go in at weekends now. I`ve told him it is too much at his age, but you know what he`s like."

She changed the subject,

"What on earth have you done to your hair, Zena?"

"Oh, that, I cut it myself that's all," she said.

Zena was starting to think she looked even more hideous now than earlier. She had always felt that nothing she ever did would ever be good enough for her mother, and not wanting to hear any further criticism, she hurriedly finished her meal and went back upstairs.

Later, her mother called to her in her room, on her return from shopping.

"Zena come down a minute, please, I've got something for you."

Zena joined her at the bottom of the stairs and watched her rummage in her full shopping bags. She eventually pulled out a white paper bag containing a white cardboard box, handed it to her, and then disappeared into the kitchen to put the rest of the stuff away, without saying anything.

Zena returned to the safe confines of her room before opening the box, intrigued at what it might contain. It contained a set of three pregnancy testing kits, which she pulled out and looked at. She had left the door ajar and jumped when her mother, who was standing in the doorway watching her, said,

"Best to know definitely if you are, or not."

She entered the room, sat on the bed, and followed Zena into the ensuite.

"You are not going to stand over me while I pee on them, are you?" Zena asked.

To her relief, she went out again and shut the ensuite door behind her. All this was stressful enough as it was, without having her breathing down her neck. After following the instructions to the letter and peeing on each tube in turn, she sat down on the toilet and waited for what seemed like an age.

Too fidgety to stay still, she started pacing up and down in the small bathroom until the three minutes were finally up. She stared hard at the results. The first one was blurry and difficult to read, but the other two were clear and confirmed that she was pregnant.

CHAPTER 29

Zena December 1985

Zena needed to drink most days; it was the only thing that calmed her nerves and always made her stay at her parents' house more bearable. By mid-December, she still had not decided what she was going to do about the baby, but her mind was made up for her when, after having way too much to drink one evening, she fell headlong down the stairs.

She awoke hearing a strange rhythmic squishing sound, cautiously opened her eyes, blinked, and saw the fuzzy outline of a baby on a small screen rigged up beside her bed. It all seemed so surreal, but that squishing noise was her baby's little heart beating away inside her, and she decided there was no way she was going to lose it.

After a stern-looking doctor explained that drinking during her first trimester was particularly dangerous, and could cause stunted growth, and other complications too, she listened and took in everything he said, and left the ward promising not to drink again, and over the ensuing weeks, realised that was easier said than done.

She had to choose the baby, or the alcohol now and reflecting on her behaviour, was aware of just how selfish she had been previously. The fall down the stairs had brought her to a real watershed, and she now understood what everyone, including Erick, had been trying to tell her. She desperately needed to do something about her drinking before it was too late.

CHAPTER 30

Zena Kerala India Christmas, 1985.

Zena's father had heard about a Retreat in Kerala, from a friend and wanting to do something to help Zena, had booked her on the next available flight. He too had often struggled with alcoholism over the years and had frequently relapsed and was aware of what a mammoth task giving up alcohol would be, particularly at Christmas. The Retreat seemed the best option, especially now she was pregnant.

She was initially unsure about the trip but enjoyed the long flight and felt elated when the plane touched down and she caught the first glimpse of her surroundings through one of its small windows. It was like a whole other world out there, and even in the half-light, everything around her looked vivid and beautiful. On the minibus ride over, she was sitting between a woman with strawberry blonde hair, who she did not know, and coincidently was Rhona, and two other dark-haired women. Although they had all smiled politely at each other, none of them spoke, and not feeling ready to talk about her addiction with strangers yet, she was glad.

When they first arrived, she gasped, because standing in front of her was an enormous A-frame design wooden building, illuminated by hundreds of flickering candle lamps, and all its glassless windows were also edged with candles. The sight before her was truly magical and beautiful, and she was even more pleasantly surprised, the following morning, after her first night in a large bright, airy suite, when she opened the shutters to find amazingly green, lush scenery spreading out beneath her for miles. Her suite, with its queen-sized wooden bed, fluffy pillows, white cotton bedding, and extra high wooden ceiling, was fabulous, and she jumped on the bed, lay back and smiled.

However, the month there was not easy. She had never stopped drinking for any longer than a week before, and by the second week, she was feeling dreadful. But Becky, the manager, was always on hand to help, taught her various distraction techniques like mindfulness, and even got her to do simple yoga poses daily.

Zena also had a treatment plan based on meditation, something she had never tried before. Being there so far from home, surrounded by such beautiful views, vivid colours, and very calming sounds, made being mindful and meditating easier. One of her favourite meditation spots was the natural pool formed from rock and the waterfall that flowed into it. Here she would swim when she most wanted to drink, usually accompanied by one of the other women, the one with strawberry blonde hair. They smiled, but never spoke, each in their little worlds.

Zena learned so much while at the Retreat, and at the end of her time there, was completely off alcohol, had lost just under a stone in weight, and looked positively glowing with health.

Amazed at her daughter's transformation, unusually, her mother hugged her as soon as she saw her.

Zena had done a great deal of thinking at the Retreat. Alcohol was always the crutch that got her through life's difficulties and had always provided an escape from things she did not want to face. But it had stopped her from properly experiencing life, living it to the fullest, and instead, kept her wrapped in a selfish little bubble. Surviving the time between one drink and the next had been exhausting, and her only way of dealing with anything outside of her comfort zone, was to get inebriated as quickly as possible, but not any longer.

Now feeling ready for new adventures, she decided to move away, leave her past life behind, and start over again as this new her, but wanted it to be somewhere with a much warmer climate than England. Concerned hearing her plans, her father suggested he discuss the situation with his younger brother Geoff, who was still living in Australia and a qualified doctor and see if he would mind her joining him for a while.

She waited expectantly while her father talked with his brother at length, and was relieved when eventually, he smiled, handed her the receiver, and said,

"Geoff would like a word with you."

Everything was sorted out during that conversation, and all she had to do, was go.

CHAPTER 31

Zena Western Australia 1986

Despite feeling uncomfortable on the long flight, now several months into her pregnancy, when she stepped off the plane and into the Western Australian heat, Zena felt sure she had done the right thing. Hating England`s long wet winters, the thought of virtually all year-round high temperatures was truly appealing.

She chatted excitedly to Geoff on the ride over to his smallholding, which was so far off the beaten track that it was in the middle of nowhere, an exciting contrast to the larger towns she was used to. Gone were the lush trees and rolling hills of Devon, replaced by dusty orange tracks transporting them deeper and deeper into the Australian Outback.

Eventually, they turned a sharp left and pulled up outside one of two large static caravans set back from the road in a clearing and she stared around her. In front of the caravans was what looked like an old scrap yard where an old red bus that had seen better days lay abandoned and half-covered by sand and dust. To one side stood old-fashioned petrol forecourt equipment, which she thought was odd. To the right of the scrap yard area were a couple of quite large chicken coups, behind which, was a kind of workshop, and Zena noticed further down from where they stood, that there were a couple of goats in a small barren-looking field.

A dog with light cinnamon-coloured fur ran out of the larger caravan and along to greet them, its tail wagging furiously. Geoff told her,

"This is Mitsy, she was a stray, we've got her and two others which were rescue dogs: a border collie-cross and an Alsatian."

They went inside the larger caravan, which Zena realised was much bigger than it looked, and found Yindi, Geoff's Aboriginal wife, stirring something bubbling away on the stove. She smiled at Zena and could see she was beautiful despite missing most of her front teeth and she warmed to her immediately. Geoff explained this was where they stayed during the gold season, the rest of the time they lived in a small house on the outskirts of Kalgoorlie.

"You've made this very homely, it's lovely," she exclaimed.

Looking around her with interest, having seen a familiar face in a photograph above the wood burner, she went over for a closer look.

"Is that Daddy?" she asked.

"Yes, it sure is. It was when we were kids, and funnily enough when we came to Australia on holiday," said, Geoff.

CHAPTER 32

Zena, Western Australia, January 1986

Zena settled easily into outback life and soon moved into the smaller caravan. She enjoyed its quirkiness and the fact she was living somewhere she could be herself without anyone judging. Despite the heat and dust, she thought it a good place to raise her unborn child. Life there was difficult, but she soon had routines to enable her to live off-grid efficiently, just like her uncle did.

Her time at the Retreat did her the world of good, and remaining off alcohol completely, she was eating fresh fruit and proper meals regularly, for the first time since her childhood.

She was returning from her uncle's house near Kalgoorlie, having collected one of his generators after hers started to play up when she and Mitch first met. He was also driving along the main route between Kalgoorlie and Perth, but on the opposite side, when he first saw her. Used to sharing the roads with the massive long-distance articulated vehicles that raced up and down that early in the morning, it was unusual to see a small Ute parked up at the roadside. After a flash of shiny red hair caught his eye, he slowed down to get a closer look.

Zena had often recalled that day in her mind, since. She remembered sitting with her head in her hands, sobbing loudly, and having pulled up level with her vehicle, Mitch had enquired through her open window,

"You all right there, Sheila?"

Startled, she dropped her hands and nervously looked across at him. Even though her face was tear-stained, and her eyes red from crying, Mitch admitted afterwards how stunned he was by her appearance and could not help but sit looking at her with his mouth open.

"Don`t do that, you'll catch flies," she said, wiping her eyes.

She was smiling at him and immediately liking her soft English accent, he continued staring back at her bright green eyes glinting in the early morning sunshine. This was disconcerting for Zena because there was no one else around, but she detected a kindness in the intensity of his stare.

Gazing shyly back at him, she studied his round face, and soft blue eyes surrounded by laughter lines. Although bald, tattooed, with a large scar on his chin, he had a kind, characterful face, bright blue eyes, and a lovely smile.

He asked again,

"You alright?"

"I`m fine, thank you," she replied dismissively.

"Are you sure?" he asked.

She nodded.

Seeing tears forming in her eyes again, and not wanting to embarrass her, he averted his gaze and focused instead on the bent driver-side rear wheel. He got out of his truck, and after putting a baseball cap on his head, said,

"Look, we are miles away from any garages out here. I can easily fix your wheel if you like. I presume you have a spare on the back. Why don`t you let me help you?"

Zena was surprised to see how tall and athletic-looking he was, and immediately feeling vulnerable, she did not reply.

Noticing how worried she was looking, he added,

"Chances are, I will be the only person you will see along here for a while. It is not safe to be out here alone."

Zena wiped her eyes and nodded.

"That would be very kind of you, thank you."

Mitch jumped back in, promptly swung his four-by-four around and parked behind her. When she descended from her vehicle and walked around to stand beside him, he was shocked to see she was pregnant. Not wanting to stare, after retrieving tools from his pickup, he got to work on the wheel.

Zena stood watching his brown arm muscles tensing as after locating the jack, he began slowly raising the right side of the vehicle off the ground. The wheel did not come off smoothly and required grit and determination. Although five-thirty in the morning, it was already around thirty degrees in the shade, and she could see him getting very hot and sweaty. Watching him and noticing his short shorts and lovely long-tanned legs, Zena could also feel her temperature rising but for different reasons, and fanned herself with her hand.

Suddenly the wheel broke loose causing him to tumble backwards and he ended up flat on his back, with the wheel on top of him in the dust.

Unable to stop herself, Zena let out a very sudden roar of laughter so contagious, that Mitch started laughing too, so much so, that he was temporarily unable to get up. He lay there laughing for about a minute until Zena stretched out her hand to help him up. Their eyes met momentarily as he stood up, but feeling her face flush red, Zena looked shyly away. But aware she still had hold of his hand, she shook it, and said in her cultured English accent,

"Hi, I`m Zena, very pleased to meet you!"

"Mitch, my name's Mitch," he replied.

He tipped his dusty baseball cap toward her and placed the dud wheel on the ground. They stood just smiling at each other for a few seconds until Mitch looked away and having put the spare wheel on, tightened the nuts.

Feeling uncomfortable standing there watching him, Zena wandered over and attempted to pick up the old wheel off the dusty road, unaware of how heavy it was.

"Here, here let me," he said at once.

"You should not be doing that in your condition."

She stood back and watched him with hands on hips, as he bounced the heavy tyre up into the back of her Ute as if it were as light as a feather. Seeing his tee shirt was completely wet with sweat, she offered him water, which he gratefully accepted and enjoyed, even though it was warm. After thanking him for his kindness, she explained she needed to be on her way. But Mitch was concerned, it was so unusual to see a pregnant woman travelling solo this far off the beaten track.

"Where are you heading?" he asked.

"Well, if I told you that, I might have to kill you," she said jokingly.

When his eyes met hers again, there was a wicked sparkle in them he had not seen the last time.

"I`m going up to the gold fields, but I`m afraid that`s all I can tell you," she said.

He went to speak, but she interjected,

"It's all right, I`m joining my uncle, he`s a qualified doctor and has been coming up here for years."

She turned her back on him, climbed into her Ute, started the engine, and after turning briefly to wave, drove off at considerable speed, leaving a cloud of dust behind her.

Mitch sighed and returned to his car smiling to himself. Zena was incredibly striking with her bright red hair and colourful clothes, and having never met a woman quite like her before, he hoped they would meet again, but the outback was a big place, and he knew it was unlikely.

CHAPTER 33

Zena`s Uncle Geoff 1976:

Geoff left England in 1976 and after interrailing around Europe, working in various cafes and bars to sustain himself, he met a blonde Australian student and returned to her native country with her. Although the relationship did not work out, he remained in Western Australia, wanting to explore the Outback and Gold Coast.

Embarking on a road trip from Perth City down to a small town on the coast, called Exmouth, he stopped at various motels and bars along the route. It was a particularly arduous journey, taking over two weeks, but Geoff found it interesting and exciting, having never done anything like it before.

On one occasion, he ended up in a strange place for the night. Initially, as an outsider in the small, rather dilapidated-looking town, he felt intimidated because people stared at him wherever he went. There was a feeling of unease as if something might kick off at any time. But after some drinks or "tinnies" as the locals called them, he realised everyone was warier of him than he had been of them, because not many people visited that area. As a stranger with a polite English accent and clean clothes, he stood out.

Very soon the proprietor of the motel he was staying in, offered him a caretaker job, which he gratefully accepted. Soon after, he was invited to supper at one of the elders of the towns` houses one evening, and not knowing them well, arrived at the extensive house, set on a large plot, on the outskirts of the town feeling rather nervous.

But after several tinnies and a lovely meal cooked by Bert Wiseman's wife Callie, he eventually discovered another reason why the locals were initially so suspicious of him, it was because they all shared a closely guarded secret. It was while sitting with Bert on the veranda drinking whisky quite late into the night after Callie went to bed, that he confided in him,

"You are wasted working in the Motel, we could do with more young lads like you out here."

Intrigued, he and Bert glugged back a little more whisky, until

Bert declared,

"There's a whole heap of gold nearby."

Geoff watched him disappear inside the house and reappear carrying an old dusty box, which he opened and produced several old, yellow-grained photos of his ancestors holding up massive gold nuggets, some of which, were worth over a million Australian dollars.

"There's more where they found that. After the gold rush in the early 1900s, all their tools and equipment were abandoned, and covered in dust and earth. But I`m telling you no word of a lie. The original gold miners did not have the capabilities we have. We can dig deeper and have extra-strength metal detectors, to locate the pockets of gold," he explained.

So enthused, Geoff resigned from his job at the Motel the following week and joined him and his team in the gold fields. It was exciting digging up the old mine workings and detecting, and after consistently finding gold, it did not take long before Geoff caught the gold bug himself. However, after early good pay-outs, the gold reserves suddenly dried up, and Bert reluctantly laid Geoff off, until he could afford even bigger diggers and better equipment. Geoff lost his main source of income and his little wooden shack on the grounds of Bill`s house, which had become his home.

Struck for cash, he decided to follow in his father's footsteps and train to become a doctor but to do that, needed to move to Perth.

CHAPTER 34

Geoff, Western Australia 1980.

After finishing his four years at university, Geoff completed his training at a practice in Kalgoorlie. He enjoyed being back there again, and on his day off from work, continued searching for gold using an old second-hand detector and panned dried-up streams and riverbeds. But found only a few small nuggets.

However, about six months after his move, he became involved in the care of a patient called Jack, who was dying of terminal cancer. Despite the high doses of morphine he was on, Jack told him one day,

"I er, know something that other people don`t round here, Geoff,"

Hearing that Geoff's ears pricked up, and he wondered what he meant.

"Oh yeah, and what's that then, Jack?"

Geoff listened as Jack explained that he had no family left.

"They're all dead mate, of this blimmin' cancer infection too," he said.

He explained that his father had been a gold miner all his life and his Aboriginal ancestors, before.

Geoff was intrigued, and unexpectedly, Jack confided in him further.

"I've got no one to tell but you now, boss," he said.

Geoff pulled up a chair beside Jack`s bed and listened intently as he explained precisely where all the gold was. He sounded so convincing that on his next day off, armed with a new and powerful metal detector and better panning equipment, he went off to investigate. The area Jack mentioned was vast, and after detecting and panning various streams for gold, he was sad to have found nothing. He was about to give up when having rounded a headland, he saw the most spectacular view down to the sea.

He remembered Jack saying,

"When you first see the sea, you know you are on the right track."

Getting excited, he continued detecting and soon found old reed beds and a small trickling stream leading down to a large estuary area. Here, he started panning for gold again but still found nothing and was going to abandon his search and go home, when he met a family of Aboriginal people who desperately needed his help. The male beckoned him over and led him around to the other side of an enormous rock, where he discovered a woman lying on the ground in the shade, obviously in the final stages of labour. After successfully delivering her baby, the woman lay exhausted, on the ground, but after a while, suddenly turned to look at him, smiled, and said,

"Me called Alinta, who are you?" in broken English.

She held out her hand, which he took, and having moved his hand over to her heart held it there and said,

"Thank you, I will never forget you, Gubbah."

Aware Gubbah was the Aboriginal term for a white man, he felt touched by her words, and was a little embarrassed when she seemed to want to let his hand go, and kept it clutched to her bosom. She only let it go when her baby was returned after it had been washed in one of the small nearby streams.

Alinta`s brother Jarli, the only man there, told him while pointing to Alinta,

"My sister thanks you, and I thank you too. Thank you, boss."

Geoff, on his instructions, followed him out onto a rocky outcrop.

"This is our holy place, and I will recite an old Aboriginal prayer to protect you. You are forever our friend, Gubbah" he said.

Hearing Jarli half-chanting, half-singing the prayer, although unable to understand his native tongue, was very moving and Geoff thanked him afterwards.

CHAPTER 35

Geoff Western Australia 1981

It was not long before Geoff enlisted his new Aboriginal friends to help find Jack's gold. They were doing exhaustive panning of the old reed bed and stream when suddenly glistening in the pan were specks of gold. Although not much, this was a start and a good indicator they were in the right location. He then invested money in second-hand digging equipment, and a large mechanical sluicing machine to rinse the gold out of the dirt they collected with the digger, leaving it embedded in specialised rubber mats at the end of the process. It was amazing how much gold the mats could hold, and this was immediately weighed and sold, and the money was used to buy more new equipment until they could work on a much more industrial level.

After learning how to clean and separate the good gold from the dirty gold, which previously affected its sale value, and how to melt it into nuggets, Geoff made a small living off what he earned part-time in the goldfields. Having originally kept his other job at the doctor's practice, juggling the two, soon became difficult.

After mining in the area for over a year, and with no indication the gold reserves would run out, he took the courageous step of giving up his job at the Practice. It was a gamble, especially as all the equipment he needed to get to this stage proved quite costly, but now beginning to pay his early debts off, although the work was exhausting and the conditions hot and dusty, he loved it. It felt like it was something he was always destined to do.

He and his men made lots of money very quickly and hoped their luck would continue, and it did, for the next five years. He went from owning a small caravan on a tiny piece of land to owning hundreds of acres of outback. In addition, after buying a plot of land in Kalgoorlie, he built a small house for him and Yindi, Alinta`s sister, to live in the off-season. He met her during one of the family's regular communal meals, and, the attraction between them was instant.

CHAPTER 36

Evelyn 1968

Evelyn first went to the Mother and Baby Home at age fourteen, accompanied by her pregnant mother, after her father left them without money. Although Sister Mary took her under her wing, after her mother died in childbirth, she treated the same as all the unmarried girls living there. She still had to get up early each day, sleep in the draughty dormitory, and work just as hard, if not harder, than the other girls, and could not appear to be getting any special treatment.

Life at Home since her mother's passing was difficult and made Evelyn feel very vulnerable and alone. With her freckled skin and pale complexion, she never regarded herself as pretty. But after mistakenly confiding in Declan the priest, also a co-owner of the Home, she was very flattered when he told her she had a lovely smile. Unused to such flattery but quite liking it, she was enamoured with him, very quickly.

Their friendship was obviously against the rules and felt very naughty, but meeting up with him secretly, provided excitement, in what were pretty dire conditions. Not only could Declan be very flattering, but he was also good-looking and appeared kind and understanding, which she presumed were typical qualities of a priest. She continued seeing him, without considering the danger she was putting herself in.

She felt awkward when he asked if he could kiss her, having only regarded him as a good-looking friend, but suggesting she sit down on the settee in his office next to him, when she did, she felt herself relax, so much so, when he lifted her chin so her lips were level with his, she did not stop him, and he started to kiss her increasingly passionately. Having never been kissed like that before, Evelyn felt like she was walking on cloud nine, and imagined them falling in love.

Later, noticing her sudden change in demeanour, Sister Mary commented,

"What`s got into you recently, Evelyn?"

Blushing, she said she was simply happy, and Sister Mary smiled, something she rarely did.

After several meetings spent kissing, late one evening, Declan coaxed her into his office and slept with her. She had just turned seventeen and very impressionable and by that time, was completely infatuated with him. She had been worried when Declan gently removed her outer garments, and she tensed up. But she let him continue after he began kissing her again until she was standing in front of him in nothing but her little flimsy slip. The actual act was unremarkable, and all over very quickly, so quickly, that she was left with a feeling she had somehow missed something. But, she enjoyed kissing him, being kissed back, and feeling the warmth of his skin against hers.

However, acutely aware that what they had just done was a sin, she hurriedly rearranged her clothing and fled, worried sister Mary would see her and somehow sense what she had been up to. She was relieved their naughty acts remained secret, and as it had been all over so quickly, as time passed, it felt increasingly surreal as if it had not happened, and she tried to forget about it.

Desperately wanting to see Declan again and to re-kindle their closeness, when he appeared to be avoiding her, her life quickly returned to its usual level of mundaneness again, and she was confused. A few months later; after she started experiencing the same symptoms as the pregnant girls at the Home, early morning vomiting, and a swollen belly, she feared terrible repercussions from sister Mary.

With absolutely no one to confide in apart from Declan, whom she was now much too embarrassed to speak to, she succeeded in keeping her suspected pregnancy quiet, disguised her new body shape in a larger robe, and it went unnoticed for several more months. But as her belly grew, so did the shame and worry.

When she saw a lot of blood splattered over the white porcelain after using the toilet one morning, she was convinced God was punishing her for what she had done. Although nearly faining at the sight of so much blood, she clutched the side of the cubicle to steady herself, unable to stop herself vomiting on top of the blood, was still retching, when she heard someone else enter the toilets. When she heard Shauna asking her if she was all right, not wanting to risk anyone else finding out what had happened, she confronted her, and swore her to secrecy, hoping she would keep her confidence.

Seeing Frank Clancy's familiar friendly face when he started working at the Home about a month later was hugely comforting. She had known him since she was a small child and always liked him. Initially feeling unable to confide in him what had happened and her predicament, when she suddenly felt faint and hot one day, she had no choice.

Frank was concerned seeing her flushed face, and after taking her temperature, diagnosed a high fever, and insisted she stay in bed until she was better, and despite sister Mary's protestations, escorted her back to the dormitory himself. Going to check on her a few days later, he was pleased to see her looking better but, she still was not right, and he sensed a nervousness about her. Having taken hold of her hand to try to comfort her, he could feel it shaking, and looked at her, worried..

Feeling overwhelmed by his reaction, she blurted out all that happened. Dr Clancy was angry, remaining more concerned about her blood loss, than how it had come about, after checking her over, satisfied it had stopped, he realised she had miscarried Declan`s child.

Although horrified at what he a man of the cloth, had done, Frank still did now know the cause of her fever and prescribed her a course of antibiotics. To his relief, she soon recovered physically but, her mental state remained a cause for concern.

Although he had not told her she had miscarried, Evelyn assumed the bleeding was connected in some way to what she and Declan had done, and surrounded by girls at the Home, who often miscarried, felt shocked to think she could have been pregnant with his baby.

CHAPTER 37

Evelyn 1970

Evelyn continued to work hard trying to impress sister Mary, but her efforts always seemed in vain, she continued to find fault with everything she did and often chastised her in front of the other girls. All the constant criticism and sneering remarks she received daily were denting her confidence, and still thinking about her miscarried baby often, she felt increasingly helpless and hopeless as time went on.

Like all the other girls, Evelyn had no money, no family, and only sister Mary as a mother figure. It was frightening thinking she may somehow discover what she had done, but at least now having Frank to confide in, she had some support and was very grateful. But as time went on, and feeling gradually worse, she often thought of Declan and the closeness they briefly shared, but with this all gone now, and with her low mood exacerbated by his continued cold reaction, she became more and more despondent.

Missing the flattery she enjoyed so much and the heart-fluttering feeling she had each time she saw him, she now had to resign herself to being left with only the cold hard reality of day-to-day life at the Home.

Seemingly unable to stop it, she hated the panicky feeling she now got in the pit of her stomach, every time she saw Sister Mary. Clutching her rosary to her chest, she prayed hard that it would all stop. But being stuck there as she was, she knew this was unlikely.

CHAPTER 38

Shauna early 1971

The Delivery Room was a room that Shauna had not been to before but had often heard blood-curdling screams and shrieks coming from there. The girls had explained that this was where all the "difficult" births were dealt with.

Entering it she found it only dimly lit, apart from one large and bright floor lamp that shone directly over the end of the bed. At the end of the bed were stirrup-like contraptions which she assumed were where the pregnant women's feet were during labour. Seeing those, she shuddered, especially as there were no sheets or blankets on the bed, just a bare plastic mattress. Protecting a person's modesty was not a priority here, either. Next to the floor lamp was a trolley, upon which were horrifying-looking metal instruments. One looked like two metal tennis rackets with connected handles, which was particularly disturbing. Besides those were sharp pincer-like tools and scalpels. There also seemed to be a big, rounded glass thing with a rubber top and tubes going in and out.

To one side of the top of the bed stood what Shauna reckoned must be a portable oxygen cylinder with a dirty rubber mask dangling from it that was touching the stained and very dusty linoleum floor. She was staring around concerned about how grubby everything was, when suddenly the double doors burst open, and a trolley was wheeled in with a woman screaming out in agony on top of it, and she had only just enough time to jump out of the way.

Pushing the trolley was a medium-height spectacled man with light brown hair who looked as if he was in his late twenties and was wearing a white coat.

Appearing surprised to see her, he hurriedly introduced himself.

"I`m Doctor Clancy and, you are?"

Shauna told him and distracted, he shouted,

"Fetch me a bucket of water and some towels, please."

He rolled up his shirt sleeves and she stared at him, trying to remember where she had seen a mop and bucket.

"Now please," he reiterated.

Seeing her looking perplexed, he tutted and added,

"The cleaner's cupboard is out in the corridor on the left. It has a plain white door, and there is also a sink in there."

She went off to fetch it and returned to find the woman on the bed with her legs in the stirrups. The doctor had his back to her and, to her horror, had one rubber-gloved hand up inside the woman and the other, pressing on her bump.

Shauna felt sick at the spectacle.

"Holy Mary Mother of God!" she had uttered under her breath.

Hearing that, Doctor Clancy asked without looking at her,

"You`re not going to faint, are you?"

CHAPTER 39

Shauna early 1971

When Shauna came around, she was lying on the dirty linoleum. Doctor Clancy was kneeling beside her, waving smelling salts under her nose. The pregnant woman was gone, but there was a frighteningly large pool of blood on the floor, immediately to her right.

"I`m so sorry," she said getting herself up, embarrassed.

"It`s ok, you`ll be better next time," he said and left the room.

Shauna went to fetch a mop from the cleaner's cupboard and, on her return, mopped the floor clean and tidied up the instruments, many of which had fallen on the floor. She then scrubbed the rubber mattress on the bed until all the blood stains came out. Unsure what to do next, she continued tidying until she could hear fast-approaching footsteps and Dr Clancy reappeared. With him was a young girl who was clutching her belly and crying. She must have only been around fourteen and appeared very frightened.

Shauna immediately helped her onto the bed and held her hand, trying to calm her down. Doctor Clancy grabbed what Shauna had thought was an oxygen mask and placed it over the girl's nose and mouth and after telling her to take deep breaths, she closed her eyes and appeared to fall asleep. Having then assisted him in putting her feet up in the stirrups, she watched him pick up the glass contraption and partially insert it between the girls' legs. After then attaching the rubber tubes to another larger bottle, almost immediately, it made a loud sucking noise, and the bottle filled with blood and debris.

The procedure was over in moments and after Dr Clancy woke the girl back up, Shauna walked her slowly back to the ward. She was in floods of tears, and she had to reluctantly leave her, rocking herself back and forth on her bed, completely inconsolable.

Upset about the girl, she quickly returned to the Delivery Room and had busied herself cleaning around the bed and wiping the mattress again, trying not to cry. Doctor Clancy had been standing with his back to her, appearing to stare at the wall. And when their eyes fleeting met when he turned around, to her surprise, he looked like he had been crying too.

"She's the same age as my niece," he said, sniffing loudly.

Shauna's opinion of Dr Clancy changed completely in those few moments. He was different from the other staff at the Home and appeared genuinely caring.

"What's that glass thing?" she asked, aware he looked embarrassed, and wanting to change the subject.

He continued to look embarrassed, having expressed his thoughts aloud, but still answered

"What you just witnessed was a textbook suction termination of pregnancy, she had been having pains for a while, and it was obvious something was very wrong when she began bleeding heavily on the ward. She is too young to wait to see what happens, which is what the nuns prefer me to do."

"Isn`t what you've just done, illegal?" Shauna asked.

He did not get a chance to answer as there was a loud knock on the door and sister Mary barged in, looking angry. She asked Shauna to leave the room, but remaining outside, she stood listening at the door.

What followed was a massive row, during which she heard
Doctor Clancy say,

"It was the correct medical decision, in my opinion."

She heard sister Mary screaming back at him,

"Yes, but it's yet another lost baby when we badly need
the revenue!"

Shauna did not understand what she meant, but not wanting to be caught listening at the door, quickly returned to
the ward.

CHAPTER 40

Evelyn early 1970

Evelyn was feeling incredibly low when she went to see Jefferson, the American co-owner of the Home's office, one evening a couple of years after her miscarriage. But he had been the only person who had asked her how she was that day and had spoken to her kindly.

Contrary to what she had told Frank and Sister, Mary, during the months and years after the miscarriage, she had been feeling increasingly more depressed and had disguised her anguish with false smiles and good behaviour. When he suggested she pop in to see him later that evening for a chat, she had innocently gone.

She had never really been that close to him before and studied the contours of his face. Struck by how his dark hazel eyes appeared to light up every time he looked at her, and realising how handsome he was, she felt her face flush when he smiled back at her. She had often thought about that day since and wondered why she had approached him so casually and touched his arm, but nothing could have prepared her for what happened next.

He suddenly stopped smiling, and in an instant, pinned her against the wall behind his desk. With no way of freeing herself, and when he lifted her robes to rape her, all Evelyn could do was stand numb and motionless, and not retaliate. When she did try to call out, he covered her mouth with his hand,

and scared and unsure what to do, she remained completely still. But when his rough thrusting started to hurt her insides, she angrily bit his hand. Wincing in pain, he tried to hit her and luckily missed when she ducked, instead, he caught his hand on the desk and cursed loudly.

"You will not get away with this, you little bitch!"

She watched him turn away, pull his trousers back up, and light a cigarette.

When he began staring out the window, smoking, she saw her chance to run and did not stop until she was back in the dormitory.

Once back there, she immediately burst into tears, seeing her, the other girls were concerned, but wanting to avoid talking about what had happened, she disappeared into the washrooms, before they could ask her anything. Here, she spent over half an hour washing herself. As usual, there was no soap, and she scrubbed herself with a scouring pad covered in disinfectant instead, and eventually returned to the dormitory, with her skin smarting and raw. Although extremely uncomfortable, the pain at least distracted her from thinking about what happened. Despite all her scrubbing, she still felt dirty and could not forgive herself for getting into a compromising situation so easily again.

CHAPTER 41

Evelyn Early 1971

Frank was surprised to find Evelyn waiting in his office early one morning when she burst into tears as soon as she saw him, he knew what she was about to tell him would be bad. After waiting patiently for her to stop crying, he rested his hand on her knee comfortingly, while she explained how Jefferson forced himself on her.

"I did not dare put up a struggle, especially after he put his hand over my mouth so tightly, that I thought I might pass out. He lifted my robes and pinned me against the wall until he had completed his dirty deed."

Frank was angry and wondered how Jefferson could do such a thing to someone so vulnerable.

Evelyn elaborated,

"I did not know what else to do, so I bit his hand hard, which at least made him stop, but it was too late. I dared to look across at him. He was standing with his back to me, smoking a cigarette and looking out the window. I felt so angry, that with every ounce of my being, so help me God, I wanted to creep up on him from behind, and hit him on the head, to punish him for what he had just done. Of course, I did no such thing, but then saw my chance to make a run for it."

She worried she had disclosed too much, especially after Frank became angry, angrier than she had ever seen him.

Thinking about it all later, Frank realised that must have been when he started seeing a change in her. To think someone so kind-hearted, could be taken advantage of again and in such an ungainly way, was awful. Jefferson had exploited her vulnerability, with the ultimate humiliation, and it was heartbreaking to see her hanging her head in shame, afraid to make eye contact with anyone. It also explained why she had overheard her reciting the Serenity Prayer and what must have been hundreds of Hail Marys every day since. She had always been so happy and carefree when he knew her as a child, but now was a different story.

Frank stormed down to Jefferson's office and hammered on the door. When there was no answer, he presumed he had fled back to America, but decided there and then, to find some way of getting back at him.

Wanting to help, he stopped Evelyn one day in the corridor and asked,

"Would you like me to go with you and tell Sister Mary exactly what happened, so she does not blame you?"

She had shaken her head and said,

"It won`t do any good, Frank, she`ll still treat me the same regardless."

She was getting increasingly worried because unlike before, the baby she was now carrying was starting to show, and she would need to give birth to it within the next few months. Aware of what happened to other girls in similar circumstances, she was scared and knew sister Mary would not take the news well.

As predicted, sister Mary was shocked to the core, and if Frank had not been with her, Evelyn was sure she would have reacted much more violently. As it was, she slapped her extremely hard around the face, called her all the names under the sun, and walked out of Frank's office in disgust. Afterwards, frightened, and cowering below her clutching her smarting cheek, Evelyn burst into tears, and concerned, Frank put his hand on her arm reassuringly,

"It's alright, I'll sort this," he told her.

After Frank ran after Sister Mary and explained what had happened, she calmed down considerably, and as the weeks and months passed, despite scolding her in front of everyone as usual, she often called her into her office to check she was all right, out of sight of the other girls, which she very much appreciated.

But as time went on, Evelyn began dreading the actual birth.

CHAPTER 42

Shauna Early 1971

Shauna did not see Doctor Clancy or Evelyn for a while and a replacement doctor was sent in his place, and was abrupt and solemn. The thought that this man, instead of him, may end up delivering her baby was worrying, and she was extremely relieved to see Doctor Clancy again when he reappeared two weeks later.

There was something different about him, that she could not put her finger on. He certainly appeared much more relaxed after his break, which was good. It had been obvious he had been working himself into the ground, before his break, but now the bags under his eyes were gone and he had got a new haircut, and she thought him quite handsome. Only after they made fleeting eye contact again she realised she may have met him somewhere other than the Home, and it bugged her.

Being in the Delivery Room with him was much more interesting than working elsewhere in the Home, he always explained everything he did and why, and although the work was often harrowing, she looked forward to working with him each day.

With her bump growing larger, she eventually broached the subject of her impending birth.

"I hope you will deliver my baby when the time comes,"
she said.

"I cannot promise anything, but I hope it's me, too," he

replied, smiling warmly.

He then told her not to worry and assured her he would try his best to be available.

Shauna had been watching all that went on in the Delivery Room with increasing interest since overhearing his conversation with sister Mary. It was dreadful to think just how many young girls had either lost their babies or had them taken away, and she decided to keep a tally in her head. When she had a chance, she asked him where all the babies went. He immediately put his finger to his lips, shut the door and speaking in a muffled voice, explained that many were taken overseas, and sold to wealthy couples who could not have children of their own. Her shock must have shown on her face, and he quickly told her,

"You must not tell a soul Shauna, you do understand?"

She nodded and listened, intrigued, as he explained he had wanted to try to stop it all for years, but could not risk losing his job. He had an elderly mother at a residential home and was paying for nurses to tend to her night and day. The owners knew this and often used it as leverage to ensure he always did what they asked and kept their sordid secrets. He had also signed a confidentiality agreement and admitted to having already divulged too much.

The more she got to know him, the more Shauna grew to like Doctor Clancy and feel she could trust him. He had trusted her with such an outrageous secret, and she was incredibly pleased when he told her,

"Call me Frank when we are alone."

She became upset after, yet another baby was stillborn overnight, and felt embarrassed, blamed her hormones and immediately apologised to Frank.

"It is fully understandable in your condition, and witnessing all you have, it`s natural to feel scared," he said.

When she looked up at him with tear-filled eyes, he produced a clean white handkerchief from his trouser pocket and gave it to her. Touched by the look of concern on his face, she blew her nose loudly and managed a smile. He smiled back and, unusually, also put his arm around her, and she felt herself relax, with her face against his chest, she felt him gently stroking her hair.

Shauna had not had any kind of human contact for over eight months when her mother hugged her, and within seconds she felt happy again, the happiest she had felt since her move there. They would have continued hugging if the emergency buzzer had not sounded, but instead, they had to hurriedly pull apart and go to collect another pregnant woman from the ward.

Later, Shauna thought about his kind embrace, often imagined it happening again and started to wonder what it would be like to kiss him. Although only too aware of how wrong this was, it was still a thrilling thought, and from then on, she could not help blushing when she saw him.

CHAPTER 43

Evelyn Early 1971

When the time came for Evelyn to give birth, she was petrified, and after what seemed like hours of writhing around in agony in the main ward, she was very relieved when pushed into the Delivery Room where Frank was waiting for her. By the time she got there, she was very red in the face, hot and tired, and the first thing he did was to take hold of her hand and try to get her to calm her breathing. She immediately relaxed, but when the next sudden contraction hit, she cried out in agony.

After checking how dilated she was, Frank returned to the top of the trolley to tell her to start panting in short, sharp pants, but not to push yet. This, she discovered, was easier said than done. When another wave of contractions came, she panted as instructed, fixing her gaze on Frank, and he counted her breaths with her. Soon she was dilated enough to push and after only ten minutes of absolute agony, she was overjoyed and relieved to hear her baby's first cry.

Frank cut the cord and immediately placed his tiny boy skin-to-skin on her stomach, which he had read in a medical journal was good for both mother and baby. Evelyn clutched his little warm body to her chest and cried tears of pure joy. Her little brown-haired baby boy was beautiful, and falling in love with him immediately did not want to let him go.

But this happiness was short-lived, as by the following morning, her baby, whom she had gently placed in its cot by her bed, and kissed on the forehead before she fell asleep, had completely disappeared. All she was left with was a fleeting memory of him looking up at her from where he had lain in his cot, the night before.

Despite only knowing him so briefly, finding him gone had been dreadful and it felt like her heart had been wrenched out, leaving only a baby-shaped gaping hole. Not knowing what else to do, she just kept crying, and could not help it.

Seeing sister Mary arrive at the ward later, despite her fragile physical state, Evelyn shot out of her bed, grabbed her arm with both hands and pleaded with her to bring her baby back.

"I know you`ve taken him, please bring him back. It`s
not fair, he`s my baby and I love him. Please give him
back to me, even if it's only for me to say goodbye to him.
Please sister Mary," she pleaded.

Sister Mary's response to her outburst was to recoil and slap her hard across the face, and oblivious to Evelyn's distress, promptly headed for the door, leaving her with her head in her hands and her face smarting. Now more distraught than ever, Evelyn screamed and cried louder and louder, and sister Mary eventually turned to look back at her from the doorway.

Hopeful she would at least comfort her, Evelyn stared at her pitifully. But instead, she told her loudly and curtly,

"I`m extremely disappointed in you for putting on such
a show. You have serious problems, Evelyn. Your child is
far better off not having you as its mother."

Sister Mary`s words were hurtful, and Evelyn was shocked by her cruelty when she needed her the most. She realised she did not care about any of the girls, but only profiting from the sale of their babies. This was hard, especially when she had regarded her as a mother figure.

She never did discover what happened to her baby boy and continued to suffer pangs of nagging guilt and feelings of emptiness every time she thought of him. But after being summoned to sister Mary`s office a few days later, she went with some trepidation, worried she may be in for another beating.

However, sister Mary rather unusually took hold of one of her hands, asked her how she was feeling, and suggested she was now old enough to take her vows and become a true bride of God. Her sudden concern was surprising, and unsure what to say, Evelyn quickly asked for time to think about it, and she agreed she could have a week.

Life had been getting increasingly harder after all she had been through, and although the idea was initially unnerving, she pondered it over and over during that week. The things she had let Declan and Jefferson do to her were sinful, and although already thinking God was punishing her, seeking redemption, she decided to go through with it, hoping to pay penance for what she had done.

Evelyn took her vows with two other scared young girls in a simple ceremony, at the small Convent chapel a few days later, and although Declan had resided over the ceremony, and seeing him again was difficult, she was soon wearing the coif and veil with pride.

Becoming a nun did have some unexpected benefits, and to her surprise, not only did it give her a break from confinement in the Mother and Baby Home, but she no longer had to sleep in that horrible dormitory, food was better and the living conditions were generally much nicer at the Convent. She even had a bathroom complete with a proper bath attached to her room, so different from what she had been used to previously.

Although trying to forget all that happened because it was still very upsetting, having to return to work at the Home each day, was a constant reminder of her son, and the brief time she had with him.

Unable to sleep during some of the long dark winter nights, her mind often wandered back to Jefferson and Declan and what she had let them do to her, which made her feel especially guilty. But try as she may, having wanted to forget particularly Declan, seeing him at the Convent chapel, she realised she still had feelings for him, but thinking such things were even more of a sin, now she had taken her vows.

Feeling dirty, ashamed and in need of further punishment, she took nightly soaks in the bath, during which she frantically scrubbed herself wanting to feel clean, but managed only to scratch her skin so badly it bled, and eventually left scars, which she saw as a permanent reminder of her transgressions, and believed she deserved.

The only thing she could do to absolve herself of this feeling was to continually recite the Serenity Prayer, accompanied by lots of "Hail Marys" several times a day, every day. Initially, doing this soothed her, but soon this ritual took over her life and she could do nothing without making the recitations. Some days she was way too anxious to leave the Convent at all.

Sister Mary must have become aware of her fragile mental state and appeared unusually kind and helpful, and trying to coax her back to working at the Home, eventually issued her an ultimatum.

"Becoming a bride of God does not mean hiding away
Evelyn, rather it is your duty to help others. I expect to
see you back on the ward tomorrow at six o'clock sharp,
do you understand?"

Not daring to contradict Sister Mary for fear of possible later repercussions, Sister Evelyn begrudgingly went back to work but remained extremely anxious and depressed.

CHAPTER 44

While they continued working together, Frank continued to confide in Shauna. He explained that the Home was owned by Jefferson, an American from Boston, and Declan Griffin, the swarthy-looking, dark-haired local priest. Jefferson dealt with the Home`s finances and set up the baby trade between the two countries and frequently arranged for prospective barren couples to visit the home to choose babies and young children to adopt and take back to America with them.

"He's the smartly dressed, smarmy American, who thinks a lot of himself, the sort of man who cannot pass a mirror without looking into it, but be very wary of him, he can be quite predatory around women," he explained.

Shauna, unsure what he meant, did not ask, but it was obvious Frank did not like him, so she decided to avoid him, too.

"Do not be fooled, Declan may be a priest and appear much kinder and more caring, but he is just as bad as Jefferson, underneath."

Shauna liked that Frank felt he could talk to her and chose to confide in her, and now viewed him as one of the few people she could trust at the Home.

As time passed, she continued to think of him often and began feeling closer and closer to him. Completely trusting him, she hoped and prayed he would be there to deliver her baby, aware that he would do his best to ensure everything went all right.

CHAPTER 45

Shauna mid-1971

The baby growing inside her was the only thing Shauna had that was hers, and although initially unwanted, with the birth looming quickly, she hoped it was getting enough nourishment to grow big and strong, strong enough to survive. But having listened to what Frank said about the fate of most of the babies, she remained worried that her baby would be taken away, just like the others.

During the final month of her pregnancy, life continued as normal, and she spent most of her time in the Delivery Room. Most of it was night work, meaning she could sleep in the dormitory during daylight hours and when it was warmer. Although missing the "crack" with the other girls overnight, she at least escaped the miseries of the ward and was no longer washing clothes or using the mangles, something she found very tiring.

One night, when called to the Delivery Room, she found Frank already there and gently stroking a very anxious young pregnant girl's hand, trying to calm her down.

She heard him saying,

"Maureen, look at me, you must take some deep breaths. Do you understand? I know you don't feel ready, but your baby wants to come out now."

Although nodding, Maureen continued to look worried, beads of sweat glistened on her face, and she was becoming redder and redder with every pant.

"That's it, Maureen, push... push. Keep going, Maureen. Clever girl, I can see the baby's head now," said Frank excitedly.

With that last push, Maureen fainted, and Frank immediately tried to resuscitate her. Shauna watched on astonished at what she was witnessing. His actions were unusual because normally in this situation, he would have removed the baby with forceps, and the mother, would often be left to die back on the ward a few hours later, something that was always very difficult for the other girls to witness. But this time, appearing genuinely concerned for Maureen, he continued trying to resuscitate her for several minutes.

When she died in his arms, he looked so pitifully at Shauna, that she felt concerned. It was unusual for him to show his feelings like this. Watching him gently reposition Maureen`s body, and brush her matted hair away from her face with his hand, she was immediately by his side when he let out a loud sob.

She only just managed to steady him as he collapsed into a chair. Kneeling at his feet on the floor, after taking hold of one of his hands, she stroked it caringly. They had been through so many harrowing things together already, and gazing up at him, seeing such a deep sadness in his hazel eyes, her heart lurched in her chest. She had never seen him like this before, but something else happened that set her heart racing even more.

As if the most natural thing in the world, he bent his head and kissed her on the lips, and although shocked, she enjoyed the kiss immensely. Seemingly rejuvenated, pulling away from her suddenly, he asked,

"Right, are you up for helping me deliver the baby, then?"

She nodded, got to her feet and immediately went to his aid. Usually, both mother and unborn baby would die and be taken to the mortuary. However, it was evident this baby was coming, even though its mother had died. She saw Frank roll up his shirt sleeves, and after saying a brief prayer, climb up on the trolley, and straddle Maureen, one knee on either side of her. With her mouth wide open in surprise, she watched him pick up a sharp scalpel, and cut her stomach open. Blood and amniotic fluid gushed out, soaking the white bedsheets between his legs, and clutching the end of the trolley tightly, she worried she might faint. But this was too enthralling to watch for her to do that, and she continued to watch wide-eyed as Frank put both hands inside Maureen's abdomen, and pulled out a baby, bottom first.

It was such a funny spectacle that Shauna could not help uttering,

"Holy Mary, Mother of God, will you look at that now!"

Frank cut the cord, lay the baby on the trolley beside its mother, and pressed its chest several times with his fingers. When nothing happened, he tried mouth-to-mouth and kept trying until suddenly there was a little cough and lots of crying. He had saved the baby, and Shauna was astounded and both of them stood smiling at each other with tears streaming down their faces.

"We have a great time, don`t we, you and I?" he said.

She nodded and continued to grin, completely unaware of the shameful secret he had been plagued with since her arrival at the Home.

CHAPTER 46

Frank late 1970

Frank Clancy had been best friends with Micky O`Brien since they were toddlers. They lived next door to each other for years, but when they reached their teens and their hormones raged, things changed. Micky hung around with a different crowd and they drifted apart. Frank was always very studious and when he returned to Dublin after graduating from Cambridge University, he bumped into Micky and his friends in the street one evening.

Micky and his new friends all had jobs locally and never left Dublin. Seeing him again, they teased and taunted him about how all his childhood, when they were out drinking and partying, he constantly had his head buried in a medical textbook. Frank always felt different from the others and very much like the odd one out, especially having remained a virgin the whole time he was at Cambridge.

He did not usually drink either, but it was his twenty-third birthday, and after deciding to meet up with Micky at the local pub later, he downed several whiskies, before drunkenly confiding that he was still a virgin. After a couple of hours of solid drinking, Micky said he needed to be somewhere, and Frank, in his near paralytic state, insisted on going with him. By the time they arrived at the playing field, they had hatched a drunken plan together.

Micky left his friend swaying in the middle of the playing field, trying to smoke a cigarette, and fuelled by the alcohol, he had drunk at the pub to give him courage; did exactly what he had told him to do.

He stood watching the girl approaching through the foggy darkness, and when near enough, stepped forward and kissed her straight away. Enjoying his first-ever kiss with a woman, he instantaneously felt aroused. But the darkness was disorientating and after laying the blanket Micky had retrieved from his car on the way there, on the ground; he clumsily tried to guide her backwards onto it, unaware some of her hair got caught in his wristwatch.

She fell backwards and, unbeknown to him, hit her head on a stone hidden in the grass and was concussed. In his drunken aroused state, Frank knelt on the rug, ripped off her panties and his trousers, spat on his hand, and moistened the hairy area between her legs, before inserting himself, just as Micky had instructed. It all felt incredibly naughty and thrusting into her, the sensations became so overwhelming, that he could not stop thrusting.

Awaking a few hours later, cold, and shivery, realising he was still lying on top of the girl, with his trousers around his ankles, he gently rolled off her. His memories of the night before were vague, with his head pounding, and his mouth dry, he was glad it was foggy, and hopefully no one saw them.

After hurriedly and ashamedly pulling his trousers back up, he looked down at the girl. She appeared deeply asleep and looked very peaceful. Studying her for a few seconds, he realised she was only about fourteen or fifteen, was very pretty and had shoulder-length dark blonde hair. But seeing her looking so young, alone, and vulnerable in the cold light of dawn, a lump formed in his throat, and he felt guilty and embarrassed about what he had done.

Attempting to make amends, he wrapped her in the blanket to preserve her modesty and protect her from the cold, kissed her gently on her forehead, and ran back to his parent's home as quickly as possible. Feeling extremely embarrassed and upset after the events of that night, he never told anyone, not even Micky, what happened.

Later, after finishing his General Practice training, and still wanting to atone for his sins, he took a job at the Mother and Baby Home, hoping working for a charity helping unmarried pregnant women would ease some of his guilt.

When he saw Shauna in the Delivery Room at the Home, and she looked familiar, it was only after working with her for a while, and having flashbacks of that night at the playing field, he began to put two and two together, and was shocked to think she was the girl from the playing field and, the baby she was carrying, was probably his.

CHAPTER 47

Evelyn mid-1971

Frank was becoming increasingly worried about Evelyn, especially when he heard her still reciting Hail Marys, an obvious sign she was struggling. After her mental health declined further, he arranged a place for her in a local asylum. Aware the whole idea was scary; it was the only place she would receive the right treatment and would give her some much-needed respite from the Home.

Although admitting she had been feeling worse as each day passed, Evelyn was still very reluctant to go, but after Frank convinced sister Mary it was for the best, she reluctantly gave in and allowed her to go. Her mental health improved considerably during the first month, she started to think much more clearly and, to her surprise, began to quite like the place.

She even befriended several long-term residents and often walked on the grounds with them. One woman called Jo-Ann appeared very pleasant and kind, but told her she had no idea why she was there, which Evelyn thought meant that she had improved and would be leaving soon. However, it became apparent this was not the case when they were sitting having a cup of tea on the terrace one afternoon. Looking suddenly very worried, Jo-Ann had turned her back on her, and whispered,

"Can you see them? Can you see the marks, Evelyn?"

Evelyn was a bit nonplussed, and replied,

"What marks Jo-Ann?"

Jo Ann looked terrified and told her,

"The blood where they stabbed me. I can feel it trickling down my back."

Evelyn quickly became aware of just how ill Jo Ann was, especially when she also told her that "they" had been listening to her through the radio in her room and were watching everything she was doing.

She was also intrigued by a good-looking younger man who, on a good day would be strutting around in a full tuxedo, and winking at the ladies, but on his bad days would be unwashed, dressed scruffily, and cowering under the nearest table, too scared to come out.

There was also an older man with a straggly beard and unruly hair, who she was fascinated by. Spending most of his time wandering the grounds by day shouting indiscriminate swear words, to everyone`s amusement, his evenings were spent at the piano playing classical tunes, amazingly well, and she was often moved by his playing.

Being there was a real eye-opener, and up to that point she had led a very sheltered life. It also gave her space to ponder sister Mary's cruel comments, and what else she had had to put up with at the Home. Now aware of how bad it was for her health, she was even more desperate to get away.

After confiding in Frank during one of his many visits, she decided although drastic, to renounce her vows and leave the Convent altogether, despite hardly having any money, and asked for his help.

"I don`t care how poor I am, just so long as I can never return," she maintained when he looked at her, concerned.

He was surprised when she explained her plans to devote her life to helping unmarried mothers, preventing them from being taken to the Mother and Baby Home, and having their babies taken from them.

Despite thinking the idea was admirable, Frank wondered how she planned to fund herself. Wanting to help in any way he could, he gave her a small amount of money and suggested she move to the far outskirts of the city, where he had a four-bed house he had bought as an investment after his father died. No one would know her there, and it would be a suitable place for her to start her new life.

She was extremely grateful to him for suggesting that and promised to look after it and pay him rent. Contrary to Sister Mary's wishes, she left the Asylum smuggled out on Frank`s car and did not return to the Home, and he later signed a discharge form, transferring her to his care.

Overjoyed to have finally been able to leave, something most of the girls, could never do, Evelyn immediately started to feel better, but with hardly any money, life was still difficult. She could only pay Frank a small amount of rent and was relieved when he did not seem bothered about the rest when he next visited.

She told him, smiling.

"Thanks to you, I have my freedom now, Frank, and that means more to me than anything, and I am doing something worthwhile."

Aware of how little she had to live on, Frank remained concerned, but not needing the rent money, decided to ask her a favour instead, which turned out to be a very big favour, indeed.

CHAPTER 48

Frank mid-1971

Frank frequently visited Evelyn and was astounded at how quickly she found young, pregnant women, to move in and live with her, and was very relieved to see her looking so much better and happier. Aware of how many catholic unmarried pregnant women ended up on the streets after being disowned by their families, she regularly scoured the nearby roads and alleys and word soon got around that she provided shelter, and food for those who needed it.

The work was hard, and the money Frank initially gave her soon ran out, but after he permitted her to plant vegetables in the back garden, prune the old existing fruit trees, and keep chickens, she at least had a well-stocked larder. Soon, she was reaping the rewards of the good growing weather the warm sunny summer brought, and had plenty of fruit and vegetables and eggs to give the girls to eat, and some of her wholesome soup and bread, which she kept constantly warming on the stove. This was more nourishing than anything they would have had on the streets.

These good deeds brought with them a newfound confidence, and she appeared much happier still, which Frank was incredibly pleased to see, especially in light of the favour he needed, when he felt she was up to doing it.

Evelyn could tell Frank had something on his mind when he next visited, he looked so serious, and she worried what he was about to say. After loudly clearing his throat, he asked,

"Evelyn, there is something that has been on my mind for some time and I could do with your help with it."

"You've been so good to me Frank, whatever you want, I`m sure I can help," she said.

She watched him sit nervously in one of the two comfortable chairs by the fire.

"I am sorry, Evelyn, but I've been keeping a terrible secret for the past nine months and no one else, apart from you, can ever know about it."

He looked so serious she stopped what she was doing and went over and sat in a chair opposite him, looking uneasy. After staring at the floor for a few moments, he explained what happened that night on the playing fields, and how the baby Shauna was carrying, was his.

Evelyn was so shocked she could not speak at first, and he felt ashamed, after admitting what he had done aloud for the first time since it had happened.

"I have been racked with guilt and shame ever since," he said.

It was obvious to Evelyn he truly meant that, and she wondered what exactly he needed her to do.

"Shauna is not very far off giving birth and when the time comes, I have decided it best that rather than hand the baby over to Jefferson, and risk it being shipped away to America, I am going to pretend it died and I want you to take it instead, Evelyn. This is an ideal place for you to bring it up for the first few years of its life, and then perhaps you could both move somewhere else when the child reaches school age."

Evelyn sat looking at him with her mouth open for a few seconds, before replying,

"I cannot believe you did that to that poor girl, Frank,"

She continued,

"I want to help you, Frank, but this does not sound right.
I do not want to play any part in covering up what you did.
What you did was tantamount to what Jefferson did to me."
She went red in the face before adding,

"You are not the man I thought you were. I have always
trusted you, and I cannot believe you would even suggest
such a thing."

With that, she uncharacteristically walked out of the room,
obviously angry. He followed and when he touched her shoulder; she turned angrily around and stared at him, and he felt
himself blush.

"I know I have disappointed you, Evelyn, but I was not
myself that night. I know it is no excuse, but I was very
drunk," he said sheepishly.

"I know what you must think of me, Evelyn, but I am
truly sorry for what I did. Every time I see Shauna, I am
reminded of it, and I have been doing everything I can to
help her since I realised who she was. I cannot bear the
thought of Jefferson giving away my baby, and I am aware
of how devastated you were to lose your baby but cannot
think of anyone better than you to bring my baby up. It is
something I will be eternally grateful for."

"Yes, but surely it should be Shauna, and not me, who brings
up your baby, Frank?" she asked.

He shook his head.

"I wondered about that, but she is too young to take on that
sort of responsibility, and besides, Sister Mary would just
remove it, and I cannot let that happen. I think you would
make a wonderful mother, and I will ensure you are both
fully supported financially and have everything you need."

Evelyn asked Frank to leave because she wanted time alone
to think.

Seeing how angry she was with him; he was worried she may not agree to his plan. But when he returned to discuss it further the following day, to his relief, she said she would do it.

A few days later, hearing Shauna had been in labour in the main ward for several hours, he felt very guilty about what he was planning to do. He hated the idea of lying to her, but it was too late now to back out of his plan, and he dreaded the moment she arrived in the Delivery Room, and the subterfuge began.

CHAPTER 49

Shauna mid-1971

When the time came for Shauna to give birth, she was incredibly relieved to see Frank waiting for her, with Roisin assisting, as she was wheeled into the Delivery Room. It felt strange being on the trolley herself this time but knew she was in safe hands with Frank. But having already spent over eighteen hours writhing around in agony without pain relief on the ward, she was feeling increasingly exhausted and worried there may be something wrong with her baby.

Frank reassured her he would do his best for her and the baby and, after placing a mask over her face, told her to breathe in deeply for the pain, and she felt herself drifting off a bit, but remained still fully conscious. She must have fallen asleep at some point and awoke back on the ward later with no recollection of what happened, which was disconcerting.

What she did not know was Frank administered something else intravenously, as well as the gas and air she remembered inhaling, ensuring she would forget everything. The birth was very emotional for him, and he cried tears of joy, meeting his gorgeous, dark-haired baby boy for the first time, but had to quickly compose himself, seeing Roisin staring at him.

But it had been a huge relief that he was alright, and was a survivor, just like his biological mother. Amazed at how perfect he was when examining him from top to toe, he felt incredibly proud of his son, despite the conditions he was conceived under.

But soon racked with guilt, holding his son, something Shauna would perhaps never be able to do, herself, made him feel terrible. It had been worrying when partway through labour, she started losing quite a lot of blood and briefly fainted. But she did come round quite quickly, and in her disorientated state, was oblivious to what had gone on.

After he deposited his baby boy in an incubator in a side room, Evelyn later intercepted it, after sneaking in through a fire exit.

When Shauna awoke much later on the ward, feeling groggy, she was worried about her baby, when there was no sign of either Frank or Roisin, but trying to remain positive, assumed they were just busy, and very much hoped to be able to see her baby soon.

But despite being in such a fragile state, she was forcibly pulled out of bed, and washed in front of everyone, but with neither the strength nor the inclination to fight back, she silently allowed them to do what they had to do. Back in her uncomfortable bed again afterwards, worried, she fretted for several hours before finally seeing Frank walking onto the ward, and it was obvious by his expression, that things had not gone how she hoped.

Not wanting to discuss it there, he called her back to the Delivery Room, where after helping her gingerly walk beside him, he pulled up two chairs facing each other and beckoned her to sit down. It was horrible watching her sitting worriedly wringing her hands, waiting for him to speak, and he felt unusually nervous. Shauna on the other hand, was even more worried when he would not make eye contact and dreaded what he was about to say.

He shifted uncomfortably in his seat, reached forward, took hold of one of her hands, and began to tell her his version of what happened.

"I am so very sorry, Shauna, but there were complications, and your baby was stillborn."

He had said it and felt terrible.

CHAPTER 50

Shauna mid-1971

Shauna cried straight away, she had clung to the idea that somehow, she would differ from the other girls on the ward, and have a strong bonny baby, that she would get to bring up herself. But that had been just a fairy tale she had concocted to get herself through the last nine months. It was so sad to think that her baby, the baby she had given birth to, the baby she had often felt kicking and moving around inside her, had died.

Reality hit hard, and, with her mind racing, she had looked pitifully back at Frank, and he leaned forward, and caringly stroked her fringe back off her face. She pushed his hand away and asked,

"Was it my fault Frank? Was it something I did, or should have done?"

He shook his head.

"Please do not blame yourself, Shauna. Sometimes these things just happen. I am so sorry."

Shauna thought back to when Sister Mary kneed her in the stomach and decided that her baby, like so many others born there, never really stood a chance. She would never know the true cause of her baby's death but felt very guilty for any part she may have played in its demise. Hanging her head in shame, it felt like she had all the woes of the world on her shoulders and could see no clear path out of her despair.

Concerned, Frank had leaned forward and gently lifted her chin.

"Shauna, look at me. I honestly did the best I could. I did, and I am so sorry. Please do not blame yourself."

She had stared straight into his eyes when he said that, and noticing the tears that he was trying to fight back, she believed him, and was glad he had been there when her baby was stillborn. Unable to stop them, tears flooded down her face again. Frank moved his chair closer and hugged her tightly, and she relaxed into his embrace, sighing. The hug was so comforting, and lovely that she wished they could stay like that forever.

But they had to pull away from each other hurriedly a few minutes later when it sounded like someone was approaching and Shauna returned to the ward feeling bereft after her stillbirth, and soft, kind human contact again. She would do anything to escape the harsh reality of the desperate life she was now left with. Her baby had provided a glimmer of hope in a dire situation, and now there appeared to be no way out.

Back again in her narrow, uncomfortable, smelly bed, she wept continually and refused to eat or drink anything. It was only when Roisin wandered over just before the lights went out, and when Sister Mary was not looking, produced an apple and half-eaten bread roll from under her skirt, that she had stolen from the nun's kitchen, that she ate something.

To her dismay, she was allocated to work back on the ward the following day, and after a week there, Sister Mary approached her. Worried that she had done something wrong, she quickly bowed her head, afraid she might be slapped again. Instead, Sister Mary explained that Doctor Clancy wanted her back in the Delivery Room because Sister Evelyn was unavailable.

Although relieved to be back working with Frank, being there meant dealing with an endless stream of difficult pregnancies, which was extremely hard so soon after her own. Frank, was wanting to keep a close eye on her, which he could not do whilst she was working was on the ward. But remained aware it was probably too soon, and wondered how she would cope.

Shauna admitted she was relieved to be back working with him again, which he found incredible, and impressed by how strong a woman she was, he hoped his son, who he had decided to call William, had also inherited that strength of character.

Curious about Sister Evelyn's long disappearance and sudden, short reappearance, Shauna questioned Frank about it one day and, was further intrigued when he appeared cagey. It was left that she had gone to take care of some family business, which knowing her history, she thought strange. Frank hated lying about that too, but had to under the circumstances, felt he must.

When she was ready to hear it and when he felt composed enough, he told Shauna she had given birth to a little boy, and when she asked why she could not see him; he stared hard at the floor, for a few seconds, before blurting out,

"It was best you did not see him because he had congenital deformities."

He had to produce a plausible reason why she could not see her stillborn baby.

"What? What do you mean, Frank?" she had asked.

As soon as the words had flooded out of his mouth, he had felt excruciatingly guilty, even though he had explained it all as simply as he could, there was now no going back, and he felt terrible for lying and giving Shauna the impression that she had given birth to a severely deformed baby.

Shauna did not know what to say and immediately burst into tears. All her worst fears about being punished for what she had done, appeared to have materialised. Trying to comfort her and feeling upset for all the hurt he was causing, Frank put his arm around her and stroked her hair, as he had done previously, and when they made eye contact, as they had done so many times, previously, for a fleeting second, he was surprised to register just how beautiful her eyes were.

Completely caught up in her grief and his shame, he instinctively bent his head towards her and kissed her passionately on the lips, and she eagerly kissed him back. But aware of the ramifications of what they were doing, they both giggled and hurriedly pulled away from each other. Shauna looked ashamed, and Frank told her,

"It is the grief, Shauna. I care about you very much and hate seeing you so sad and upset. Forgive me, but I could not help myself. I`m so sorry, to do that when you are so vulnerable, was extremely unprofessional."

Although difficult to process, over the weeks that followed, Shauna came to accept what had happened as God's will, and further punishment for her sins, but remained incredibly sad and upset about losing her baby boy. Life quickly returned to normal, and she and Frank continued to work closely together and grew even more fond of each other.

Although they never mentioned it, both often thought about that kiss.

He never let it show, but Frank remained racked with guilt about what he had done.

Shauna, still grieving for her lost child, and completely convinced it was all her fault and she deserved God's punishment, remained completely unaware Frank`s sinful secret.

PART TWO

Chapters 51- 63

CHAPTER 51

Spending long hours away from home working at the Centre, Rory was finding it increasingly difficult being at the cottage alone. Aside from Dougal's occasional snore in his sleep and the odd bark or pant, the place felt extremely quiet and soulless without Rhona and Erick. Having initially been comforted surrounded by all Erick's paintings in his studio, that room now felt more like a shrine to the father he had so suddenly lost, and he quickly became quite depressed.

Although often tempted, he resisted the urge to raid Erick's Poitin cupboard and, after finding his old yoga mat in the back cupboard, started practising some of the yoga moves Rhona had taught him years earlier. Doing this made him feel considerably better, and quickly became his usual early morning routine, cheering him up as the longer, darker mornings of winter approached, and helping him relax and sleep better.

In addition, he walked Dougal across the fields and down to the lighthouse and back, before work, and did a route up and around the Beacon after returning from seeing Rhona every evening. The exercise and fresh air were good for him, and he especially enjoyed being out with Dougal early enough to catch the sunrise and sunset, just as he had done with her. The top of the Trevaunce Beacon was one of his favourite spots to think. The view from up there was amazing, it always brought a smile to his face and seemed to soothe him the most, just as it had done, Rhona.

Everything on the family front had gone noticeably quiet. He had not heard anything from Belinda since the funeral and, while glad, hoped it meant she was finally coming to terms with everything. But an uneasy feeling in the pit of his stomach remained every time he thought of her.

It took a while and was hard, but by late September, he felt he had properly settled back into his old life. He was enjoying working at the Centre again, which also proved a good distraction from the disturbing memories that had haunted him since the accident. Now looking forward to a bright happy future at the Trevaunce cottage too, Rory's life was sent completely off course, when something unexpected happened.

CHAPTER 52

Rory October 2014

On one unusual weekend off, Rory was sitting in the kitchen reading the paper with Dougal at his feet, when there was a loud rap on the door. He opened it to find Belinda standing on the doorstep. Seeing her was a shock, and he was caught off guard. She looked very angry, which was worrying, and when Toby came into view carrying a large suitcase, Rory felt very uneasy about what was going to happen next. His heart sank and before he could say anything, Belinda pushed past him and disappeared inside.

He remained where he was and asked Toby,

"What's going on, mate?"

Toby looked embarrassed and answered,

"I`m so sorry mate..."

His voice trailed off when Belinda returned and handed him a sealed letter, and not looking at him, said,

"Read this and everything will become clear."

Concerned, he had returned to the kitchen, and having detected the sound of menace in her voice, not wanting to open the letter immediately, he offered them both tea, which Toby accepted straight away, but Belinda just scowled back at him and impatiently asked,

"Well, are you going to read it then or not?"

Disliking her ordering him around, Rory glanced at Toby, who looked away, embarrassed.

"Better do as she says, mate," said Toby without looking up.

Both disappeared into the snug, leaving Rory anxiously holding the letter, and he quickly opened it after taking a deep breath, and began reading its contents. To his horror, it was an official letter giving him notice to vacate the property within the next four weeks.

Angry, he leaped up from the table and went off to find Belinda, and eventually found her in the studio room, gazing around at her father's paintings.

"You cannot do this, Belinda, you cannot. This is my home just as much as yours."

"Unless you can legally prove that you are my brother, this letter will stand, and if you cannot, then you are out. I do not want you sponging off my parent's estate anymore," she said.

Feeling shocked and angry and worried he might do something stupid, he decided to take Dougal for a walk, to try to calm himself down. Having fetched his lead, he returned to the studio went straight up to Belinda, and through gritted teeth, told her,

"I`m going to take Dougal for a walk and expect you both to be gone by the time I get back, do you understand?"

He was close enough to see small flecks of his spittle had landed and were glistening on Belinda's cheek. But she did not move and stared back at him with her hands on her hips.

"How dare you! How dare you order me around? You are in the wrong, and I will prove it."

He attached Dougal's lead and, after slamming the front door, quickly marched up to the field above the lighthouse and was out of breath by the time he got there.

CHAPTER 53

Rory 2014

Dougal was overly excited as it was his second walk that morning and ran around Rory in figures of eight, barking at him to play, but he continued walking until nearing the lighthouse. Here, he sat down on the grass and wept, while Dougal sat and looked at him. Having always known Belinda disliked him, he never expected it to go this far and was so angry and upset, that he punched the air furiously many times, and passers-by gave him funny looks.

Dougal snuggled up to him, wanting his tummy tickled, and he lay there with him, thinking, imagining the old Rhona's reaction to what Belinda had done; one thing was certain, she would have been very cross with her daughter. After wiping his eyes his jumper sleeve and getting up, he hurried to the cliff edge, where he stood gazing around him at the view, just like he used to do regularly with Rhona and Erick. It was a bright day, and he could see right the way down the coast and stood watching the gently rippling blue waters of the sea lapping the rocks beneath him and herring gulls dancing above it in the sky.

He remembered Rhona telling him that looking at a wonderful view, makes your worries seem less significant and she was right, but the worry and knot in his stomach remained. Halfway back, remembering the large suitcase Belinda and Toby had brought, he turned tail and ran back to the cottage with

Dougal as quickly as possible. Although relieved to see their car gone, he was concerned what they may have taken away with them, in his absence.

CHAPTER 54

Scouring the house, Rory ended up in Erick, and Rhona's bedroom, which had been ransacked. The photos on the dressing table were all gone, many of which he had intended to take into Rhona at the Care Home, and pictures had been removed from some of the walls. Horrified, he went back downstairs again to Erick`s studio room, which he thought was left untouched, and discovered his favourite painting of the coral beach near where he grew up, was also gone, which was heartbreaking.

His stress levels increased further after Padraig phoned to tell him they had a date for the reading of Erick's Will, and wanted everyone to attend, including him. Not wanting to ever see Belinda again, he was very reluctant to go, but the others insisted he was a part of the family and should be there. He still felt like he was an outsider whilst the Will was read and felt he was encroaching on something that was none of his business. This was not helped by seeing Belinda scowling at him the whole time, which made him feel even more uncomfortable. She annoyingly smiled, when it was confirmed she inherited the Trevaunce cottage, meaning the terms of her letter giving Notice would stand. Orla and Padraig inherited the Cullenmara cottage and Rory was unsurprised he was not mentioned.

Although he had lived with Erick and Rhona as their lodger and friend for over two years, it had only been a couple of weeks before the accident, that Erick and Rhona discovered he was their biological son, and way too soon for any Will changes. The real blow was when Belinda announced she now had a full Power of attorney over Rhona, something she had hidden from everyone and did not go down well with Padraig and Orla.

Much to their relief, Belinda had to get back to London, leaving just him, Padraig, and Orla together. The solicitor`s office was in Trezance, and he suggested it would be fitting to go along to the Fishing Boat Inn, in nearby Treggenhow, and have bowlfuls of fish chowder and Guinness, one of Erick's favourite things to do.

It was strange being back there without Rhona or Erick, and from the moment Rory bent his head to enter the old traditional stone pub, memories of his times there with them came flooding back as vividly as if they had only just happened. To distract himself from getting emotional, he asked Padraig and Orla what they would like to drink and from the bar, watched them go over and sit at a table in the corner by the window.

Seeing them in deep in conversation, and not wanting to intrude, he waited with the drinks at the bar, until he saw Orla get up and go off to the toilet, and then carried the drinks over on a tray, and sat himself down opposite Padraig.

"I`m not sure what I`m going to do bro, I have only got another couple of weeks at the cottage. I`m toying with the idea of turfing the long-term tenants out of my old flat in Camluggan, which holds loads of bad memories, but it`s good to have the income from that and my job at the Centre now," he confided.

"We feel terrible about what Belinda has done, it is so cruel of her to chuck you out when you are grieving too," Padraig said, looking genuinely concerned.

"I just do not get it at all. Belinda should be pleased she has another half-brother and not behave like this.

I do not know what has got into her lately. We were talking about her. She had no right to go behind our backs and get the Power of attorney over Rhona. We should have been involved, all of us. I`m not sure she even followed the correct procedure. She would have needed Rhona's consent, and in her current state, she would not be unable to give it."

Orla returned and the fish chowder arrived at the table.

"I've just been telling Rory how disgusted we are with Belinda's behaviour," said Padraig.

She shrugged her shoulders,

"I guess there's not much we can do about it, especially as she now officially owns the cottage."

They all went silent apart from letting out the odd slurp, as they hungrily ate the soup and big hunks of bread that accompanied it. Rory finished his first and, after wiping his mouth with a serviette, asked,

"How's life on the farm then Padraig?"

Not wanting Belinda to remain the sole topic of conversation, it was good to think about something else. He, Padraig, and Orla were still getting to know each other and had not seen each other much.

Padraig explained how busy he and Lou, his partner, were at the farm, but did enjoy the work, even though it meant early starts and long days.

"I love the solitude," he said.

"What do you mean? I always thought farms were very noisy places," Rory remarked, intrigued.

"It is Dad's fault, he got me so used to living in the middle of nowhere, surrounded by countryside in Cullenmara when I was young, and I`m now in my element at the farm, with just the surrounding cows, and no people for miles. I still crave that feeling of freedom and calm, I suppose."

Having grown up in Cullenmara himself, Rory knew exactly what he meant.

He was thinking about that when he suddenly remembered the piece of land Heidi, one of Rhona's best friends, had beside her house. Erick's campervan was left there while he was in hospital previously, and there had been a caravan on it when he collected the van before they all went off to Cullenmara together.

"Talking to you has given me an idea. I wonder if Heidi would let me rent her caravan. I think she might appreciate the extra revenue."

He sat back in his seat and smiled.

"That sounds like a plan," said Orla.

Neither Orla nor Padraig could stay long, as both had commitments, but Rory enjoyed spending time with them again and continued to feel closer to them than he had ever felt to Belinda. Extremely aware of how easily they could have disowned him too, he appreciated them caring about him and wanting to help.

CHAPTER 55

Belinda October 2014

Belinda returned to London triumphant, after their Trevaunce visit. Unbeknown to Toby, while rooting around in the cottage when Rory was walking Dougal, she found one of his combs and removed strands of hair to send for DNA testing.

So wrapped up in defaming Rory, she had been blissfully unaware of how all this was affecting Toby, and how distant she had become. He had been feeling very unsettled and often thinking about their relationship, wondered what he could do to save it.

He had fallen in love with Belinda soon after they first met, and reflecting, he wondered if they had rushed into living together too quickly, especially now he was seeing such a different side of her. He had initially been drawn to her directness, her "go-getting" approach to life, and the fact that nothing ever seemed to phase her. Those qualities had been exciting and attractive, compared to the other women he had met at university, who had seemed so timid. But over time, had increasingly become aware she was pushing him further and further down on her list of priorities. He understood her family meant the world to her, and that they should be uppermost in her considerations, but since her father's death, living with her had become almost unbearable. All they seemed to do was argue, and when they were not arguing, there was a cold atmosphere between them.

He had made various attempts to deflect their conversations away from Rory and encourage her to confide in him about how she was feeling about her father's sudden death, hoping that allowing her to express her grief, instead of directing anger toward Rory, would make her feel better. But she appeared unwilling and unable to do that and remained angry. However, recently she seemed not only just angry with Rory, but with him, and the whole world too.

From Belinda`s point of view, before the accident, she had always had Rhona to go to, to talk things through with, and she had always provided a wise old shoulder for her to cry on. Now she could no longer do that, she felt lost. The accident had knocked everything off-kilter and she felt isolated and upset, and that no one understood her anymore, not even Toby, who she had always relied on previously. Aware that their recent difficulties were seriously impacting both their lives, she assumed he loved her enough to weather the storm. But when her relationships with colleagues at work also became affected, she felt even more isolated.

To then see her mother confused and not recognising her, when she had visited the care home, had been the last straw. Both her parents had been brilliant over the years, a formidable team that had guided her through all life`s difficulties, and without them, she was rudderless, swaying from one mood to the next, unsure what to do to feel better.

When one of her only remaining, long-term friends suggested she needed counselling, she had initially been very reluctant, but now, realisation was dawning, that she needed to do something drastic to sort herself out. The scariest thing was that out of desperation, in an attempt to blot everything out, she had started drinking regularly, and was soon also snorting cocaine, which was surprisingly easy to get hold of locally. Although aware this was a slippery slope and could end her legal career if caught, the exciting, buzzy feeling doing this gave her, not only pepped up her mood and made her feel euphoric, but helped ease the grief. But incredible lows followed every euphoric episode. Luckily, she could only afford to buy cocaine now and then, and after going out clubbing with her friend one evening, she had returned home, obviously very high.

Toby recognised the signs straight away, and although not saying anything at the time, watched her closely, from then on, worried what she might do next. As usual, she had awoken the following day feeling groggy and experienced the worst low she had ever had, a low so low that she decided she would rather be dead than ever feel like that again. Feeling like this frightened her, and in utter desperation, she phoned the counsellor her friend had told her about. She told no one, not even Toby, and had begun to have regular sessions.

Unaware of her decision to have counselling and feeling totally fed up with her never listening to him, Toby decided he had had enough, worried that if he stayed with her, his mental health would also suffer. But Belinda was feeling too overwhelmed with enough grief and loss already, to try to get him back, and despite still having strong feelings for him, in her current state of mind, she just let him go.

CHAPTER 56

Rory 2014

Rory visited Heidi at her smallholding above Trezance on his way back from Treggenhow, and after explaining his predicament, was relieved when she said she was happy to let him, Dougal, and Tigger live in the caravan on her land. There was something about him she had always liked, and she was glad to have someone trustworthy to help her look after her animals whenever she went on holiday. She had been wondering how she would cope on her own after recently splitting up with her long-term partner, and so he appeared a godsend.

Heidi was one of Rhona`s closest friends. They had met when she volunteered at the Refuge in Trezance, and it had been her who had convinced Rhona to do her full counselling training, and they spent many happy years working together. Heidi had been there for Rhona after her partner Bryn fell to his death while climbing in Wales, and also after she lost Bryony the daughter she was carrying, and they had been good friends for over thirty years.

Rory was pleased because Heidi did not charge much at all, for the caravan, and although scruffy on the outside, it was quite warm and cosy inside. He was delighted after having managed to rig up a rudimentary ariel and borrow a small television from the Centre, he had something to do during the cold long nights of winter.

Before meeting Rhona, he had frequently drowned his sorrows in the pub, but she taught him the importance of looking after himself properly, especially when life got difficult. She had explained that, although seeming like a temporary solution, alcohol was a depressant and would play havoc with his sleep patterns and make him even more depressed and unable to cope, so he cut down his intake dramatically. Since heeding her advice, his life had certainly changed for the better, and indebted to her for all she had taught him, he still visited her whenever he could.

But as things turned out, he soon had other things to keep him occupied, too.

CHAPTER 57

After receiving a phone call from his tenants telling him he had some post, Rory drove up to his flat in Camluggan, and seeing most of it was addressed to Josie, was a surprise. He had long ago accepted that her and Lottie`s disappearance from his life was permanent, and given up trying to find her and her mother on facebook, and other social media platforms since they disappeared. He had missed her terribly and often wondered where she and Lottie were, hoping wherever they were they were happy, healthy, and maybe missing him a little, too.

Unable to face opening the letters straight away, he quickly stuffed them in his coat pocket and returned to the caravan, where after making himself a cup of tea, he initially stared at them, trying to decipher the postmarks, and began opening them one by one, to read their contents, hoping they would indicate where they had gone.

Three were unpaid bills, that he promptly threw in the bin, one an advertising circular, and another was a letter from Josie`s old GP advising her smear test was due. It was the last one that was the most interesting, it was from a Somerset-based cleaning company, informing Josie that she had not got the job, but they would keep her details and be in touch if another position came up.

Rory could not remember Josie ever having any connection to Somerset, and it was particularly interesting to think she and Lottie might not be so far away from him as he originally thought, and he had gone to work the next day feeling a lot more positive.

Coincidently, he was sent to collect a man with complex care needs from Bristol, and Angela the manager, would accompany him on the drive and look after the man. It was highly unusual for them to take clients from so far away, but he had relatives in the Treggenhow area.

Rory was apprehensive because although working for Angela for over two years, they had never spent time alone together before. But he need not have worried because, despite her ultra-professional appearance, she shared the same dry sense of humour, and they chatted happily for most of the way.

After stopping off at a supermarket to buy chocolate and other things to eat on their return journey, Rory was heading back across the car park when something stopped him in his tracks. He recognised them both straight away, the golden brown curls, so unmistakably Josie and Lottie, and he stared at Lottie, so grown up in her jeans, little boots and baggy jumper, and was grinning as she helped her mother carry the shopping bags. Peering around a large pillar, he watched them smiling together. They appeared deep in conversation while walking to the edge of the car park, where they stopped and seemed to be waiting for something. All Rory`s impulses were telling him to go over, but wondering what sort of reception he would get, he held back.

"Feck, I`m going over to them," he said aloud.

But before he had the chance, a small black convertible car with a personalised number plate pulled up in front of them, and he watched a tall man with longish dark hair get out, run over and help them put their bags in the boot. Rory hoped it was a taxi, but there was no signage on the vehicle to indicate this, and he continued watching as the man put his arm around Josie, kissed her on the cheek, and cuddled Lottie and they all got into the car and drove off. This was mortifying. He had been so excited to see them again, particularly his little Lottie, who did not look so little anymore, but now all his hopes were shattered.

Seeing them looking so happy, he realised how selfish it was of him to think they would want a sad, grieving man, with no money and prospects like him, back in their lives again. They were obviously both very settled and happy with this other man, and he was glad to see that, but it did not make it any less painful and he felt a tremendous sense of hurt and sadness afterwards.

Angela detected there was something wrong when he returned to the van and asked,

"Are you alright Rory?"

She was sitting in the back of the van beside the new client and after checking he was comfortable, squeezed herself between the two front seats to sit next to Rory, worried.

"You look like you`ve seen a ghost."

"I`ve just seen my wife and child," he replied quietly, not wanting to wake the client.

having already told her a little about his past on the journey up, she looked concerned.

"That must have been a bit of a shock, " she said.

"What did you do? Did you go over to them?"

He shook his head.

"Don`t think I want to talk about this now, Angela."

He switched the radio on low and, sensing how upset he was, she changed the subject and soon had him laughing again. But seeing Josie and Lottie again had unsettled him, and he could not get them out of his mind. Lottie looked so beautiful and was glowing with health and vitality and seeing her like that made him realise that her happiness was far more important to him than anything else, but he just wished he could still be a part of her life.

He recalled the chats he had often had with Erick about Padraig and Orla, and what he had said about never giving up hope. Although it had taken years, he had eventually managed to have them back in his life, and this thought inspired Rory.

About six weeks later, an official-looking letter, delivered first to the Trevaunce cottage and redirected by Belinda, arrived at the Centre. It was from Josie`s solicitor asking him for a divorce. After witnessing what he had in the car park, he was not surprised, but it still came as a massive blow. But thinking back to a conversation he had with Rhona when she pointed out that the most important person in all this was Lottie and her well-being. Hard as it was to let them go, it was the best thing he could do as a father, and he signed the letters quickly and returned them in the past before he could change his mind.

It had been hard closing that chapter in his life, but he could now fully concentrate on his situation and try to work through his grief. He also remembered Rhona telling him,

"Grief is love with nowhere to go, and with each day

that passes, you develop better ways of coping with it."

He knew he would get through it all eventually, and thinking about what Rhona had also told him about being kind to himself, he now needed to focus on the things in his life that made him the happiest, and not dwell on the past anymore.

But that was easier said than done.

CHAPTER 58

Rory and Angela October 2015

Since their return from Bristol, Rory's relationship with Angela changed, and they became good friends. He knew she was married and did not want to overstep the mark; her friendship was more important to him than that. But as the weeks passed, she confided in him, and he realised things in her private life were not what they appeared to be on the surface. He had met her husband, Roger, several times, and they had occasionally gone for a beer together. But although a nice guy, Rory did think he was a bit of a know-it-all.

One evening Rory arrived back late at the Centre after collecting a patient from Truro and went to the office to return his keys to the key cupboard in Angela`s office as usual. He put the light on and was surprised to find her sitting at her desk in the darkness, her eyes looking red from crying. He felt embarrassed for barging in,

"Oh, sorry Ange, I did not know you were in here," he said.

She continued to cry, and he went over to comfort her.

"Whatever is the matter?" he asked.

He leaned in close to her to reach the key cupboard and return the keys, and being close to her, instinctually placed a comforting arm around her. She buried her face in his armpit and continued crying.

"I do not think I can take any more. Hold me, Rory, please hold me," she said.

Having never seen her like this before, he was concerned.

She stared back at him, teary-eyed as he continued to hold her, so close that he could feel her warm breath on his neck. Suddenly, with feelings intensifying, feeling her heart beating against his, he hugged her tighter. At that moment, nothing else mattered, and they began hungrily kissing each other and pulling at each other's clothing. Rory swept several items off her desk and onto the floor and after pulling Angela's knickers down her long legs, threw them to one side. Staring into her eyes, looking for an indication he should continue when she lay back and seductively parted her legs, he had got his answer and was on top of her straight away.

She grabbed him around the waist, pulled him toward her, and began kissing him more and more ferociously. There was no going back now, and both were soon letting out increasingly louder, ecstatic moans, until they simultaneously orgasmed. They laid back giggling, still out of breath, and Rory snuggled up to Angela, and she brought her leg up over him, and they continued to kiss, giggle and hug and soon lost track of the time.

Rory was the first to break away.

"Well Ange, that was a surprise..." he said, breathlessly.

She smiled and cheekily replied,

"I do not know what came over me."

"I do," he said winking.

Realising the time, they both hurriedly dressed, and after one last long lingering kiss, went their separate ways. But from then on, met up whenever they could in secret, and Rory thought he had found his soul mate.

CHAPTER 59

Rory and Angela 2015

It was surprisingly easy for Rory and Angela to meet up after work and she told her husband she was doing an evening class in Trezance. After their regular love-making sessions in her office, they sometimes went down to the pub on the quay in Treggenhow for a couple of drinks and to talk, at a time when they knew it was quietist. Although they tried not to think about Roger, he often cropped up in conversation. Angela explained how she had fallen for him almost immediately. He was tall and slim, had a thick head of hair, a long Roman nose, and she liked the way his top lip curled up slightly when he spoke.

Noticing how sad she looked when talking about him one evening, Rory commented,

"Are you ok Ange, only you look tired and not really yourself tonight?"

"Oh, thanks for telling me that, you do know how to make a girl feel good!" she exclaimed, smiling.

He immediately apologised.

"It's ok, I was only kidding,"

She averted her gaze to the floor, and Rory was worried he had said or done something else wrong. When she eventually looked up, she said,

"They say that you can`t choose who you fall in love with, and it should have all been fabulous. We both loved each other and had lots in common, and I got on very well with his grown-up children. But after we married, everything changed, Roger seemed constantly in a bad mood. All I ever wanted was for him to be happy, but he seems disinterested in everything I do, and anything about me. For some reason, he seems to deliberately sabotage any good times we have, by suddenly losing his temper over the stupidest things."

She sighed.

"I feel like I`m walking on eggshells, and I never know what mood he will be in from one moment to the next. When I start relaxing our good times, it is like he senses this, and suddenly rears up at me and says such awful things that I usually end up in tears. I`ve tried speaking to him about it, but he says he cannot change. But it comes out of nowhere, leaving me feeling shaken and shocked to the core."

Rory took hold of her hand and gently stroked it.

"It sounds a bit like what living with Josie was like."

She continued,

"Don`t get me wrong, he`s been kind to me and I`m very grateful for that. But every time he blows up at me, he acts like nothing has happened, and never apologises for upsetting me. What is the worst is when he then blames me for his behaviour and says I made him do it! It's been get-ting me down, I`d hoped things would improve after he retired, but they only got worse. Now, all he seems to want to do is pick apart everything I say and constantly contradict me."

Tears welled up in her eyes.

"I do not know how much more I can take."

Rory was shocked hearing how bad things had got.

"He`s never physically hurt you has he?" he asked.

She shook her head and he was relieved.

Although they continued to meet regularly in secret, sleeping together, and talking sometimes for hours, Rory sometimes felt bad about what they were doing. But he had fallen head over heels in love with Angela and, as time went on, was increasingly wanting to be with her and to go public about their relationship. But Angela had other ideas, and he had to go along with them. She said she still loved her husband, which he understood, and although she said she could see a much brighter, happier future with him, she was not wanting to rush into anything and hurt Roger any more than necessary. So Rory had to wait until she was ready, and having no idea how long that would be, was exasperating.

Another issue was that Angela knew so many people through her job, and feared being seen when they went out. Desperate that Roger never finds out about them, they end up just staying in the office and stopping going to the pub.

Rory viewed this as a big backward step, and not having many friends in Cornwall, had no one to confide in about it. Instead, internalising his feelings, frustrations and the growing insecurity about the affair, started to affect him. He hated all the subterfuge, and with Angela so adamant she did not want to hurt Roger, he often wondered where exactly the relationship was heading.

Aware constantly having to hide his clandestine affair was preventing him from going out and meeting new people, and making new friends in the area, in case they knew Angela or Roger, he often worried that he was doing the wrong thing. But convinced, she was his soulmate, hoped for some kind of divine intervention that would make Angela leave Roger, but worried that might never happen. Having found her, he could not envisage life without her and certainly did not want to go out and meet any other women.

It was insidious at first, but the feelings of isolation combined with the uncertainty of how the affair would pan out, along with Angela seeming to be calling all the shots, really started to take its toll. But not wanting to end the relationship, they continued seeing each other whenever they could, convinced they were being discreet, and no one would ever know about the affair.

But someone had seen them together and things soon quickly deteriorated.

CHAPTER 60

Zena Late 1986

Although aware that she was getting closer to giving birth, Zena jumped at the opportunity to get a tickets for the Peter Frampton concert in Perth, and had been on her way there by train, and just disembarked, when her waters broke on the station platform. A woman, waiting on a seat nearby, rushed to her aid, concerned. But loving live music, gripping her stomach tightly, Zena cursed, and asked,

"Can`t I still go to the concert? I`ve always wanted to see Peter Frampton. I`m sure I`ll be all right. I don`t think my baby`s ready to come out yet."

She eventually gave in after the paramedics arrived and convinced her it was not only dangerous for her, but also her baby, to wait, she went with them to the nearest hospital.

The most memorable thing about the birth, apart from Geoff arriving not long after she was transferred to the Delivery Suite, holding her hand, and telling her to remain calm, was the pain. She had never experienced anything like it before.

Adamant she wanted a natural birth, just like her Aboriginal friends, she managed to be very brave early on, but when the labour pains were increasing and seemingly going on forever, she eagerly accepted everything the hospital suggested to make her more comfortable, but remained in considerable pain.

"I am never ever doing this again!" she shouted at Geoff, after he had told her several times to calm down.

"Calm down! How would you feel if something the size of
a large melon was trying to force its way out of a hole
the size of a ping pong ball?"

Although shocked at her uncharacteristic anger, finding
what she said amusing, he chuckled to himself, while continuing to hold her hand and try to calm her, while she gripped
it tighter and tighter with each contraction. As a doctor, he
was used to dealing with difficult births and was also used to
women hurling abuse at their partners during labour.

When she was eventually dilated enough, the midwife gave
Zena permission to push with all her might, which she did several times, shrieking, grunting, and panting loudly. Exhausted
by this point, she glared at Geoff, red in the face, grimacing,
sweating profusely, and feeling sorry for her, after making eye
contact with the midwife, he told her quietly and calmly,

"Just one more big push now Zena."

Suddenly, having summoned up the energy to give one last
big push, Zena felt the baby slide out, gripped Geoff`s hand
even tighter than she had been, and then held her breath,
waiting for her baby`s first cry. But there was silence at first,
which was worrying, and she was just going to ask what had
happened when her baby let out a very loud, robust cry.

Although completely exhausted, the very first time she held
her baby in her arms was incredible, and she could not stop
teas of absolute joy from streaming down her face, at seeing
her gorgeous and perfectly formed baby girl blinking up at her.
It was overwhelming to think she could feel so much love for
this baby, whom she had only just met.

Breastfeeding was initially difficult but after a couple of days,
her baby daughter latched on, and Zena was relieved, knowing
that as a nurse, this meant she could go home soon, she could
not wait to be back in her own bed again. But when her blood
pressure was taken and was higher than it should have been,
she was forced to remain in hospital until it stabilised.

The extra time at the hospital gave her more chance to think of a name for her baby girl. Having painstakingly gone through all the usual names, not one to stick to convention, she decided,

"Janis, I`m going to call you Janis, after Janis Joplin, she was a strong, feisty woman and that`s what I want you to be like too."

CHAPTER 61

Mitch 1986

Mitch had long given up on the idea of ever seeing Zena again. But having bumped into his sister, Franny, who excitedly told him how she helped a pregnant woman on the railway station platform when she was waiting for her train, his ears pricked up.

Franny had said,

"It was so funny. She was more concerned about missing the concert than having her baby, and in fact, she still contemplated going!"

"Where was this?" he asked.

"East Perth, "she replied.

The coincidence was too great. It surely could not be her, he pondered. She had only been a few miles south from where he had seen her that day.

"Do you remember what she looked like?" he asked.

"She was striking, had red hair and green eyes, and wore very brightly coloured clothes."

Mitch knew immediately it was Zena, and after searching the local hospitals pretending to be her partner, he eventually found her. To say she was surprised to see him was an understatement. She had just finished breastfeeding and had laid Janis on her cot when there was a knock on the door.

A nurse entered and told her that her partner was there to see her, which was confusing.

She had barely enough time to respond before Mitch peered around the door awkwardly, looking embarrassed, seeing she was breastfeeding her newborn baby.

"Oh, sorry! I know you will think this strange, and I certainly don't want to freak you out, but when my sister told me she had helped a pregnant woman with red hair at the railway station, I had to check if it was you and make sure you were all right. I hope you do not mind?" he said.

After hurriedly pulling her dressing gown back on, she glared at him, speechless.

"I'll understand if you think I've overstepped the mark,"
he said.

He could feel her green eyes on him, as he stared nervously back at her and then, half smiling, she said,

"Well, being as you are here, you might as well stay a while."
Mitch immediately relaxed.

Zena was secretly pleased to see Mitch, having often thought of him over the last three months, and had never expected to see him again. Forgetting what he looked like close-up, she welcomed the warmness of his smile and the way his hazel eyes sparkled when he looked at her. Although they had spent over an hour together previously, she had forgotten how ruggedly handsome he was, and after giving him her best attempt at a sexy lingering stare, he responded by asking,

"You alright Zena, only you looked deep in thought?"
She smiled, and he remembered just how beautiful her smile was.

"Yes, I was deep in thought, maybe one day I will tell you what I was thinking about."

She gave him a mischievous wink, which made him even more intrigued. Both jumped at a sudden knock on the door and in walked Geoff.

"Oh, er sorry mate, did not realise she had any other visitors."

To Geoff, it felt like he had walked in on something he should not have, and Zena quickly interjected,

"Mitch, this is my uncle, Geoff,"

"Geoff, this is Mitch, the chap who helped me change my wheel that time on the main road."

"Alright, mate? Geoff asked, looking him up and down.

Mitch put his hand out and shook Geoff's hand firmly and he liked him straight away.

"Good to meet you, mate."

Zena could tell Geoff was impressed by Mitch's politeness and directness when immediately both men started chatting about everything, including where they were from, what they both did for a living and how well the Ozzie side had done in the rugby against England.

She sat quietly watching them, enjoying seeing how easily Mitch built up a rapport with people, and warmed to him even more.

Geoff invited Mitch over for supper the next day, which coincided with her finally being discharged from the hospital. It was great how her family accepted him into the fold straight away, and she remained completely captivated by him. This was scary, as it had been a while since she last felt that way about someone, and that had been Erick.

Being constantly surrounded by big strong guys working in the goldfields, there had been opportunities over the last few months, but they usually did or said something that put her off them, and it was exciting to think she may have now met her perfect match.

CHAPTER 62

Zena and Mitch 1986

Mitch Crosby had always lived in Western Australia, and his parents Jon and Joan, ran a local hardware shop. He left school at sixteen and decided to become a carpenter, just like his father. He loved working with wood and often spent hours in the workshop at the side of his parents' house. Enjoying being creative, over the years he became well known in the Perth area for his ornately carved bannisters and balustrades, and had a reputation for being able to turn his hand and lathe to anything a customer commissioned him to do.

Living in a suburb near Perth with his parents was all right, but he yearned to get a place out in the sticks in the Outback. Preferring the peace, quiet, and simpler life there, aged twenty-seven, he moved out of their house and rented a place in Kalgoorlie, with a large outside shed for him to work in, and lived there until an ideal plot of land became available.

When he first met Zena, he was on his way down to the plot far into the outback, where he was part-way building himself a log cabin. When he finished it only a few months later, he could not wait to move in. It was strange, but for the first time in his life, he wanted to settle down, and ever since meeting Zena, had daydreamed that the two of them would meet, fall in love and live together there.

There had always been a constant flow of women through his life, but none of them had been as independent, driven, determined, and yet so feminine, as her, and he had been enthralled with her straight away. It had been wonderful seeing her in the hospital not long after Janis was born, and he had driven her and her daughter back to their caravan and later went for a meal with her, Geoff, and Yindi.

Mitch, had suffered from a stutter as a child, and been quite an introvert, and the thought of meeting all Zena`s family and friends, was quite daunting, when he did, it felt like they had all known each other for years, and they had a very enjoyable evening eating, drinking, and talking, and he and Zena were inseparable from then on, and Mitch was overjoyed that his idle daydream might in fact, come true.

His cabin was less than five miles away from Geoff`s homestead, which was close by outback standards. Although she always liked her little caravan, Zena did not need to think twice about her and Janis moving in and living with Mitch in the log cabin, long-term. It was a much better environment to look after a small baby, and although there were times when Mitch went up to Perth to work, Zena and Janis were happy there alone, just the two of them. The cabin stood nestled in a little valley, from which it was about an hour's walk to the sea, and she was in her element there. It was not long before she had Janis swimming with her and walking the dusty track alongside her, and had to admit that being there was bliss.

Zena had enlisted Yindi`s help in planting a small vegetable garden and fruit trees around the back of the cabin. These took a while to grow, but in the meantime, she learnt how to forage for food in the outback, and was shown where to find useful medicinal and nutritious plants. This was all extremely interesting, and Zena loved the idea of living off the land, without the need to do weekly shopping in Kalgoorlie, which often took a day and was very tiring.

Since leaving, she only returned to Riverton once, about a year after Janis was born. It was a flying visit to see her father when he was ill. But by the time she reached Riverton Station, and walked up to her parent's house, he was already in bed and deeply unconscious. It was such a shock seeing her usually strong, jovial-spirited father in such a state, but she was still glad she had gone and had at least been able to talk to him, stoke his hand, and spend precious time with him, even if he was unaware she was there.

It was a very emotional time, during which she also made peace with her mother, who admitted how sorry she was for how she behaved the last time she saw her. Although showing her mother photos of Janis, now in her seventies her mother appeared disinterested. This, Zena found strangely comforting because it meant that all those years she had spent feeling like she did not measure up, and that her mother was always cross with her, were nothing to do with anything she had done, but purely down to her mother just not ever feeling maternal. The way she behaved towards her over the years, had been no reflection on her, but said more about her mother.

Her father passed away peacefully with them both at his bedside and after her mother broke down into floods of tears, despite her previous attitude to her, Zena hugged her tightly and consoled her.

Acutely aware she now needed to be the strong one, she set about sorting everything out, aware she was in no fit state to do it herself. She arranged funeral directors, collected the death certificate, and registered the death.

After remaining inconsolable for days, her mother eventually started to calm down, and told her, for the very first time in her life, how much she loved her, appreciated her help, and continued to open up to her about herself. It was hard to think of leaving her, now that she had apologised and their relationship was so improved, and also remaining concerned about her, Zena stayed on a bit longer, during which time she managed a quick trip down to Cornwall, where she met up with Erica. She had hoped to also track Erick down, tell him about his daughter, and apologise for leaving him like she had. But discovering he had left the Newlyn house; she had no idea where he had gone.

Although still very sad about her father's sudden passing, after some further really good conversations with her mother, she returned to Australia, feeling more confident and relaxed. So much so, that she took the bold step of deciding to home-school Janis. Although a bit of a chore at first, with time she felt she got better at it and continued until she turned eleven, when she was extremely pleased and proud to see her pass the entry exam for the nearest High School.

CHAPTER 63

Janis 1997

The remainder of Janis`s school years seemed to fly by and due to her unconventional upbringing, she was unusually independent and confident for her age. Despite having beautiful long red wavy hair and a smile which lit up her entire face, she remained quite the adventurous tomboy child. Although boys showed interest in her, they often bored her quickly and she preferred her father and Uncle's company to any men her age. One boy became so besotted with her, that Zena had to tell his parents that what he had been doing was tantamount to stalking. Most girls of her age would have been frightened, but she was unconcerned and just shrugged it off.

Janis left school at seventeen and got a job in a local motel a few miles away up the main Kalgoorlie Road, which entailed a long walk there or back. But after Mitch found an old mountain bike and did it up for her, it was just over half an hour's cycle. Although often tired when back at the cabin after work, she rarely moaned and just got on with it.

Zena was proud that her daughter had inherited so many of her traits, her devil-may-care attitude to life and her resilience. She was also strong-willed and capable like her and was often found out in the goldfields with her Uncle Geoff on her days off from the Motel, working alongside the other men.

Janis had also inherited Erick's witty sense of fun, and although not her real father, Mitch's presence not only helped build her confidence but also calmed her down considerably, although she still had a very mischievous streak.

Both Mitch and Geoff were concerned to discover her on several occasions, in bed with any man that took her fancy, but never embarrassed about being caught, she would smile at them, and assure them,

"We are not doing anything wrong, and I`m careful. And besides, it's not like I`m going to marry any of them or anything."

"Just so long as it does not interfere with your work..." said Geoff, aware that if he told her off, she would be more likely to do it anyway, and more covertly.

For Janis, this way of life was perfect. She loved the thrill of finding gold and never seemed bothered by how dirty or hot she got, none of that was an issue for her as it had been for some of the men.

"There's no doubt about it, Janis. Gold mining is in your blood too," Geoff remarked to her one day.

She just smiled and said,

"I love it, Uncle."

The job in the Motel was alright, but all she wanted to do was work full-time with her uncle in the goldfields. He was reluctant to offer her the full-time position that recently came up, but having badgered him constantly, he finally gave in, and she resigned from her job at the Motel.

Working in the goldfields required careful handling of dumper trucks, precise manoeuvring of large lorries, something which she was particularly good at, along with running errands into town on Geoff's old quad bike. But Janis had other ideas of how she could be even more useful to Geoff. Despite never learning how to drive formally, she could often be found behind the wheel of many of Geoff's off-road vehicles and driving around the immediate vicinity of the homestead, and now, reckoned she was old enough and experienced enough to take her test and made her driving official.

She failed on the first attempt, but remaining undeterred, after some lessons with a local instructor, and aware she had driven a little too fast the first time, she drove much more slowly the second time and passed without any problems.

Geoff was immensely proud, and after accomplishing that, she then badgered him to teach her how to ride a motorbike. Although unsure if it was a good idea, she jumped at the chance of helping him strip down the old Norton motorbike that he kept in one of his sheds. Expecting her to get bored, he was surprised at how much she loved doing it, and eventually, he let her also take her motorbike test.

She rode the Norton for another two years until Mitch and Geoff clubbed together to buy her a Harley Davidson Fat Boy for her eighteenth birthday. The freedom she felt riding through the outback with the wind blowing in her hair was exhilarating, and Janis often ferried her mother around pillion, and she also thought it great fun. The bike brought Zena and her even closer together, and Janis was pleased to have the sort of mother who shared her passion for speed and excitement.

But as time went on, it was becoming increasingly obvious to Zena from her barrage of questions about her father, that Janis was contemplating taking a trip over to the UK to try to find him. Although a little dubious about her doing the journey alone, Zena and Mitch agreed she could go and funded her trip.

Just before she left, really hoping she would find him, Zena wrote Erick a heartfelt letter and gave it to Janis to take with her. Janis had set off excitedly, but by the time her plane landed in Heathrow, she had butterflies in her stomach. But seeing the gleaming Harley, that was her rental bike, she had set off with a newfound determination to find her father.

PART THREE

Chapters 64 - 73

CHAPTER 64

Shauna early 1971

Continuing to grieve for the baby boy she lost, Shauna often wondered what it would have been like if he had been born healthy. Certainly, the Mother and Baby Home would have been a dreadful start to its poor little life, but she had grown to love the baby growing inside her and recalled being particularly delighted when she first felt him kick. Now he was gone, all that remained was a horrible empty feeling, that she suspected would never be filled again. The constant Hail Mary's, and recitations of the Serenity Prayer ever since appeared not to help, but at least distracted her from some of the pain of her loss.

Still feeling very ashamed of her wanton actions the night her baby was conceived; she became increasingly depressed and worried that she may never be able to leave the Mother and Baby Home. Loving working with Frank, had made it difficult to leave the Delivery Room, but aware of how detrimental dealing with the streams of fretful mothers of stillborn babies, all constant reminders of what she had been through herself, was for her, she had to go.

With a heavy heart she concluded it best she return to working on the ward again, and having gained Sister Mary's permission, and also seeking new ways of redeeming herself, she worked extra hard and often cleaned through the night, when she should have been resting.

Frank returned from a little breakaway, surprised to discover she no longer worked in the Delivery Room. He had been getting more and more worried about her when he last saw her, and when she passed him in the corridor, she looked very pale, and when he tried to speak to her, appearing unable to look at him, she stood with her head down, playing with her apron strings, which was so unlike her, and heart-breaking. Seeing her like that, brought home how badly his lies had affected her, and he felt **terrible**.

Although desperate to keep seeing her and to make sure she was all right, he had to be content with only catching brief glimpses of her as he passed the ward each day, but it soon became obvious by her demeanour, that she did not want to see him anymore. He guessed he was too much of a reminder of what had happened, and it hurt to think about it, but he missed terribly and still cared about her a lot.

CHAPTER 65

Shauna 1973

Shauna remained working on the ward and in the washrooms for the next two years, and saw saw Frank only occasionally, usually when walking down the main corridor, but each time, they smiled politely at each other, and both kept walking.

Roisin had become a great friend and always tried to visit whenever she could, under Sister Mary`s radar. She was like a breath of fresh air, always had a funny story or a piece of gossip to tell her, and never failed to make her smile.

One day she beckoned to Shauna from the door to the ward and whispered that she had just heard that Doctor Clancy was on mourning leave for a few days because his mother had died suddenly. Knowing extremely well what it is like to lose a parent, Shauna was sorry to have not had a chance to commiserate with him and hoped he was all right.

In Frank`s absence, Sister Mary insisted Shauna go to clean the Delivery Room, which was left in a bit of a mess after he left so suddenly. This happened to coincide with the arrival of Jefferson, on one of his regular visits back from America.

Aside from what Frank had told her about him, Shauna always felt uneasy around him and always tried to keep her distance. But, on this one occasion, seeing her alone in the Delivery Room, Jefferson called her to his office, wanting an update on the latest baby count.

She entered his wood-panelled, very grand office, to find him standing with his back to her in front of his leather-top desk, smoking a potent-smelling cigar. He was wearing an expensive-looking suit, and standing with one hand on his hip, looking out the window.

She opened her mouth to speak, but having inhaled the smoke, ended up coughing instead.

He turned to look at her and enquired about the latest birth figures.

"I`m afraid I don't know, it`s been a while since I last worked in the Delivery Room sir," she said, shyly.

The cigar smoke still hung in the air and Shauna continued to cough.

"Are you all right there?" he enquired in his strong American accent.

Shauna nodded, and keeping her head bowed, sensing he was moving closer, promptly backed away.

"I do not believe I`ve had the pleasure of meeting you properly before, have I? Let me have a look at you," he said.

He eyed her up and down, put his left hand under her chin, and lifted it until her eyes were level with his, and she felt extremely uncomfortable.

"My my!" he exclaimed.

"You surely are a fine woman, aren't you?"

"Please step away from me sir," she said forcefully.

"Wow, a filly with some grit, I like that," he said, grinning.

His grin sent a shiver up Shauna`s spine, and when he lunged in her direction, she managed to dodge his advances but ended up with her back against the wall. Frightened, she instinctively folded her arms across her chest, but in an instant, he was grabbing at them and trying to pull them away.

To her relief, at that point the door suddenly flew open, and in walked Frank, having seen what was going on from the car park.

"Oh no you do not, Jefferson! I know exactly what you did to Sister Evelyn, you wouldn`t want me to tell everyone about that, now would you, eh?" he said, loudly.

"Shush, man there`s no need to shout," said Jefferson.

He was now squaring up to Frank and appeared undeterred.

"We do not want any trouble here, do we Frank? I`m sure you want to keep your job. What with your ma and all."

He was unaware that Frank`s mother had died, and Shauna stood watching, wondering what Frank would do next. She had never seen him this angry before.

"You can`t use that against me anymore, Jefferson, I don`t care if you sack me on the spot, just please let Shauna go."

"Now hang on, don`t be too hasty now Frank, I`m not going to sack you."

To Shauna`s surprise, Frank let out a loud belly laugh and replied,

"Yeah, I know too much, don`t I?"

Before Jefferson could answer, Frank grabbed one of Shauna`s hands and escorted her out of the room, leaving Jefferson standing looking at them with his mouth open. They headed straight back to the Delivery Room and once inside, burst into fits of giggles, and glad to see each other again, had hugged each other.

After she had composed herself, Shauna asked,

"What exactly did he do to Sister Evelyn? I`ve been worrying about her ever since she disappeared."

Although reluctant to divulge much, Frank relayed what Jefferson had done, and this explained why she had behaved as she had when Shauna found her in the toilets.

She was horrified to think what she had witnessed, was Evelyn miscarrying her baby.

"Poor Evelyn, to think what she went through. It makes me wonder how many other girls he has done the same to," she said.

"Yes, but at least we have more bargaining power over him now," said Frank, smiling.

CHAPTER 66

Shauna 1973

Shauna returned to work in the washrooms and ward again and often smiled to herself, remembering when Frank had stood up to Jefferson, and rescued her that day. She also frequently recalled what happened at the moment they shared afterward, when safely back at Frank`s office.

She had turned to leave after thanking him for stepping in and saving her from Jefferson`s clutches, when he unexpectedly took hold of her hand, pulled her towards him, and hugged her very tightly, and during that warm embrace, they kissed again.

She remembered what it was like to feel his arms around her once more, and for that split second, felt herself melt in his arms. But feeling suddenly embarrassed and ashamed, she had excused herself and left and felt bad about doing that now. She had missed Frank a great deal, but having gone through the loss of her baby, still could no longer bear the thought of returning to work in the Delivery Room, ever again. But seeing Frank and being close to him again, had unsettled her, and fed up with life at the Mother and Baby Home, she prayed hard every night for guidance, and a reprieve from her horrible life there.

CHAPTER 67

Shauna July 1973

Guidance came in the form of a dream. One night when lying in her narrow bed, just as she was drifting off to sleep, she saw a vision of the Virgin Mary, and she was beckoning to her towards a magnificent panorama stretching out endlessly for miles, in front of her. She awoke convinced this meant she should do something more purposeful with her life, but unsure what, spent the next few months feeling torn and deliberated about what she could do.

But then, something unusual happened. She was visited by a serious looking smartly dressed man, who she reckoned was in his mid-forties. He explained he was an executor of her parent`s estate, and hearing that, she had gasped and asked,

"Has something happened to them? "

She held her breath until he answered.

In all the years since Shauna had been forced to leave her childhood home, she had not heard anything from her parents or received any news of the twins. Unbeknown to her, her parents had recently died in a car crash, the twins had been fostered, and being as she was now over eighteen, she had inherited the house. Over the years she had already become resigned to the idea she would never see any of them again, and this just confirmed that, but it was shocking to hear that they had both died so suddenly. The full ramifications of what had happened did not sink in at first, and it was only after the solicitor had gone, that she burst into floods of tears.

She remained inconsolable for days and was even allowed a break from her ward and washroom duties, to rest in the dormitory during the day. Still in shock from the news, lying in her bed in the dormitory, she often thought of the last time she had seen her family and replayed what had happened, over and over in her mind. Although she had still not forgiven her father for what he had done, it was heartbreaking to contemplate never seeing her parents again, and maybe her sisters too. But as time went on and the heavy fog clouding her thoughts began to lift, she had a light bulb moment. Her parents' house could be her key to getting away from the Mother and Baby Home, and she needed to visit it as soon as possible.

The idea of being able to leave was very compelling and fuelled with extra confidence, she went to see Sister Mary, to ask her permission to go. As usual, not making things easy, she informed her she could only let her have the weekend away, and that she needed to resume her duties by Monday morning, and Shauna had to be content with that.

CHAPTER 68

Shauna 1973

When she turned the key in the latch and the door to her parent`s house sprang open, Shauna felt very uneasy. The place still looked the same as it had always done, and she half expected to hear the shouts and laughter of the twins playing upstairs and smell her mother`s cooking. But instead, what greeted her was a musty-smelling silence.

Wandering around and exploring the place again, she spent an uncomfortable night in her old room in her narrow single bed. The following morning, entering her parent`s room for the first time, somewhere out of bounds, when she was a child, felt very strange. She stared around her nervously, and her glance landed on a silver-framed photograph of her father, taken when he was young, and one she had never seen before. He was wearing a full army uniform and was, she thought, taken during the war, and before she was born. She wandered over to her mother`s dressing table which, like all the furniture in the house, was covered in a thick layer of dust. She picked up one of her hairbrushes and stared at the clumps of grey hair between its bristles. Sighing, she felt her eyes fill with tears, and was compelled to remove some loose strands, and put them in her pocket, to keep as a form of remembrance.

Wiping her eyes, she searched the dressing table drawers for anything important and discovered a large pile of letters at the bottom of one of them. The letters to her surprise, were all written in her mother`s handwriting. On each one was the Mother and Baby Home`s address, and "Return to Sender," stamped at the top. It was heart-breaking to discover that, contrary to what she had assumed, her mother had not completely abandoned her for all those years. Instead, she had written to her every month since she left, but every letter had been returned by the Home.

Feeling anger rising within her, she pondered how cruel it had been for Sister Mary to do that to her and her mother and climbed onto her parents' bed to begin to read the first letter. It was all so much to take in, and after slowly reading each one thoroughly, she felt a much bigger connection to her mother than she had ever felt before. Having long ago accepted what she had done had been unforgivable, it was now obvious that despite that, her mother had still loved and cared about her. The letters indicated she had been clearly missing her and she had chatted away to her regularly, in them. Amidst the mundane everyday life stories, her mother had recounted in the letters, were little pearls of wisdom to pass on to her daughter, famous book quotes she hoped would inspire her, and other little ditties copied from the local newspaper, that she hoped would make her smile.

After having read each letter again, she had put her head in her hands and sobbed, and felt better for doing so. It was as if all the pent-up sadness, frustration, and guilt, she had been carrying with her for so long, had suddenly lifted, and she could tangibly feel her mother`s love for her, as if she were there with her, in that room.

Later, after having nipped along to the shop for some food and set the oven going, she wandered around the rest of the house. She had intended to sell it, but decided there and then, to rent it out cheaply to young pregnant girls, who would have otherwise ended up in the Mother and Baby Home. The house held too many bad memories for her now, and the idea of it being put to beneficial use, really appealed.

After telephone calls from the payphone up the road, and with the help of the serious-looking solicitor, she assigned an agent to manage it all for her, all paid for by her parent`s estate.

CHAPTER 69

Shauna 1973

Shauna only briefly returned to the Mother and Baby Home to collect the remainder of her things, and say goodbye to Roisin, and was worried when Frank was not in his office, and she could not tell him her plans. She then headed to Sister Mary`s office with some trepidation, her decision to take her vows and become a nun was not one she had taken lightly, and as she watched her long wavy hair fall to the ground in big clumps, as Sister Mary shaved her head, she wondered if she was doing the right thing. Her scalp felt extremely tender afterwards and it took a while to feel comfortable wearing the coif and veil, but regarding the discomfort as further penance, she remained determined to atone for her sins.

It was such a strange experience, lying completely prostrate on the cold wooden floor of the chapel that smelt of a mixture of old wax polish and damp, with seven other girls dressed all in white, waiting for Father Declan to pronounce them, "Brides of God, "and she was very relieved when the whole ordeal was over and they were shown around the convent.

She was very pleased to see how much better conditions were there, for a start, she had a room all to herself, with a comfortable-looking bed and clean white cotton bedclothes. There were even French windows opening onto the garden, quite different from the small narrow bed, and dirty, itchy bedclothes she was used to at the Mother and Baby Home.

There was, however, still a strict daily routine and after the five o'clock bell rang, she joined the other nuns in the chapel for early morning prayers, followed by a breakfast of porridge and tea, in a small room off the main kitchen. There was then an hour of completely silent contemplation, and when that ended, she had to start work. She liked the new structure to her day and was particularly pleased when assigned cleaning duties there, instead of working at the Mother and Baby Home.

Although quite laborious, she enjoyed her new role, and the much-needed solitude and peace enabled her to get her thoughts about everything that had happened, straighter in her mind. The overall atmosphere was also much better at the Convent, and her mood began to improve very quickly.

By the end of her first year there, she was starting to feel ready to take on another challenge and wanted to do something more meaningful and helpful with her life, and wished she could talk to Frank about it.

She often thought of him and regretted not being able to tell him where she had gone, but never wanting to return to the Mother and Baby Home again, she presumed she would not see him again, and felt very sad about that. He had made a big impact on her, and together they had made the best they could out of horrible circumstances. She missed his smile, sense of humour, and above all, his kindness. It had been so lovely to meet a man like him, after her horrible experience on the playing field, and he had restored her faith in men again.

CHAPTER 70

Rory Spring 2015

Rory continued to visit Rhona regularly and sometimes took her out. She loved seeing her old Jeep and would eagerly climb into it and chat away with him, just like she used to before the accident. It was great to have part of the old Rhona back.

On one occasion, they drove down to Seachapel, parked in the car park beneath the old Fishermen`s Chapel, and walked along the coast path, until they reached Rhona`s favourite bench and sat down. Sitting there happily watching the wild waves crashing against the rocks below, Rhona told Rory all about Bryn again, and how they had often sat together and watched the sea.

It was good to see her in such a good mood and when Rory suggested they round off the day at the Fishing Boat Inn at Treggenhow, with fish chowder, Rhona was extremely excited. They entered the old stone pub and gazed around its old familiar fishing photograph-covered walls, and Rhona said very lucidly.

"This takes me back."

Rory nodded, but noticing that although smiling, she had tears in her eyes, he instinctively took hold of her hand and stroked it, and was surprised by her response.

"I know my brain isn`t what it was, but one thing`s for sure, I`ll never forget you, Billie."

Hearing her say that Rory felt quite choked, and fighting back tears himself, he said,

"Look at us, we`re a right pair aren`t we, Rhona?"

He wiped his eyes, put his arm around her, and hugged her tightly.

There was a vacant table by the window and Rory left her staring out at the view, while he went up to the bar, and ordered the chowder and soft drinks for them both. He could see her still sitting contentedly staring out at the old stone harbour and disappearing to the toilet, where he splashed his eyes and composed himself when he returned to the table, he was horrified that Rhona was nowhere to be seen. Trying not to panic, he looked worriedly around the pub and asked people if they had seen her, and luckily, someone said,

"Is that her, out there?"

She was standing in front of the railings across the road and appeared deep in thought, and after he tapped the window, she did not respond and continued looking out across the harbour. When she eventually turned to look back at him, he beckoned her back inside. She looked much happier after her venture outside, excitedly told him about the pretty sailboats she had been watching in the bay, and exclaimed what a lovely colour the sea was. It was as if her mannerisms had suddenly become almost childlike, and she appeared filled with awe and wonder at what she had just witnessed. This was good to see, and Rory realised just how shut away she must have been feeling, now living at the Care Home, and vowed to try to take her out much more frequently in the future.

As usual, their chowder was delicious and Rhona wolfed hers down very quickly, and to Rory`s amusement, let out a little burp, afterwards. Back outside after he had settled the bill, Rhona returned to her childlike state again, and now grinning from ear to ear, watched a flock of guillemots as they swooped, dived, and flew high up into the brilliant blue sky above them. Still smiling, she stretched out her arm and pulled him close, and they remained entwined like that until finally he gently pulled away.

"Come on Rhona, think I need to get you back now, it's getting cold," he said.

He was a bit nonplussed by her response,

"Can we go to my real home this time, please Rory?"

she looked at him with pleading eyes.

"I`m sorry Rhona, but we can`t go there, I`m afraid."

Immediately feeling bad, he wished he could take her back to the Trevaunce Cottage, but he no longer had any keys and knew Belinda had already let it out.

Remaining silent for the whole of the drive back, when they eventually pulled up outside the Care Home, she said,

"I hate it here."

When he tried to explain this was now her home, to his horror, she became suddenly angry and before he could stop her, she lashed out at him with her hand and struck him across the side of his face. This was a nasty shock after her lovely earlier mood, and flinching, he held his hand against the smarting area on his cheek, in disbelief. Although she had gone quiet, she still looked angry and unsure what to do, he sat for a while thinking. Rhona had never done anything like this before, and aware her dementia was playing tricks on her, he decided to apologise for upsetting her.

But instead of acknowledging his apology, she silently and determinedly clung on to her seat belt and did not make eye contact, and when he eventually got out of the car and went round to open the passenger door, she remained sitting where she was, and said defiantly,

"No, I`m not going back in there, do you hear me? I`m never going back in there, again!"

With no other option but to lock Rhona in the car and go inside to get help, Rory stood watching as the staff coaxed her out of the car and virtually frog-marched her up the path, and inside the care home.

As they were passing, one of the carers turned to him and said,

"Probably best if you just go."

This was an upsetting, shocking and horrible end to what had otherwise been a lovely day, and he returned to the caravan feeling despondent.

CHAPTER 71

Rhona May 2015

When she visited Rhona at the care home not long after she had moved there, Belinda was upset when she did not appear to recognise her, and seemed very confused. Vowing never to return at the time, she now felt guilty for not returning for so long, and desperately wanting to see her, she decided to try visiting again. The counselling sessions were helping and feeling like she was back on an even keel again, she still knew that seeing her mother again would be difficult.

She pulled up in the car park with butterflies in her stomach, and sat for a while, hesitant to go in. No one was expecting her, and she could easily drive off again, but no, after getting that far, she had to go through with it. Deliberately bypassing the Nurse`s Station, she had gone straight up to Rhona`s room and found her sat with a care assistant, who appeared to be feeding her her supper with a spoon. After instinctively going over and hugging her, it was obvious she still did not know who she was, and witnessing this again was very upsetting. Battling back tears, she had to be content with sitting and watching the care assistant spooning Rhona`s supper into her mouth just like you would a baby. To her, this was new and completely unnecessary, no way was her mother to be treated like this when fully capable of doing it herself.

Annoyed, she stormed out of the room in disgust and went straight to Erica`s office. Erica did not recognise her at first, after only meeting her once, and quite a long time ago. When she asked what they had done to her mother to make her like that, and began a tirade of abuse about her not needing help eating, because she was fully capable of doing it herself, Erica sat quietly, waiting for her to finish.

Having worked out who she was, she asked,

"I presume you are talking about Rhona?"

Belinda was by now, very red in the face and answered,

"Yes."

"I know it`s stressful seeing her like that but getting angry with me is not the answer."

Belinda looked stuck for words and shook her head, and when Erica pulled up a chair for her, she sat silently, trying to hold back tears. Seeing she was upset, Erica phoned the kitchen and requested tea for them both. While sat with tea in hand, Belinda calmed down a little and Erica explained that Rhona had a nasty urine infection, which she had told Rory about, but as she had never left any contact details, she **had been unable to** inform her. She explained how urine infections tend to cause increased confusion and Rhona was temporarily, unable to feed herself. She was on a course of antibiotics, and when that ended, she would improve.

Belinda felt guilty when Erica mentioned how good Rory had been in her absence.

"Whatever`s happened between the two of you is  no concern of mine but, what I`ve witnessed is that Rory loves Rhona very much and has visited her virtually every couple of days without fail, since she moved here, and has even taken her out to some of her favourite places."

She continued,

"Don`t forget that he, like you has also been grieving over Erick. He was so upset when you chucked him out of the cottage, and with nowhere else to go, ended up living in a small, draughty caravan. It was very thoughtless and

unkind of you to do that."
Belinda, now with both her hackles and voice raised, replied,
"You can`t talk to me like that! None of that is any of your
business."
But Erica, who was now feeling riled, was not backing down.
"I wouldn`t be doing my job properly if I wasn`t looking
after my resident`s relatives too. If all you want is to vent
your anger on me, it is not what I`m here for and I think
you should leave. I`ve got twenty-nine others to deal with,
whose needs are greater than yours."
Aware she may have been a bit harsh, Erica immediately
apologised, but seeing the look of shame on Belinda`s face, it
was obvious her words hit home. She went noticeably quiet,
and after solemnly scribbling her number on a piece of scrap
paper, sheepishly handed it to her, and mumbled a quick,
"Thank you for everything," before hurriedly leaving,
without bothering to say goodbye to her mother.
Belinda hated that Rhona had ended up in such an insti-
tution and was having trouble accepting the mother she loved
and appreciated so much, was now a shadow of her former self.
Feeling embarrassed about her behaviour, she returned to
London, more determined than ever to continue the counselling and to get back to her usual bubbly self again.

CHAPTER 72

Sister Shauna 1974

At the Convent, Shauna was able to fully mourn the loss of her parents, and over time, felt able to forgive her father for what he had done to her. Also feeling much more at peace within herself for her childhood transgressions, and her part in what had gone on on the playing field, she was still unable to rid herself of memories of the terrible things she regularly witnessed at the Mother and Baby Home.

Still missing Frank, she often reflected on how much he had helped her over the years, and felt guilty for not having thanked him, and for leaving without saying she was going. As the months flew by, she found herself becoming increasingly overcome with waves of despair and anxiety, far worse than she had suffered as a child and just wanted to hide herself away.

Shauna had only met Mother Superior once, and unlike Sister Mary, she had appeared kind and likeable, but when she was called urgently to her office one day, she felt uneasy.

She sat down opposite her and gazed at her hands nervously.

"I think it`s time you came clean with us Sister, there has been something on your mind for a while, has there not?" she asked.

Shauna nodded and still not wishing to make eye contact, bit her lip, anticipating a reprimand. But instead, Mother Superior sat quietly, awaiting a response to her earlier question.

Eventually, she looked up from her lap and told her,
"You are right Mother Superior; I have been having disturbing thoughts recently, and try as I may, I cannot
break away from them. I have prayed and prayed, asking if I could do anything to improve things for all
those wretched souls at the Mother and Baby Home,
but nothing has come to me."
The old lady tutted, shuffled in her seat, and sighed loudly,
and Shauna held her breath, thinking she had displeased her.
But instead, she asked,
"Would you like a change from being here all the time?"
Feeling quite taken aback by her question, Shauna peered
back at her curiously, wondering what she was suggesting.
"God`s work does not just go on inside these four walls.
I`m aware that you rent your parent`s house out to
unmarried mothers, which is admirable, and wondered
if you might consider taking a position at the new
Catholic Children`s Adoption Centre, instead of wor-
king here?"
Not fully understanding what she was suggesting, Shauna
stared back at her blankly.
She went on to explain,
"A dear Sister from this Parish, Sister Frances, recently
set up a separate Catholic Adoption Home and has been
working closely with unmarried mothers, helping them
take care of their illegitimate offspring, providing some
paid employment for some, and finding suitable local
couples to take unwanted babies. Some women have
also been taken into another local convent, where they
have found a new vocation and salvation through penance. We need your help because although we have found
new and more suitable homes for most children, many
remain at the Adoption Home. With limited space and
what appears to be a sudden increase in demand, we must

keep the Adoption Home running, because we have recognised the Mother and Baby Home is unsuitable for older children."

Although initially quite taken aback at the thought, Shauna wondered if this was the answer to the prayers she had been seeking. But worried that it would also be like working at the Mother and Baby Home, she quickly replied,

"Oh, I`m not sure I`m cut out for that."

"Sister Shauna, I can assure you that the Adoption
Home is nothing like the Mother and Baby Home.
It is a lovely place, full of very caring people."

She insisted that Shauna go there for a month to see how she got on, but could tell she was still unsure, and added,

"You will still be able to live a pure life there, but not
under such strict routines. You will have more
personal freedom, yet still be doing God`s work."

Before she could answer, Mother Superior jumped up from her seat and stated loudly,

"Well, that`s sorted then, be ready tomorrow morning
at six."

CHAPTER 73

Sister Shauna 1974

Shauna apprehensively approached the entrance of the Catholic Adoption Home, pulled on the doorbell, and when the door clicked and opened, she went inside.

Greeting her was a jolly-looking nun with dark ginger hair and a red freckled face.

"Hello, I`m Sister Frances. It is lovely to meet you,

Sister Shauna. I`ve heard only good things about you,"

She was grinning from ear to ear and Shauna immediately relaxed.

As Sister Frances showed her around, it soon became apparent how different working there would be compared to the Mother and Baby Home.

The Adoption Home was light blue throughout, and pretty pictures adorned its walls. The children looked happy playing together, well-fed, cared for, and were smartly dressed. She noticed there were inside toilets and separate shower cubicles, and in place of a horrible stench filling the air, was the clean smell of disinfectant mixed with the aromas from large vases of pretty flowers, that had been placed in every room.

Sister Frances continued the tour and they entered a large, grand room with expensive embossed wallpaper on its walls.

"This was the original ballroom, but we mainly use it for fundraising activities now," she said.

Peering around, Shauna`s attention was drawn to what appeared to be a large plaque halfway along the wall and wandered over to it.

Listed on the plaque were the names, of all the benefactors of the charity, and right at the top, was

"Dr Frank Clancy ....1960."

The whole time that they had known each other Frank had never mentioned his work at the Adoption Home, but it was strange and yet comforting to realise how personally invested he was in the place she would now be working.

She had often wondered what he did on his regular Thursday off, from the Mother and Baby Home, and now she knew.

During the two months since she left the Home, although she had often thought of Frank fondly, she had tried to put their time together behind her. He was a part of something she wanted to forget, but seeing his name again, reminded her of when she had last seen him.

Aware of how difficult it was for her to continue working with him, she guessed he had thought she would never be able to leave, so it must have been a shock to find her gone.

While standing looking at the plaque, feeling a lump rising in her throat, she swallowed, and asked,

"Does Dr Clancy still ever visit?"

Sister Frances explained,

"He`s been a real godsend. We`ve struggled to get enough funds to do the place up before he came along, and the money he so kindly donated has made all the difference. He has been incredibly generous and has continued volunteering here every Thursday, his only day off since we first opened, I don`t know how he does it, it`s so kind of him."

Sister Frances continued guiding her along corridors accessed from a door at the end of the old ballroom, where they reached a large Victorian kitchen with flagstone floors, a massive Aga, and a scullery, behind which, was a very well-equipped laundry and drying room.

To the right was Sister Frances`s office, which to her surprise, was an elaborately decorated, wood-panelled room.

When taken to the back of the building, she was shown the nun`s rooms, which even had ensuite facilities. Astonishment must have shown on her face, and Sister Frances said,

"As I told you, God has bestowed many blessings on us here, my dear."

PART FOUR

Chapter 74 - 78

CHAPTER 74

Evelyn, 1973

Evelyn had been finding life as a mother, challenging, and after having never really been treated well in her own life, she did not understand what to do when William became very clingy. When he was a baby she had felt different, and if she wanted to, could hold him at arm`s length, but a two-year-old, was a different kettle of fish.

It took her a while to accept that close human contact, was what calmed him when he had a tantrum, which he appeared to do frequently. But so unused to close physical contact with anyone, cuddling him like she had seen Frank do, felt like an alien and awkward thing for her to do. She was relieved when the tantrums gradually lessened, and William`s little person-ality began to grow. But trying to avoid hugging and cuddling him, was proving very difficult.

When he had screamed,

"Mammy, Mammy!" at the top of his voice from outside

One day, she went to him.

He had fallen and badly gashed his knee on an old broken bottle at the top of the garden. Seeing the blood gushing from her son`s knee, she became suddenly very emotional and in-stinctively wrapped both arms around him, and he hugged her tightly back seeing she was also crying.

"It`s alright Mammy, don`t cry," he said.

Frank appeared about ten minutes later and while he sutured the wound, William had been astonishingly brave, and at that moment quite naturally, she had smiled, kissed his head and felt very proud of her son. It was as if she needed that to have happened for her to fully appreciate how vulnerable her little boy was, and how much he needed her, and she needed him.

This was a complete revelation, and from then on she cuddled and kissed him often. William never had another tantrum, and over time, turned into a lovely, kind, gentle boy, and she was even prouder to be his mother.

CHAPTER 75

Frank 1974

Frank continued to miss Shauna, and although other young girls were sent to assist him in her place, it was not the same without her. But some things did improve in her absence. After his altercation with Jefferson, he was able to negotiate a salary increase and was given some better, more up-to-date equipment. This was all well and good, but he remained unsure how much longer he could remain complicit in all the terrible things, still going on.

Feeling extremely guilty for his part in it all, he continued obtaining evidence of what had been happening, whenever he had the chance, hoping that it could all be stopped. at some point. The opportunity to get hold of more damning evidence considerably improved, when he successfully negotiated an administrative day each week, "to help" Jefferson with the paperwork, while overseas. He could also reduce his hours in the Delivery Room, when another doctor was employed. Most importantly, he now had access to the records, and before disappearing back overseas again, Jefferson showed him where they were all kept.

Not long after he had gone, Frank made an exciting discovery. In addition to the filing cabinets Jefferson had shown him, he found another cabinet key taped to the underside of one of his desk drawers. After unsuccessfully trying it in several different cabinets, he had been about to give up, when he suddenly realised there was a cabinet partially hidden under one of the desks. The key fitted and having hurriedly opened it, he found it contained even more birth and death certificates.

This a strange, but significant find, and he deduced they must be important because someone had gone to so much trouble to try to hide them. After comparing them with those in the main filing cabinets, it soon became obvious they were forgeries. There were glaringly obvious irregularities in the typeface and style of the entries, and the signatures authorising them also appeared different. He had unearthed compelling evidence that confirmed exactly what Jefferson, and Declan the Priest, had been up to at the Home. This was vital because although he had been aware what they had been going on was morally wrong, he now had proof that it was also legally wrong.

Desperate to tell someone what he had found, he wished he could somehow track Shauna down. He had heard about her parents via the local grapevine, and although sad to have no clue where she was living now, he was very pleased she had managed to leave the Mother and Baby Home. She would have been extremely excited about his discovery, and in her absence, all he could do was tell Evelyn.

"He`s always been a slimy character, that Jefferson," she said when he told her.

He had gone to check on her and his son, William, aware he was fast approaching primary school age, and they would shortly be moving away.

"You must be missing her, Frank," she said suddenly.

He stared at her blankly, and she explained,

"Shauna, I know how much you cared about her, have you not heard anything from her at all?"

Shaking his head despondently, he stared at the floor, and she watched him, fully aware of how hurt he had been discovering Shauna had left without even saying good-bye. Evelyn could read him like a book and was amused he never mentioned his restless nights, spent thinking and wondering about her, since she had gone. The dark furrows under his eyes, and jaded manner, were a testament to that, and she hoped he would hear something from her soon.

Frank did not think he could ever forgive himself for the lies he had told Shauna, what he had done and said was shameful; and he felt very guilty and upset for letting her think her baby was deformed and had died. How could he have done that to someone he had cared about so much? Was a question that often went around in his head.

Feeling a strong compulsion to put things right with her in any way he could, he wanted to find her but had no idea where to start. For now, he had to be content with the knowledge that what he was doing, collecting all this evidence, was somehow going to make amends. Following his big breakthrough with the birth certificates, he continued to gather and document every thread of evidence he could find against Jefferson and Declan, and logged it all in the evidence ledger, that Shauna had already started before she left. Even if all this did was prevent more babies and their mothers from dying in the future, those who were lucky enough to survive, being taken miles away from their biological parents, would at least be something.

But, shouldering all this on his own was hard, and he often felt overwhelmed, powerless, and unsure what to do that was constructive, with the latest information yet. In addition to his wavering confidence about it all, the guilt about his terrible secret weighed heavy on his mind, clouded his judgment, and made it impossible for him to think clearly.

Noticing a change in his demeanour, and realising he was now struggling with working there and at the Mother and Baby Home, Sister Frances arranged for one of the new nuns to transfer over to help him out.

CHAPTER 76

Sister Shauna and Frank, 1974

Shauna had come to trust Frank over the years and one day, plucked up the courage to confide in him about the night she was raped when her baby was conceived. She noticed he went rather pale and appeared shocked, hearing her account of what happened.

Feeling touched by his concern, she told him,

"Ah, bless you for caring so much Frank."

Although he looked uncomfortable and seemed poised to say something, he instead changed the subject, and they never discussed it again. But the reality was that Frank had broken out in a cold sweat, and had been worried that she would see and question his reaction; and had been extremely relieved when Shauna cut the conversation short. But unexpectedly hearing her talking so frankly about that night, he teetered on the brink of confessing all but distracted himself by changing the subject. Memories of that night at the playing field came back so clearly as if it had only just happened, and he struggled to stop himself from breaking down in front of her and begging her forgiveness.

Shauna often thought about the baby boy she carried inside her, and his death played heavily in her mind. Convinced she still needed punishment for her sins, she wanted to follow a path of full redemption, and continued praying hard every day and strictly kept her nun`s vows.

After befriending a very timid, elderly nun called Sister Clara, who manned the switchboard at the Adoption Home, and was the first point of contact for any unmarried mothers throughout the Irish Republic needing to put their babies up for adoption, Shauna asked if she could see the list of mothers waiting for their babies to be collected.

Reading the names and seeing their geographical locations gave her an idea, and aware that Sister Clara did not like driving, she took the opportunity to offer to go and collect the babies for her. With Sister Clara backing her up, she also managed to get Sister Frances to agree to her collecting them, leaving Sister Clara to deal with the babies at the Adoption Home.

This was an exciting breakthrough and trying not to look too pleased, Shauna hatched a plan to intercept as many babies as possible, and instead of taking them back to the nursery, planned to place them instead with local couples, desperate to have babies and unable to conceive themselves.

CHAPTER 77

Sister Shauna and Frank 1975

Shauna`s first trip out into the more rural areas of Ireland proved very fruitful. Not only did she succeed in collecting vulnerable babies, which ordinarily would have gone to the Adoption Home, but with the help of a Vicar called Tomoltach's, from Tullyvaughn, Cullenmara, she succeeded in finding suitable childless parents with which to place each one. On her return, she told the Adoption Home they had been stillborn. Although feeling very guilty for lying, feeling she was now taking control of a small part of a very unpleasant situation, she continued to intercept as many babies as possible, preventing them from being sent away to America.

One day, something unexpected happened. She had been at the vicarage with Tomoltach, when Máired, Tomoltach`s wife, opened the door to find a bedraggled woman on the doorstep. Inviting her in straight away, when she removed her cloak hood, Shauna gasped.

"Roisin! Oh, my goodness, are you alright?"

Roisin proceeded to drop her cloak to the floor and reveal a tiny baby boy wrapped up in a blue blanket in her arms, sleeping peacefully.

"I finally did it, Shauna," she said excitedly.

Shauna stared at her in disbelief, and startled by how pale she looked, only just managed to prevent her from falling onto the hard floor, when she collapsed. Luckily, the baby was unharmed and remained cushioned in her blanket, but having awoken, it began bawling loudly. Máired retrieved the baby from Roisin`s clutch, Tomoltach tried to bring her around with smelling salts, while Shauna knelt beside her good friend, trying to comfort her.

Bursting into floods of tears when she came around, Roisin said in between sobs,

"I`d thought I wasn`t going to be able to do it, I`ve hardly any

money but managed to dodge the ticket inspector on the Cullenway train, by constantly moving around for the whole of the journey. I only just had enough money to catch the last bus to Tullyvaughn. I`m exhausted, so I am, but relieved to get here."

Shauna hugged her and determined to help in any way she could, to repay her for the kindness she showed her at the Home, years earlier. She was pleased when after asking Tomoltach if there was any paid work available locally, he suggested Roisin could help Máired clean the vicarage, in return for her bed and board.

Shauna went back to the Convent later, feeling proud of what Roisin had done. She had sacrificed so much to save that one baby and was glad she had managed to escape that terrible place.

Initially assuming that the baby was Roisin's when she next visited, Tomoltach explained how Roisin had acted on the spur of the moment, after discovering it alone and crying in a separate room from all the others. Quickly taking matters into her own hands, with no idea who the mother was, she had fled, without even considering the consequences.

A doctor called Eamon, from the islands in the far west of Cullenmara, contacted Shauna one day to tell her about a special case involving his two good friends Rhona and Erick, and she agreed to help. Getting to them meant a much longer journey than usual, and she was pleased to break her journey and stay at the Vicarage, part way down, until Eamon called her when the baby was ready to collect.

She arranged to meet him at Canla, which was on an easy bus route from the vicarage. From there, he would drive her the rest of the way down to Lochálainnin. Having never been that far west before, she was impressed by the long road bridges, transporting them further away from the mainland, and how rocky the terrain around her was becoming, as they drove. It was so remote and rocky, that it reminded her of the surface of the moon. The drive up the narrow and very winding boreen had felt perilous, and she was glad to get out of the car and into the safety of the cottage.

It was always difficult to separate mother and baby when the time came. But on this occasion, Rhona, the baby`s mother, had named her baby Billie, which was unusual and seemed particularly reluctant to let her take him. It was quite late, by the time she let Shauna have him, and she was worried about how she would get the baby to its new parents and catch the last bus back to Dublin that same day.

To her immense relief, Eamon very kindly suggested he drop her at Cullenway Bus Station first, and agreed to take Billie over to Tomoltach`s daughter Lizzie and her husband, on his way back home, as they were near neighbours of his. He said he had also found adoptive parents for the baby boy Roisin brought, and collected him from Tomoltach, the following day.

CHAPTER 78

Sister Shauna and Frank 1978

Over the years, Shauna continued to track unmarried mothers from all over the Irish Republic, retrieve their babies, and arrange their transfer to suitable local parents. But it was hard, having also to occasionally return some of the babies to the Adoption Home, knowing they were going to be sent away to America, but to pretend all the babies she collected were all stillborn, would have aroused suspicion.

Although missing Frank, she did enjoy being away from the Adoption Home, and was comforted by the fact he was continuing to collect and collate evidence in her absence, with the idea of presenting it to the authorities later.

One day when out and about, Shauna spied an intriguing headline on a local newspaper stand and went and bought a copy of the paper. It was another very busy day and she did not have time to read it until on her bus journey back to the Convent. She had turned the first page and read the first line, and was absolutely astonished at what she read.

"1000s of babies thought to have died at Dublin Mother and Baby Home."

When she reached her stop, she quickly descended from the bus, hurried up the road to the Adoption Home and along to Frank`s office. Where, relieved to see him still there, she showed him the article immediately, worried about the ramifications for them both.

Frank went silent while he read, and afterwards, removed his glasses, rubbed his eyes, and said,

"Well, at least it will all be properly investigated now."

"But what about us, we`ve been part of it all for years, aren`t we both culpable, too?" Shauna asked.

"Well, I reckon the best thing we can do is gather up all the information we have and send it to the Gardi, anonymously. Then there won`t be any comeback on us in particular,"

From that moment on, the atmosphere at the Adoption Home completely changed. Sister Mary stopped visiting altogether, and Sister Frances was confined in the Convent with a mystery illness. There was also a fire in one of the offices, which the Gardi thought was arson, after which Declan the priest appeared to have disappeared, but luckily the filing cabinets containing all the forged documents had survived.

After sieving through all the paperwork they had collected, and removing anything that might incriminate them, Shauna and Frank did what they planned, and sent it anonymously to the authorities, and anxiously awaited the repercussions.

Mother Superior remained in position and now more than ever, relied on Shauna to help her with the day-to-day running of the Adoption Home. In addition to Sister Frances`s sudden departure, Jefferson had vanished, and The Adoption Home was soon swarming with plain-clothed Gardi who removed files, patrolled the area, and watched everything that was going on with interest.

Through the local grapevine, Shauna heard that Sister Mary and Sister Frances had been remanded in custody, after both being instrumental in how the two Homes were run, and the whole local area was shocked by the scandal.

The Gardi, local council, and Adoption Authorities arranged for the excavation of part of the back grassed area of the Mother and Baby Home, where they discovered human adult and baby remains, many of which local experts confirmed had been there for over fifty years. Another area to the right of the building was also being excavated and more decomposed remains were found.

The Gardi gave a statement saying,

"This is probably only the tip of the iceberg."

Hearing this made Shauna shudder, she had walked over that grassy area so many times in the past, completely unaware of what lay beneath her feet.

Although taken in for questioning, both she and Frank were cleared of any involvement in hiding the bodies and viewed as just doing what they were ordered to do, especially when Frank explained how Jefferson had abused him and threatened to sack him if he did not do what he wanted. The other younger nuns and unmarried mothers working at the Home were also absolved of any responsibility for what had happened.

Now that it was all out in the open, and with the threat of closure of both the Mother and Baby Home and the Adoption Home, Frank and Shauna were finally able to leave their positions.

Shauna, now completely disillusioned with the Catholic Church, renounced her vows and returned to her parent`s house to continue supporting unmarried mothers there. Frank returned to work at the local GP surgery where he had done a placement during his medical training. It all happened so fast, that neither had very long to think about it, let alone make any plans between them.

Both soon lost touch and although sad, Shauna appreciated how invaluable Frank`s friendship had been while they had been thrown into working together under such gruesome circumstances, and decided that outside of the confine of the Homes, their relationship would probably not have worked anyway, but she did miss him terribly.

Although a new life now awaited him, Frank was carrying with him a lot of guilt and sadness about all the lies he had told Shauna, and now unable to be with her, which was something he had dreamed of whilst at the Home, his life felt empty. But, he now had the opportunity to become involved with his son`s life, and after reluctantly cutting all ties with her, not wanting her to ever discover his terrible secret, he very much looked forward to the future.

PART FIVE

Chapters 79 - 101

CHAPTER 79

Shauna 1978

Initially, Shauna felt like a fish out of water when thrust back into normal life again. She had become so used to her life at the Mother and Baby Home and later, at the Convent and Adoption Home, over the previous twelve years, that she felt very anxious about leaving. But it did not take long before the apprehension she initially felt, soon ebbed away, and she was glad to be free at last.

It was, however, strange to be back at her parent's house, and although thankful for the company of other women there, during the hours of darkness, she often thought of Frank and wished they had not lost touch. Someone had told her he had gone down to Dorset to live, which she thought was strange. But another bit of local gossip was that he had got Evelyn pregnant, and she had made him marry her. The latter, Shauna could not believe and would often smile to herself at the absurdity of the thought.

She also often wondered what happened to her twin sisters, but all she knew was that they were fostered somewhere locally, but she had no idea how to go about finding them. She also increasingly missed Frank and would often lie awake thinking back to when he kissed or hugged her closely, and fondly re-membered what it was like to be in his arms. But sadly, she had to resign herself to him being gone from her life for good, and that she would probably never see him again.

CHAPTER 80

Evelyn 1979

Evelyn left Dublin when Willliam reached school age, and having tracked down Michael, her second cousin in England, arranged for them both to go and stay with him and his family for a while in Dorset. She hoped to secure herself a job, and a school for William, and find a lovely place for them to live there.

Her first-ever plane journey was a hair-raising experience, and several times during the flight she grabbed hold of the seat in front of her and held on to it tightly. William by comparison had not seemed at all bothered and had slept most of the way, which had been a relief because she did not know what she would have done if he had been scared too. She was glad when the plane eventually came to land at Bournemouth Airport, and she could get off it and back onto solid ground again. After they had completed all the usual airport formalities, they emerged through the double doors of the Arrivals building to find her cousin waiting for them outside.

Evelyn had not seen Michael since before she went to the Mother and Baby Home, and would have never recognised him, had he not approached and introduced himself. He stepped forward and hugged them both straight away, and helped them get their luggage in the car, before beginning the drive to the little Purbeck hamlet where he and his wife lived.

Evelyn studied him as he drove, he was a lot taller than she remembered, his dark hair now had specks of grey around his ears, giving a distinguished look, and he looked as if he kept himself fit.

The journey was interesting and after bypassing Bournemouth, they headed for the coast. Before long, they were boarding a little chain ferry, much to William`s delight, which transported them over a body of water and onto a little peninsula called Studland. From there, they drove along what seemed like a wide straight road surrounded by heathland, and lush green countryside for a few miles, before going through a little village, where they turned off down narrow country lanes until they finally came out on top of a hill.

Michael pulled off the road into a clearing from which he pointed out Arne Nature Reserve, Brownsea Island, Poole Harbour, and where they had driven from, far in the distance.

"Wow, what a view mummy!" William exclaimed, excitedly, loving being so high up.

They then continued downwards towards Corfe and having gone under a bridge; heard a steam train chugging above them. William had never seen a real steamtrain before and craned his neck to look backwards at it and the steam trail it left behind. Evelyn grinned watching, as with his eyes wide with amazement, he excitedly pointed out various landmarks along the way.

He was particularly captivated by the ruins of Corfe Castle, which stood majestically atop a small hill to their right, its uppermost walls enshrouded in mist. This was an amazing adventure for a young boy who had only known nothing but a very sheltered life in Dublin, and she loved seeing him so animated.

She was, however, desperate to get to Michael`s house, having never been a good passenger, and after the nauseatingly rough plane flight, and the winding Dorset lanes, she had been feeling very queasy. They soon pulled off the main road, drove up a steep hill, and through a little hamlet called Kingston, and the road suddenly bent sharply to the left and it was here, that Michael pulled over into a small driveway.

She gasped, he did not live in any ordinary cottage as she had assumed, but in a beautiful converted old church on a plot with far-reaching views from all sides.

"Welcome to our humble abode," he said, smiling proudly.

He leapt out of the car, dragged their suitcases from the boot, and up a small path leading to the large wooden ornately carved front door, and Evelyn and William followed.

Having never really left Ireland before, Evelyn felt nervous when introduced to Michael`s wife Betty, and their dog, Bounder. But Betty quickly made cups of tea and ushered them out to the back garden, where they could sit in the sun and chat, and she started to relax.

The garden, sided by old stone walls, was a real suntrap, full of wildflowers. An old, twisted wisteria, covered in dusky lilac blooms framed the building`s large arched windows, and she could look down over a blanket of green fields towards the ruins of Corfe to her left, and the sea, shimmering blue in the distance to her right.

"What a beautiful place you have here," she exclaimed.

She sank back into her chair in the sun, sipping the tea Betty had handed her in a bone china cup. Meanwhile, William was down in a lower part of the garden playing with bounder, his giggles being carried on the gentle breeze toward them.

All afternoon, Michael and Betty, who Evelyn was surprised to discover was very petite in stature, recounted stories of how they met, found the church, **did it up** and all about their life there, while she listened, enthralled. They explained that when the two of them met, they both had their own houses and after deciding to buy the dilapidated church and restore it, had rented out Betty`s seafront flat.

"The tenants have only recently given Notice to end their tenancy, so we thought it would be ideal for you both."
"Oh, my goodness. That is so kind of you. But we will pay our way," said Evelyn, hurriedly.
"No really it`s fine, you are family, after all," they replied.

Evelyn was shocked by their generosity, and felt a bit uncomfortable, but remembering the envelope Frank insisted she take with her, she hurried along to her room and opened it. It contained twenty thousand pounds in £50 notes, meaning they had enough money to live on and could pay their way for the next few years, and told Michael so.

"Well, the offer stands if you ever need it," he said.

CHAPTER 81

Evelyn and William, 1979.

Michael drove them down to Swanage to show them the flat the following day, and they liked it so much that they moved in immediately. It was lovely, and right on the seafront in a building that was originally a hotel. It had walls at least four feet deep and had been built in 1837, and Evelyn was excited to discover, after talking to one of her new neighbours, that Queen Victoria had stayed there when a child, having stopped to break her carriage journey back to London from Dorchester.

Evelyn was always pleasantly surprised each time she opened the flat door. Although not large, the soaring high ceilings gave it an airy, spacious feel and its three large sash windows provided stunning views not only of an expanse of sea, stretching out for miles, but also to the far left of the seafront and her right, down as far as Poole and Bournemouth. Her favourite view, however, was the one immediately across from the flat, of an expanse of flat-topped rocky cliffs lapped by the sea and topped with dark greenery.

Although the part of Dublin she had grown up in was only a stone's throw from the sea, she had not remembered ever going there as a child, so it felt like she was making up for lost time, now. After making herself a cup of tea in the little kitchenette each morning, she would often pull the wicker chair in the window into a good vantage point, and stare out at the rippling waves, in awe. This always calmed and soothed her and was a lovely way to begin her day. Usually back there again after walking William to school, she remained there for at least an hour most days, mesmerised by the changing sea in front of her.

One morning, just as she was getting up from her chair, she noticed something bobbing around between the waves. She stared at it trying to decipher what it was, and to her surprise, realised it was a seal. Unable to contain her excitement, she put the front door on the latch and ran out and across the road taking her mug of tea with her, over to a little old stone pier that jutted out into the sea from the main thoroughfare. The seal had disappeared but re-emerged right in front of her one more time, before disappearing completely from view, and returning elated, further reinforcing how being there, made her and William so happy.

It was surprising how quickly she settled into life in Swanage, and William appeared to be enjoying school and had made some new friends. When the weather was nice, she would don a long warm coat, take her early morning cup of tea to the pier, and sit and watch the sea. Sometimes William went with her and dangled a crab line over the edge, but now a typical young boy often preferred to stay in bed until she returned.

CHAPTER 82

Evelyn and William 1979

Evelyn had passed the local corner shop often, and one morning noticing a card in the window saying they needed staff, she went in and introduced herself straight away, and after a day`s trial, was taken on. Working there was great and positioned where it was, in the main High Street, she felt like she was in the very hub of the local community. She met lots of local neighbours, and wherever she went everyone seemed very smiling, happy and friendly.

It is only a short walk down into the town and the seafront from the flat, and she would often walk from one end of the bay to the other, enjoying the sound of the sea and breathing in the fresh, salty air.

There was only one downside to the flat, and that was that the sash windows, had been painted shut at some point, and it was impossible to open the top part of them at all, they were stuck solid. This had not mattered over the winter, but as the new year dawned, and the days began to get longer and warmer, she needed to be able to open them. The other issue was that the bottom ones although openable, would never stay open and would often gradually slide down and close. She and William had resorted to using bits of wood to prop them up, which not only became a chore but was also dangerous and could accidentally hit someone walking by underneath if one were to fall out.

After mentioning the issue to Michael, he sent a man called Jim, to look at them for her. After what had happened at the Mother and Baby Home, Evelyn still felt very shy and uneasy around men, but there was something about Jim, that from the first moment she saw him, struck her. It was strange, but it felt as if they had already met, but they could not have done so, as he had no connection to Ireland.

Usually very standoffish and shy around men, she felt different around him, and she could feel herself relaxing, as she listened to him talk. He explained how he had moved down to Swanage from London over thirty years earlier and, later his other brothers, and eventually his parents, also joined him in the town.

Virtually straight away, Evelyn had felt like she could trust him, and they had chatted away as if they had known each other for years. She liked his easy-going manner and sense of humour and often felt quite deflated after he left. Her last experience of being enamoured with a man had been so completely different, and she shuddered, remembering what Jefferson had done and how he had made her flesh crawl. But Jim was stirring up a range of emotions and feelings she had laid dormant for some time, and she could not get him out of her mind.

Picturing his long legs, slightly longish dark blonde hair, and penetrating turquoise-blue eyes, she often found herself unable to sleep. But, putting it all down to her feeling a little lonely, and just being silly, she tried to forget him, but the windows needed more work when the weather changed, and he returned.

This time, she summed up the courage to tell him,

"I don`t know why, but I have a strong feeling that we've met before."

She had said what she had been thinking aloud, and Jim`s reaction surprised her.

"I know, I`ve been thinking the same thing. It`s strange isn`t it?" he said.

He had met her gaze and smiled, but feeling her face flushing red, she had averted her eyes and looked shyly away.

Jim needed to be at the flat for the rest of the day and after having composed herself again, Evelyn continued to chat to him as he worked. She discovered that they were indeed similar in many ways. After all, she had been through with men in the past, it was a real pleasure to meet someone so nice, and after getting to know him better and better while he was working at the flat, he restored her faith in humanity again.

Although suddenly nervous when it was time for him to leave, she managed to ask,

"Do you fancy doing something this week, maybe going to the cinema or out for a bite to eat?"

He had appeared a little taken aback, and Evelyn was worried she had been too forward. But he smiled and remarked,

"I was just about to ask you the same question."

CHAPTER 83

Rory September 2015

One evening Rory arrived at the Care Home a little later than normal and found Rhona in bed. He had brought her favourite freesias and placed them in a vase, where she would see them the next morning. Although she had stirred slightly, looked at him and the flowers, and smiled, before dropping back to sleep, he had returned to the caravan later, sad that he had been unable to properly talk to her.

The following morning when the staff started their early morning rounds, Rhona was not in her bed, and after searching the whole building, they still could not find her. Realising her clothes were gone, Erica instructed the staff to search the area around the Home, by car and on foot and was getting increasingly concerned when she was still not found.

Rhona had awoken from a long deep sleep with a smile, seeing the freesias on her bedside table. Remembering back to when Bryn had brought them specially for her when they were in the flat on the Wharf at Seachapel, and how divine they smelt, she felt very contented. Laying on her bed, staring at the sunlight seeping around the curtains, she pictured him standing in her bedroom window with his back to her and gazing across the water towards Seachapel. He was wearing his motorcycle leathers and carrying his helmet in his hand.

When he turned towards her, she saw he was wearing the red spotted handkerchief he always wore and caught glimpses of his much-loved rainbow-coloured woolly jumper, under his leather jacket. He grinned in her direction, the same grin she had always pictured since his cruel removal from her life. But by the time she had sat herself up, he had vanished.

The sun was now streaming through her thin curtains even more brightly and without hesitation, she got out of bed, dressed, tidied her hair and after grabbing her handbag, crept out into the corridor where, finding the side fire door unlocked, she snuck out.

There was a crisp chill in the air and not wanting to get cold, she walked as quickly as she could along to the village, where she knew she could hail a taxi. She had only £10 in her purse, which she thought should be enough, and was soon speeding along in the back of a taxi down the back lanes, across the Ayer Estuary and on towards Seachapel.

After driving through the town, Rhona directed the driver to the car park nearest the footpath leading to the Fisherman`s Chapel, where she had her marriage to Erick blessed. From there she walked down to the lower coast path, just as she had done so many times with Bryn. Her legs soon got tired from walking, and when near enough, she grabbed hold of the thin metal railing to steady herself on the steepest bit of path, that led down to the sea. Back on a flat piece of footpath again, she stood trying to catch her breath and gazed around her.

It was a gorgeously sunny day, with a bright blue sky above and the crispness of the blowing wind felt invigorating, and she breathed it into her lungs in large gulps. It felt so good to be out of the overpowering warmth of the Care Home and in such fresh and familiar air again.

After watching the roughed-up white-topped waves as they crashed against the rocks below her, in awe for a while until her breathing steadied, she wandered a little further along the path and was glad to be able to sit down on her and Bryn`s favourite seat for a while to rest her legs.

Looking around her, completely enthralled and smiling, she took it all in, savouring it all for one last time. Sitting there, it felt like a huge weight was suddenly being lifted off her, and despite only being there a short while at that moment, she could have been there a whole lifetime.

With happy memories playing over and over in her head, she felt an incredible lightness, and as if a gust of wind could blow her away. She had never felt this way before, and feeling a bit tired now, she was the most relaxed, calm, and happy as she had ever been.

Suddenly, looking over to her right, and stretching out her hand, she said aloud,

"Hello Bryn, I was hoping you would be here for me."

Sighing, she smiled contently and engulfed in a floating feeling of weightlessness, she suddenly felt free.

CHAPTER 84

Rory September 2015

Rhona`s body was found considerably later by a jogger. Other people had seen her but assumed she was asleep and did not try to wake her. The jogger later admitted that although initially shocked by their discovery, she had been looking so peaceful and was smiling, when she went.

The news of Rhona`s death was a terrible shock for Rory, and he wished he had properly woken her when he visited the evening before, instead of just going home. Beside himself with grief, not even Angela could do or say anything to comfort him.

Eventually plucking up the courage to phone Padraig and Orla to tell them the news, he had completely broken down, as the words tumbled out of his mouth in a rush. Padraig, although incredibly sad to hear the news, did not get that emotional on the phone, but Rory could hear Orla sobbing loudly in the background, which made him start crying again.

Aware that Belinda also needed to know, Rory dreaded ringing her after a year of no contact and was very relieved when Padraig rang back to say he had already told her. Padraig told him how upset she had been, but had got Toby there with her, to comfort her.

Not knowing anything about Angela, Padraig asked,
"Are you going to be ok on your own, Rory? It must be so hard for you, especially as you saw her so frequently."

Touched by his brother`s comment, Rory thanked him and told him not to worry he would be fine, but that was not strictly true.

He also received a phone call from Erica at the Care Home, who was full of compliments about Rhona, and said they would all miss her terribly. She had been very apologetic about Rhona leaving the Care Home unseen and said she wished she had been able to stop her.

To which he had replied,

"It`s not your fault Erica, Rhona was always very strong-willed, and if she had made up her mind to do something, not much would stop her.  Please don`t blame yourself."

She told him,

"We will miss her Rory, she was such a character. I know several staff would like to go to the funeral if that`s alright?"

She sounded choked when she said that, and he told her,

"When I know what`s happening, I will let you know."

Feeling exhausted after he ended the call, and with all the ramifications of Rhona`s passing suddenly hitting him, he collapsed into bed and cried all night long. Awaking early the following morning, after having dreamed that Rhona was in the caravan, he recalled hearing what sounded like a radio being turned on loudly in his ear, and Her voice said loudly,

"Rory, don`t worry. Everything will be all right. Believe me Rory, and it will all be ok," and then everything went quiet again.

This was strange, and unlike anything he had every experienced before, but was so typical of her and he had got out of bed filled with a new sense of hope. Although remaining incredibly sad about her passing, he felt convinced that she was somehow still with him, just like he had believed his mother and grandma had been, since they passed, and that everything would indeed be all right.

CHAPTER 85

Rhona`s Funeral, September 2015

As per her wishes, Rhona`s cremation service was open to anyone to attend and followed by a short service at the Woodland Burial Ground, for family only, the following day. She had stated in her Will, that after cremation, she wanted half of her ashes put in a casket and buried next to Bryony at the Woodland Burial Site.

"So that she would no longer be alone."

Then, the other half, she wanted to be scattered above the cliffs between Treggenhow and Nansmorrow, and the rest, taken over to Cullenmara and scattered around Erick`s favourite rock.

Feeling a strong sense of foreboding when Rory joined Belinda in the front pew of the Crematorium Chapel, he had been worried when he heard the others could not go to the service, and it would just be the two of them for both ceremonies. Apart from really appreciating all the efforts the local women`s institute had gone to, in decorating the inside of the chapel with his mother`s favourite freesias, everything was a bit of a blur for him. The chapel was more crowded than he had expected and before the service started, people he did not recognise, approached, shook his hand, and offered their condolences.

One man appeared particularly upset, and introduced himself in a broad Scottish accent, as Angus. With no idea who he was or what he had meant to Rhona, he had looked at him blankly. Angus had patted him on the back, and said,

"I`m so sorry for your loss, I want you to know that Rhona was a wonderful friend to me, and I will always be indebted to her, she saved my life but sadly, we lost touch years ago, I had to come when I saw the funeral announcement."

He was fighting back tears when he walked off and joined a tallish woman with blonde hair, who appeared to be waiting for him.

Although grateful for everyone`s condolences, wanting to shut everything out and pretend it was not happening, he kept his head bowed, it was all so surreal, and he felt closed off and numb.

He hoped Heidi would come, but aware she had new clients at The Refuge, he knew it was unlikely she would be there. It would have been nice to have her there for moral support, but Erica and other staff from the Home had managed to come, which was comforting.

Rory got to his feet immediately after the service ended, and was starting to walk back up the aisle when Belinda called after him. Pretending not to hear her, he continued walking purposely out of the church, but when she shouted after him even louder, he stopped, and stood watching her extricate herself from a small crowd of mourners, and hurriedly walk towards him.

This was the first time he properly looked at her since Erick`s Will reading, and she looked quite different to how she had done at his funeral. She was dressed all in black again but he noticed she had a ladder in her tights and her dress looked very creased, and when she got closer, could see her complexion was very pasty and. she had dark circles under her eyes.

Strangely, the first thing she did was to touch his arm affectionately and apologise for not visiting her mother more. She also thanked him for all he had done for "her mother," since she went to the Care Home.

"No worries, Belinda, I was right here, and you live much further away. It`s all right," he said quietly.

Her behaviour was uncharacteristic and disconcerting, and although annoyed by her insistence on calling Rhona, "Her mother," he could not bring himself to confront her about it.

The music started up, although Rhona had picked an arousing tune, as he watched the curtains slowly closing around her coffin, he became so suddenly overwhelmed with emotion, that he put his head in his hands and broke down sobbing.

Belinda moved closer, squeezed his hand, and waited for him to compose himself.

Unused to this sort of attention from her, he shrugged off her hand and told her abruptly,

"I`m ok, and don`t need your false commiserations."

"I`m sorry Rory, sorry for everything!" she said.

She left Rory standing pondering her apology, which was also very out of character.

The next day the journey from the cottage to the Woodland Burial Site took about half an hour, and having previously booked two different funeral cars because Belinda was staying with a friend, she and Rory arrived separately.

"We could have planned this better, it`s not very green, us using two cars is it?" she said.

Rory nodded silently as they wandered silently along to Bryony`s plot.

There was no sign of Heidi, and Rory hoped she would turn up because being alone with Belinda was making him feel very uneasy again, especially when she was behaving so strangely.

Knowing Rhona so well, the vicar stood by the graveside and spoke much more personally about her in this address, before lowering the little casket gently into the recently dug hole, adjacent to Bryony`s grave. After reciting a little prayer, he shook Rory and Belinda`s hands and left them to contemplate alone.

"I miss her so much Belinda," said Rory and she nodded.

"Yes, it's so hard to imagine our lives without her in it, isn't it?"

She sniffed and having found a tissue in a pocket, blew her nose very loudly.

Seeing, and seeing how upset she was, Rory offered her his handkerchief which she took, and mumbled a quiet,

"Thank you."

Although now seeing glimpses of her more relaxed and kinder side, he still did not trust her, and typically she went quiet and distant, and after checking her watch, hurriedly told him she needed to catch the four o`clock train. With that, she left without even saying goodbye, or returning his handkerchief, leaving him standing alone at the grave.

This was a kick in the teeth, and falling to his knees in the mud, he sobbed his heart out. He loved Rhona so very much that he could not believe that so soon after having found her, she was now gone, and he was back on his own again. To lose both parents in such a short time was absolutely devastating.

CHAPTER 86

Rory and Heidi 2015

Rory was knelt in the mud in a trance-like state, until it began to get dark, when he had felt a gentle tap on his shoulder.

"Excuse me sir, but we`ve been waiting to finish up," said a man with a deep Cornish accent.

It was one of the gravediggers, and he apologised for keeping them, and stiffly got to his feet. He was cold right down to his bones and the knees of his suit trousers were muddy and damp, but he did not care. Now that both Rhona and Erick were gone from his life, nothing else mattered anymore.

Heidi arrived at the Woodland Burial Ground late, feeling bad after having promised Rory faithfully, that she would be there, and had hurriedly walked down to Bryony`s grave from the car park. Recognising Rory`s crumpled outline in the dim light of dusk, she watched him stumble precariously up the winding concrete path toward her. Seeing the sorry state, he was in, and how much he was shivering with the cold, she quickly returned to her car, retrieved a blanket from the boot, and took it down to him.

He looked at her so blankly at first, and then back down at the ground, and in that split second, Heidi was reminded of how Rhona looked, the day after Bryn died. Back then, and so caught up in her grief, she was oblivious to the fact that Heidi was there with her, and when she realised, all that had happened suddenly hit her, and it was horrible to watch her, one of the strongest women she knew, completely go to pieces.

Sighing, she placed **the blanket** around Rory`s shoulders, and hugged him for a few minutes, trying to get him warmer. She then apologised profusely for being late, and he did not look up from the ground straight away, but when did so, seeing how pale he looked, the deep dark hollows under his eyes, and his tear-streamed face, she wished she could do more to help him.

"Better late than never, eh Heidi?" he mumbled.

From where she was, Heidi could see the gravediggers filling in the hole where the casket was buried. It seemed strange to think of one of her best friends, now reduced to ashes in a little box. The thought made her shudder, and she started to cry, something she had done a great deal of, since first hearing the news. A friend like Rhona was irreplaceable and her loss was difficult to bear.

She took hold of one of Rory`s hands and as they silently walked hand in hand back up to the car park, she told him,

"I`m always here for you, you aren`t alone in this, you know that don`t you?"

He nodded and after stopping to hug her, began sobbing again, and with his voice shaking with emotion, managed to say,

"I don`t know what I`m going to do, without her, Heidi."

"I know, it feels like that now Rory. But the thing is, she wasn`t happy was, at the Care Home, and she`s gone to be with Bryony, Brynn, and Erick now."

When they reached the car, she guided Rory into the passenger seat, and when he did not speak. at all on the journey back, she was concerned. Instead of taking him to the caravan, she helped him out of the car and into the warmth of her house, where she insisted he ate some hot, homemade nourishing soup and bread, and was pleased to see the colour returning to his cheeks.

He told her,

"I just didn`t think she would be leaving us so soon, Heidi," and looked forlorn.

"I`m sorry, the last thing you need now is to have to contend with me, you`ve known Rhona a whole lot longer than I have, and I know you loved her too."

Hearing that Heidi struggled to keep her tears at bay and tried to be strong, and having put her arms around him, let him sob until he could not sob anymore.

She told him,

"Yes, I did love Rhona very much, she was one of my best friends and I am so sorry, I wasn`t there with you, at the service. But you know what Rhona was like, I mean the *old* Rhona, before the dementia, she would not have wanted any of us to be sad for long."

He managed to give a slight smile before saying,

"Do you know what? The jogger who found her said she was smiling when she went."

Heidi half laughed back and told him,

"It was what the old her would have wanted, Rory. There were times when I visited her at the Care Home when it was obvious, she was aware, she wasn`t herself and hadn`t been since the accident. Although it`s been a terrible shock, Rory, she died on her terms, and you`ve got to admire her for that and she remained rebellious to the end."

It was as if this had suddenly struck a chord with Rory, and now properly smiling, he added,

"She wouldn`t have wanted to die in that little single bed in the Care Home, I can see that now. I guess she did go to find Bryn."

"Let`s hope she found him then, Rory," she said.

Rory felt so much better after talking to Heidi, and although remaining incredibly sad that Rhona had gone, and he was on his own again, he appreciated having one of her best friends to count on.

CHAPTER 87

Frank 1981

Frank was getting itchy feet after five years working in General Practice in Dublin, and having recently turned forty, decided to holiday in Dorset. It would be a chance to spend some more quality time with his son, and if possible, rekindle his friendship with Evelyn, and do something he felt he should have done years earlier.

Having always kept loosely in touch with her by letter, and with no close family, he yearned to see his son again, after having only briefly seen him after he left his job at the Homes.

After writing to say he would be arriving in a month, he eagerly crossed off the days until he could go. Feeling it was high time that he stepped up and did right by Evelyn, when she had done so much for him, in taking William, he boarded the earliest flight from Dublin that day.

The plane journey was soon over, and after having been through Bristol Airport and out of Departures, he picked up his hire car from the car park. The journey cross-country towards Swanage was interesting and very picturesque in places. Passing Corfe Castle so closely had been exciting, especially as despite the early sunlight, its grey castle walls remained enshrouded in mist, giving it an almost ethereal feel. He was also impressed by the pretty grey stone buildings in the lovely village beyond and was tempted to stop and have a cup of tea in one of its cosy-looking teashops. But eager to reach his destination as soon as possible, he continued onwards.

Soon, as Evelyn had directed, he veered off the main road and up a winding hill past a gorgeous-looking ivy-clad stone pub, and the road bent sharply to the right. This took him up to a high upper road, where he gasped at the patchwork view of fields stretching towards the coast, and could see the Swanage sands in the distance, and an expanse of blue-green sea, beyond.

He soon reached another pretty village, full of little stone cottages that having driven through, took him back onto the main road into Swanage. Where, heading for the seafront, it did not take him long to arrive at the imposing Victorian building, that Evelyn had described. It was in an area signposted as "The Old Quay," and where he could park in the road outside.

While he was retrieving his holdall from the boot, he absentmindedly patted the top pocket of his jacket, to check the little box he had brought with him, was still there. Evelyn had sacrificed so much for him, and he was convinced that seeing each other again, and this time doing the right thing by her, that love would eventually blossom between them and the three of them could become a proper family.

However, he was unprepared for what happened next.

CHAPTER 88

Rory End September 2015

The evening after the funeral, Rory returned to the caravan appreciating his chat with Heidi. It had been a difficult day, and although she was not at the service, she had looked after him when he needed it the most. He hated that Angela could not risk attending the funeral with him. Knowing Rhona well, after having been involved in Erick`s care for two years at the Centre, after his nasty head injury, she had wanted to go, but this was one of the downsides of having an affair with a married woman.

Desperately wanting to see her, although risky, he bravely rang her at her home. Luckily, she answered the phone after seeing his number, but was unhappy with what he had done, and told him,

"Rory, Roger`s only in the next room."

Annoyed, she listened as he quickly told her,

"Angela, please come over, I need you. Please can you stay the night this time, I can`t face being on my own?"

Rory knew he was expecting a great deal, but feeling so upset to have lost both Erick and Rhona he needed her. Detecting the emotion in his voice, to his relief, she arrived about half an hour later, expecting to only spend a couple of hours with him and make sure he was all right.

Seeing her, Rory immediately grabbed her and pulled her close to him, and they enthusiastically embraced, and were soon ripping off each other`s clothing. The chemistry between them was more intense than usual, and with their passion remained fully ignited, until they both let out ecstatic groans and flopped on the bed, exhausted.

Rory lay, hot from their frantic lovemaking, watching Angela nakedly walk over to the fridge, retrieve two beers which she quickly opened, and bring them over to him. Wolf whistling as she approached, he had made her blush, and she shyly handed him a bottle and clinked hers against it, before thirstily swigging it back.

Sighing contentedly, she lay beside him and rested her head on his chest, and hearing his fast-beating heart beneath her, immediately fell asleep. So glad that she was there with him, Rory gazed dreamingly down at her and felt his whole body completely relax, having also fallen asleep, he was suddenly awoken by something hours later. Gently shaking Angela awake, he clicked the bedside light on, his alarm clock was next to it and seeing the time, and panicking, Angela quickly sat up.

"Oh my God. Roger will be wondering where I am!"

Rory watched her scurrying around, trying to find her clothes. She had only managed to get her underwear on when there was a loud knock at the door. Both looked at each other worried and with that, the door flew open and to their horror, Roger was standing in the doorway glaring back at them.

All three stared at each other in complete silence. Angela did not move but could see everything computing in Roger`s eyes. He suddenly and very violently launched himself at Angela, grabbed her legs, and pulled her out of the bed. She lay startled and afraid on the floor and looked up at him pitifully. Rory, still naked, immediately got to his feet, and after squaring up to Roger, a horrendous fight ensued.

Managing to scramble back onto the bed, Angela pulled the duvet around her to protect herself. But, unable to bear watching the men fighting, when the doorway became clear, still wrapped in the duvet, she ran over to Heidi`s house in a state of panic.

Initially, there was no answer when she knocked, but to her relief, a window opened above her and Heidi stuck her head out. Looking down at Angela, bleary-eyed, and with her curly hair stood on end, obviously still half asleep, she eventually managed to exclaim,

"Angela, why are you here, what on earth`s going on?"

Angela ignored her question and instead asked,

"I`m so sorry Heidi, but can I come in, please? I think we may need to call the police."

Heidi came downstairs and let her in.

CHAPTER 89

Rory and Angela September 2015

Angela explained all about their affair and what had happened, before bursting into tears, and Heidi, although trying her best to comfort her, was more worried about Rory, and phoned the Police, and joined Angela, who was standing in the cottage doorway, just in time to see Roger being roughly manhandled into the back of a waiting police car, which then drove off at some speed.

Heidi, still concerned about Rory, went over to the caravan and found him sitting on the bed looking dazed, nursing a bleeding lip and a black eye. Blood was also pouring from his nose, despite his attempts to stop it.

Gasping in horror, she ran over to him, and after grabbing the nearest tea towel, held under the cold tap, wrung it out placed it across the top of his nose and squeezed it.

"It`s ok Heidi, I`m alright," Rory said hurriedly, seeing her distraught expression.

Angela appeared and immediately told Rory off,

"Look at the state of you! I was so worried. Roger is a strong man and having grown up in London, enjoys a good fight."

"Yes, but did you see the state of him? said Rory with a cheeky wink.

Heidi left them, knowing they needed to talk.

"We've got to get away from here, Rory," Angela said.

"I can handle myself and look after you, you can see that,"

he replied. But, she remained insistent that her husband would be back and would want to make both their lives a misery.

Unsure what to do and after an extremely restless night with hardly any sleep, Rory suggested he phone Padraig to see if they could go and stay at the farm. He was only too happy to have them go and stay, in return for helping him through one of the busiest times on the farm. It was comforting to have the opportunity to get as far away from Roger as possible, and as Angela had the weekend off, they would have time to decide what to do next once they got there. They packed the car up early and after popping in to see Heidi and check she could look after Dougal and Tigger; set off on their journey to Somerset.

Heidi was concerned and surprised hearing their plans and was worried Rory was not thinking straight. Running off with Angela, so soon after Rhona`s death, she reckoned was a mistake. But she could not say anything to stop him when he had already decided.

Seeing Rory at the graveside the previous day, her heart had gone out to him, and all she wanted to do was hug him tightly. It had been a while since she had felt like that about a man and had been thinking about him after he returned to the caravan that evening. But discovering the affair had been shocking; after having thought he felt the same way about her, as she did about him. She had been imagining them doing more things together, and even embarking on a relationship, but that dream had been suddenly shattered.

She shut the cottage door with tears in her eyes and suddenly felt very alone.

CHAPTER 90

Rory and Angela September 2015

Angela explained all about their affair and what had happened, before bursting into tears, and Heidi, although trying her best to comfort her, was more worried about Rory, and phoned the Police, and joined Angela, who was standing in the cottage doorway, just in time to see Roger being roughly manhandled into the back of a waiting police car, which then drove off at some speed.

Heidi, still concerned about Rory, went over to the caravan and found him sitting on the bed looking dazed, nursing a bleeding lip and a black eye. Blood was also pouring from his nose, despite his attempts to stop it.

Gasping in horror, she ran over to him, and after grabbing the nearest tea towel, held under the cold tap, wrung it out, placed it across the top of his nose and squeezed it.

"It`s ok Heidi, I`m alright," Rory said hurriedly, seeing her distraught expression.

Angela appeared and immediately told Rory off,

"Look at the state of you! I was so worried. Roger is a strong man and having grown up in London, enjoys a good fight."

"Yes, but did you see the state of him? said Rory with a cheeky wink.

Heidi left them, knowing they needed to talk.

"We've got to get away from here, Rory," Angela said.

"I can handle myself and look after you, you can see that,"

he replied. But, she remained insistent that her husband would be back and would want to make both their lives a misery.

Unsure what to do and after an extremely restless night with hardly any sleep, Rory suggested he phone Padraig to see if they could go and stay at the farm. He was only too happy to have them go and stay, in return for helping him through one of the busiest times on the farm. It was comforting to have the opportunity to get as far away from Roger as possible, and as Angela had the weekend off, they would have time to decide what to do next once they got there. They packed the car up early and after popping in to see Heidi and check she could look after Dougal and Tigger; set off on their journey to Somerset.

Heidi was concerned and surprised hearing their plans and was worried Rory was not thinking straight. Running off with Angela, so soon after Rhona`s death, she reckoned was a mistake. But she could not say anything to stop him when he had already decided.

Seeing Rory at the graveside the previous day, her heart had gone out to him, and all she wanted to do was hug him tightly. It had been a while since she had felt like that about a man and had been thinking about him after he returned to the caravan that evening. But discovering the affair had been shocking; after having thought he felt the same way about her, as she did about him. She had been imagining them doing more things together, and even embarking on a relationship, but that dream had been suddenly shattered.

She shut the cottage door with tears in her eyes and suddenly felt very alone.

CHAPTER 91

Rory September 2015.

Rory relished the opportunity to spend time with his half-brother Padraig on the farm, and enjoyed meeting Lou his partner, and appeared to take to farming life easily. Excited to also be starting a new life with Angela, he was in his element there, well aware she was not her usual bubbly self, he assumed she was only tired because working on a farm, was different from anything she had done before.

Angela had rung the Centre to say she had car problems and the local garage in Somerset needed to order a part which would take at least a week to arrive. Unable to face telling Rory the truth, she had told him she had quit her job, and he was pleased because this was another big step in the right direction for them both. Even Padraig, who was not good at reading people at the best of times, noticed how cheerful and happy his brother now was, and was pleased he had found his potential soulmate and taken her there with him.

Most days Rory would be off over the fields on a quadbike, securing fences, herding animals, moving feed, hay baling, and helping Padraig with general maintenance chores. Loving being outdoors in breathtakingly beautiful countryside, he would often take his lunch up to a particularly nice area on the hillside behind the farmhouse, near Ham Hill, from which he could see even more of the Somerset Levels, spreading out beneath him for miles while he ate.

Angela on the other hand, was working in one of the larger barns, often tending to motherless lambs, feeding them bottles of warm milk until they were big and strong enough to join the others. She loved how their eyes opened wide when they saw her and they came gambolling over, and looked forward to seeing them each day.

However, she was shocked one morning, to find one of the smaller lambs lying dead in a pen, with its mother nuzzling it and trying to get it to move. Unsure what to do, she picked its little body up and hugged it.

"No time for sentimentality, I`m afraid," said Padraig, who had crept up behind her.

She turned to him with tears in her eyes, and seeing she was upset, he said.

"I`m sorry, for my insensitivity, I guess I`ve become rather used to it all over the years."

He took the dead lamb from her.

"This little one`s death won`t have been in vain," he said.

She looked at him,

"It`s going to save the life of that little fellow, there."

He pointed at an emaciated-looking lamb, seen visibly shivering, in a straw bed immediately under one of the heaters.

Disappearing with the dead lamb, he returned about half an hour later, carrying something. Curious to see what he was doing, Angela went over and watched him pick up the skinny shivering, obviously very poorly, lamb, wrap it in the dead lamb`s skin, and secure it with string. After dropping it into the pen with the dead lamb`s mother, soon after wobbling about near her, the newly dressed lamb found the ewe`s teats and began suckling away her milk.

"The ewe now thinks the lamb is hers," Padraig explained.

"That dead lamb saved its life."

Witnessing this gave Angela renewed enthusiasm about working on the farm, and Rory was relieved. Early September was a lovely time to work, and she began to feel more positive about being there, so much so, that she requested the Centre let her take her remaining annual leave and extend her stay beyond the first week. HR had been understandably unhappy, but after she reminded them how infrequently she usually took time off, they agreed to find a temporary replacement.

But as the days started to shorten, and darkness often enveloped them sometimes as early as three-thirty in the afternoon, the work suddenly became much harder, and the barn was cold to work in. It took virtually all of Angela`s energy to drag herself out of bed and leave the cosy warmth of the farmhouse, during the endless cold, dark, and bleak, early mornings, and an icy wind greeted her on her way over the yard to the barn. As someone who loved any chance of a long lie-in, particularly in the Winter, the early mornings were becoming increasingly difficult, and when working in such freezing conditions, started to affect her physically and mentally, she started having second thoughts again.

Often, she hardly saw Rory all day, and although Lou was lovely, she was not like any of the friends she had back in Cornwall, the ones she had always been able to confide in so easily. Also, regularly seeing Jemma, the farm border collie, was a constant reminder of her lovely dog back home, whom she had looked after since a small puppy, and missed very badly.

Rory, remaining blissfully unaware of how she was feeling, continued on as normal, and it was annoying for Angela, that he seemed unaffected by the cold dark bleakness.

Struggling increasingly more each day, and unable to pluck up the courage to tell Rory, having run out of holiday leave, Angela needed to decide if she would stay or not. She did love Rory, and in the beginning, their relationship had been great fun, but all the lying and deceit that came with it, had made her feel extremely uncomfortable. Feeling guilty about all the lies she had been telling Roger and all the subterfuge, assuming the affair would fizzle out, she had never considered it marking the end of her marriage, her life in Cornwall, and all its trappings.

Knowing Roger so well, and how they had joked about what would happen if either of them was unfaithful, she genuinely believed their marriage was over, and that there was no going back, running off with Rory had seemed her only option, but it had been a huge risk.

Rory was the absolute opposite of Roger, and that had been one of the reasons why she had been so attracted to him, and every time she saw him, her heart leapt in her chest and she wanted to be with him, touch him and make love to him. No man had ever made her feel quite like that before.

All this was going around in her head, when Roger suddenly and surprisingly texted, informing her he had stomach cancer. Although a complete shock, suddenly everything became clear in her mind, and her gut reaction was to check the train times and to return and be with him as soon as possible.

Now knowing how ill Roger was, she felt dreadful about all the hurt, pain, and stress she had caused. Issues aside, under his harsh exterior, she knew he was vulnerable, and now, more so than ever, and in the text, he made it obvious he needed her and still loved her; despite everything she had put him through.

It was heart-breaking to think of leaving Rory, and the pain she was going to cause him, but seeing how happy he was to be there with his brother and Lou; she was sure he would be all right without her, but dreaded ending the relationship, and in the end she took the coward`s way out.

CHAPTER 92

Rory and Angela October 2015.

Although Rory heard Angela get up at night, he was unconcerned as she usually needed to visit the toilet at least once, and dropped back off to sleep. But, finding her gone when he awoke later, and after frantically searching the farmhouse, he returned to the bedroom, and realised he had missed a note she had left propped up on the top of the chest of drawers. On a piece of A4 paper, she explained how much she missed Cornwall and had decided to return after talking to Roger, wanting to give their marriage another go, but did not mention his cancer.

Feeling so completely shocked and dismayed Rory immediately blamed himself. He had been so busy that he had just not seen that coming, and struggled to come to terms with what she had done. It was incomprehensible Angela could do that to him, especially by letter, and so soon after he had lost Rhona.

Managing to continue working at the farm through the winter, and until the next Tupping season, he had plenty of time to think about it all and concluded that Angela could not have genuinely loved him, or else she would not have left so suddenly and cruelly. She would have also found a way to attend Rhona`s funeral, knowing how much she meant to him, and how upset he was, but no, she had not done that either.

Now taking off his rose-tinted glasses and looking at the relationship a whole lot more clearly, he could see how he became so caught up in all the excitement of having an illicit affair, that he let his emotions take over, leading him to believe Angela was the key to his future happiness.

Although his first thought after reading the letter was to follow her back to Cornwall, seeing things more clearly now, he was glad he had not done that.

He thought back to a conversation he had had with Rhona about his relationship with Josie, and remembered her saying,

"As adults, we are all responsible for our happiness and no one can make us happy, we must be able to do that our-selves, and then it's a bonus if we meet someone who we can truly be ourselves with, can trust and love."

She had also said,

"As adults we have choices, we can either let our emotions run rough-shod over us and control us, or take control of them for ourselves. We can choose to be happy within ourselves and not rely on anyone else for that. Once we can be happy within ourselves, we have better relationships-ships can create boundaries and control how we react to things."

Realising how true this was for their relationship, and that Angela had provided him with a lovely distraction from all the grief and upset he was feeling after losing Rhona, and meeting her, had given him hope when everything felt hopeless. But sadly, he had come to depend on her and their relationship to make him feel better, make him feel needed and loved, and could see now that it had become more of an addiction, than true love. Rhona had coined the term, "Co-dependent relation-ship," and said it was something to be avoided because it was always dysfunctional for both parties involved.

After taking Padraig to one side to talk, he admitted how much it had all hit him, and although not wanting to let him down, had decided to either go back to Cornwall, or pursue something else, because being there, he was constantly reminded of Angela, and the mistake he had made.

Padraig completely understood and was very sympathetic; he had already been watching his brother gradually withdraw into himself and was worried about him. Wanting to help, he asked him if he could go over and care for the Cullenmara cottage, for them. He and Orla had been worrying about it being left uninhabited since they were all there. Brenna, their family friend from the end of the loch, had been checking on it, but concerned about the maintenance of the property, they said they **would pay him for doing it**. He also suggested that while there, he could scatter Erick and Rhona`s remaining ashes, something else neither he nor Orla had time to do.

Initially taken aback contemplating returning to Ireland, and the same area he had fled after leaving prison, Rory wondered if he would feel better or worse over there. But the more he thought about it, the more he wanted to go. It would be a chance to catch up with his best friend Diarmuid and his family, whom he had missed a great deal, and was also a chance to contact all the other people he had lost touch with over time, and probably enough time had elapsed since.

CHAPTER 93

Frank 1981

Frank entered the outer hall of the imposing Victorian building, pressed the bell for number three and after a click, was able to push the big glass-pained door and enter the main foyer. Seeing a sign showing that the flat was to the right and upstairs, he soon found it and after taking two deep breaths to compose himself, knocked loudly on the front door. Standing on the welcome mat, his heart pounding in anticipation, he heard movement and muffled voices emanating from inside, and the door opened and in front of him stood Evelyn, and beside her, was who he assumed was William.

Instantly overjoyed to see them both, Frank could not get over how different his son looked and stood on the threshold for at least a minute with his mouth open until Evelyn ushered him inside.

She immediately went to the kitchen to put the kettle on to make tea, and he watched her nervously, pleased to see how lovely she looked. Her auburn hair was longer than he remembered, and she had put on a little weight since her move, her clothes were fitted and showed off her figure nicely.

He complimented her,

"You certainly are looking very well, Evelyn."

She blushed, which he hoped was a good sign, and not wanting to embarrass her further, by continuing to stare, he went over to look out of one of the flat`s large sash windows at the fabulous views.

Meanwhile, William remained silently watching by the door and appeared unsure of what to do next. Noticing, and wanting to include him, Frank turned to him and asked,

"Well William, you have certainly grown, boy. I`m
your father, do you remember me at all?"
William stared at him, frowned and then shook his head.
"No, sorry, I don't remember you at all," he said.
Frank watched him sit awkwardly down at a table positioned in the next window, where head down, he continued with a jigsaw he had started earlier.

The kettle boiled, and as she made tea, Evelyn commented on how long it had been since they had last seen each other. But Frank was not listening and was staring at his son, feeling sad that he had not recognised him.

Raising her voice above the sound of the whistling kettle, Evelyn rearranged her previous question,

"How long has it been since we last saw each other, Frank?"

He admitted it must have been at least five years, and seeing he was looking a little uneasy, she beckoned him over to sit on the settee, carried the pot and cups over, and began pouring the tea. Frank relaxed back and remarked how lovely the flat was. Evelyn nodded and having poured herself a cup, sat down in a comfortable chair to one side of Frank.

"So, how have you both been?" he asked, nervously.

Evelyn told him about her job at the corner shop, the walks she took every day, and how well William was doing at school, and Frank smiled; pleased to hear that. After drinking his tea, and devouring the biscuits Evelyn also brought over on a separate plate, after clearing his throat, Frank asked,

"Would it be possible for the two of us to speak in private please, Evelyn?"

Hearing him say that made Evelyn nervous, reluctantly, she got up and asked William to go to his room, which he silently did, but remained listening at the keyhole. Aware Frank looked a little hot under the collar and uncomfortable, Evelyn stared at him, without saying anything. Although he had prepared a little speech beforehand, Frank had not anticipated how nervous he would feel and began speaking after taking a deep breath,

"Evelyn, I am so indebted to you for all you have done for me, and for keeping my secret all these years. You have also been doing a very decent job looking after William on your own; despite the struggles you must have had as a single woman, with a child."

He was looking intently at her, and she blushed again.

"You are indeed a marvellous woman, Evelyn," he added.

Still not good at handling compliments, to distract herself, Evelyn got to her feet and asked,

"Would you like more tea Frank, there`s plenty in the pot?"

"No, sorry no thanks," he said.

The interruption was unwelcome and affected his thought processes. He had to get this right, and after taking another deep breath, continued,

"Please sit down beside me Evelyn," he said, patting the settee cushion beside him, and Evelyn did as he asked.

"There is something important I wish to ask you."

Feeling even more worried than she had earlier, Evelyn put her hands in her lap and gazed at the floor.

CHAPTER 94

Evelyn and Frank 1981

Frank moved the coffee table out of the way and got down on one knee. While down there, he retrieved a tiny box from his jacket pocket, opened it, and proudly displayed it in front of her with glee. The box contained a beautiful opal ring, rimmed with tiny pearls and Evelyn gasped.

"It was my mother`s," he said gleefully.

"Will you do me the honour of becoming my wife, Evelyn?" he asked.

Evelyn looked flummoxed and stumbled over her words,

"I`m sorry Frank," she said, with her voice trembling,

"But I can`t, I can`t marry you."

Not knowing what to do next, Frank knelt awkwardly at Evelyn`s feet, trying to take in what she had said and what it meant, he had certainly not been expecting that reaction. He sat back down on the settee again, and she watched him hurriedly return the jewellery box to his pocket, looking crest-fallen.

"You`ve got to understand, Frank, we've not seen you for over five years and have made a life here It wasn`t as if you and I were ever romantically linked."

She was trying to sound convincing but wanted to say that she had met someone else, and was incredibly happy with him, but felt that would be too cruel. Frank continued to look crestfallen, but having come to his senses, quickly got up from the settee and said abruptly,

> "Well, are you going to take me on one of those walks you do regularly, Evelyn? I would like that. William can come along as well?"

He continued, and his voice sounded choked,

> "If it`s all right with you, I passed a very nice-looking hotel on the way into the town and will go and check in there for the week. I don`t want to waste this opportunity to spend quality time with you and William."

Frank saw them both every day for the next seven days. Evelyn thought it best not to tell him about Jim, and after phoning him beforehand to explain the situation, he agreed to stay out of the way until Frank had gone.

Although incredibly sad that his time down there didn`t turn out as he had planned, Frank was grateful for Evelyn`s continuing friendship and companionship and took her and William out for lavish meals, locally. Before he was due to drive back to the airport, Evelyn had taken his hand and squeezed it, and for a second, he hoped she had second thoughts about his proposal, but instead, she said,

> "I`m sorry if I`ve hurt you, Frank, but glad we`ve had some time together, the three of us, it has been lovely to see you and catch up."

She added,

> "Any news about Shauna, I did hear that she had left the Adoption Home. You always liked her Frank, didn`t you?"

Frank nodded, and the conversation ended there. He quickly said his goodbyes and left.

On the drive back, he started thinking about Shauna again, he had tried putting her out of his mind over the years, but Evelyn was right, he was still very fond of her and missed her a great deal, and decided there and then, to try to track her down when he got back.

CHAPTER 95

Rory March 2016

Rory briefly returned to Cornwall to collect Dougal from Heidi and got her to agree to keep Tigger, while he was in Ireland because it would be too unsettling for him to go on a ferry, let alone travel to a completely different country. Heidi had been genuinely concerned when he phoned from Somerset to say he was on his way back again and invited him in for a cup of tea, as soon as he arrived back. Still having strong feelings for him, when he told her the sorry story of what Angela had done, she instinctively leaned forward and hugged him, and he went limp in her arms and began crying again, something he had done a lot of on the journey back. They stood like that for a while, before he broke away, embarrassed to be crying.

She did not let on but felt relieved his affair with Angela was over. She had a bitter experience of being involved with a married man in the past, and it had left her feeling lost and vulnerable. The man at the time, had promised to leave his wife so they could be together, but had eventually decided to stay with her. Having already invested two years of her life in that relationship, she realised later, that she had become so swept along with it all, that she was powerless to stop it.

Her feelings for that man became strong so suddenly, that she had turned a blind eye to the fact she was never his priority, never the one he properly confided in, and had accepted his regular and very sudden coldness and lack of communication, as normal because he was married. It had taken her a long time to realise how much she had been at his disposal, and how he had never been there for her, especially when she had slipped and broken her wrist, one frosty winter, and all he had been concerned about was if he had gone to her aid, his wife would have found out.

Rory on the other hand, was kind, caring, and sensitive, and just the sort of person easily taken advantage of, and she feared the same fate awaited him. But having been through what she had, she now understood how impossible it is to see things clearly, when in the middle of it.

She told him this and he squeezed her hand, and said,

"You have always understood me better than anyone else, I need you to know, that I`ve always appreciated everything you have done, Heidi."

He gave her a quick hug and a peck on the cheek before driving off.

She watched him go with tears in her eyes, and been touched by what he said. Although sad to see him go, she realised that had he stayed any longer, liking him as she did, she may have done something she might later regret. Their friendship was much more important to her than any quick fling, and besides, it would have been way too soon after his break with Angela.

But Rory was her last link back to Rhona, and she would miss reminiscing with him about her, and their chats. It was good to have Tigger with her though, who as he was getting older, was becoming more attentive, and liked to sit on her lap, something he never usually did. and she wondered if it was because he was missing Rhona. He was a beautiful cat, and she often admired his thick ginger coat, and how perfectly his stripes lined his body, down to the end of his tail, just like Rhona had. It was such a comfort to have him there and she fondly remembered how much she had loved him too.

CHAPTER 96

Rory March 2016

From the moment the ferry docked at Dun Laoghaire Port, and as he drove Rhona`s Jeep down the gangplank, Rory felt a mixture of emotions. The journey down to the Swansea ferry terminal had been good but unable to prevent his mind from wandering back to Rhona driving with her hair blowing about in the breeze, and remembering the constant smile she always had on her face, as she sped through the Cornish countryside, he had felt sad. Now being back on Irish soil again, different memories came flooding back of his childhood, his grandma, and Siobhan, who had died so tragically.

Leaving the port traffic behind and now en route to Dublin, and having joined the new motorway, just as he had done with Rhona and Erick, less than two years earlier, a lump formed in his throat. It was a longish journey ahead, and the wrong time to get emotional, and he quickly wiped the tears away, wanting to save those for his arrival in Lochálainnin, which he knew would be difficult.

The motorway journey down to Cullenway went very smoothly, and after skirting the city, past all the brightly painted pubs, and grey stone houses, he was soon on the Wild Atlantic Way, the main coastal route down to the cottage. Passing the Cullenmara Court Hotel on his left, reminded him of when he was a bell boy there, one of his first jobs, and passing through Tullyvaughn, he remembered the nearby factory where he had also worked until he got caught with a girl from the office, literally with his trousers down, which had cost him his job. He smiled, that all seemed such a long time ago now and in another life.

As he continued, the roads became quieter and he passed Canla, and the signpost to Snáithecoiréil. He had loved living there with his grandma as a boy. It was only five miles now, to the cottage, and he was feeling unsure if he had done the right thing, going back. But he could not turn back now and did not want to let Padraig and Orla down.

Soon crossing the first long winding road bridge, transporting him further and further away from the mainland, and over rocky, seaweed-covered shorelines to the remote island of Aitmháith, he passed what had been his parent`s old pub, and focussed on the road ahead, when tears welled up again. But soon he was on the second bridge to Killeileana and passing Bauch`s Supermarket on his left.

Just as Rhona and Erick had done previously, when having been away from the area for a while, he pulled over in front of the large grey stone catholic church that sat majestically on the top of a small hill about a mile from the cottage. From here, he surveyed the fantastic view of wild rocky and hilly terrain, stretching endlessly around him. Although by this time the sun was descending low in the sky, perched high on a hillside ahead of them in the distance, he could see the outline of the cottage.

Minutes later, he turned off up the narrow and winding boreen and eventually stopped outside the cottage gates. Everything looked the same and although comforting, this was also hard to see. They had all been so cheerful when they had last driven out, and all he felt was sadness now.

Getting out to open the gate, he recalled all the times he had held it open for Erick so that he could drive the campervan in, and by the time he reached the front door, tears were streaming down his face again.

CHAPTER 97

It was as if time had stood still and his memories of leaving the cottage after Erick`s birthday, remained intact, so much so, that he half expected the door to swing open and to see both he and Rhona drinking Poitin and giggling together inside. He turned the key in the lock and tentatively pushed the big thick wooden door open, and what greeted him instead, was a much mustier smell than usual and a coldness that hung in the air.

To quickly contain any warmth in the building, he pulled the door too and wandered into the main room, where he collapsed into Erick`s old, battered leather chair, sobbing loudly. It had never entered his mind that he would be back again, without them both.

Feeling cold, grabbing handfuls of turf from the basket Brenna had left, and placing them vertically in the grate, he lit it, and it started smouldering in seconds. The familiar acrid smell of burning turf filled the air and reminded him of his grandma`s cottage, where he had grown up. It was so sad to be back in Cullenmara without her, Rhona, or Erick.

Soon feeling warmer, he wandered around the cottage, reminding himself of happier times. Peeping into the far bedroom, he gazed at the bed he was born in and smiled. Rhona had been so proud to show him, immediately after they had discovered he was their son, Billy. It had been nerve-wracking breaking the news, which had been confirmed by a flimsy little copy of his birth certificate, he had found in his grandma`s jewellery box. It clearly showed he had been registered as Billy, and not Liam which his adoptive parents had named him, and when he had told them, Erick and Rhona had been dumbfounded.

After explaining he had been brought up as Liam, the Irish version of William, and had changed his name to Rory, which had been his middle name, when starting his new life in Cornwall, they had shrieked with absolute joy, having never thought they would ever get to see their son again.

His gaze landed on Erick's rudimentary shelving, fashioned from planks and rope, and his clever idea of using bamboo as a curtain rail and smiled. Erick, just like him, had always been so creative. He came out of that room and needing to pee badly, headed across the flagstone floor into the tiny, damp-smelling bathroom, to the left of the front door. Afterwards still sitting on the old wooden toilet seat, too tired to stand any longer, from there he stared at the wooden bath panel, behind which he knew Erick kept his Poitin still.

Grinning to himself, he flushed the toilet and after washing his hands in chilly water in the sink, returned to the now much warmer front room, where he sat himself down again in Erick`s favourite old, battered leather chair, by the fire. The earlier smoke had dissipated, and the turf he had placed vertically in the grate was cracking and popping as it burnt.

When darkness began to fall, he got up and lit the two oil lamps positioned high up on a shelf above the fireplace, and was immediately soothed by their gentle hissing, and their shadows dancing on the bare walls around him. Hanging high above was one of Erick's early abstract-style paintings, one which Rory had always been curious about. It consisted of a series of views, all broken down into minute segments to reflect the rugged greenery, rock, and water of the area, the centre of which was a solitary man, with an angular face, wearing a flat cap and an old scruffy, brown suit. The man was staring out of the picture and into the distance, and painted in Erick's inimitable style, in hundreds of tiny segments, the colours of which cleverly highlighted the contours of each of his facial features. Rory wished he had asked Erick about it, and would have loved to have known who it was, but it was too late now, and unable to stop them, tears poured down his face again.

Trying to stop them and distract himself, he wandered out to the kitchen, where he familiarised himself with the water butt with the dogy lever, that would soak you if you were not careful, and checked the calor gas-powered fridge, and was pleased to see Brenna had kindly left him provisions.

Feeling hungry, he made himself a bacon sandwich and a cup of tea, which he took back into the main room and sat in one of the wicker-covered carver chairs, surrounding the large stripped wooden table. Through the windows from where he was sitting, he could see the path down to the lake, the island on it, and another rock-strewn, gorse, and heather-covered hill, over which was wild Atlantic Sea, was buffeting the shores in the distance. He was as transfixed now by that view as he had been when he had first set foot in the cottage, the day before Erick`s seventy-second birthday.

He remembered him suggesting they go fishing, but had to distract him from that idea, because of the planned surprise party, and regretted not going now. It had been a shame and feeling tearful again, Rory realised he needed time to come to terms with it all, and that what had gone on since Erick`s death, had prevented him from properly grieving all that he had lost.

The next few days were a bit of a blur and if it had not been for Brenna filling up the turf basket, and leaving provisions, Rory did not know what he would have done. He certainly did not want to go out or see anyone. But after two days of crying, he was worn out, and what followed were prolonged periods of sleep in what would have been Rhona and Erick`s bed. Maybe it was strange wanting to sleep in there, but it was where he felt particularly close to them.

By the third day, and after having awoken to sunlight pouring into the bedroom, he began feeling more positive. Looking around him from the bed, he smiled. Erick`s old, short off-white cotton bathrobe was still hanging from a hook on the wall. He had always worn it when sat on his favourite rock each morning, with his coffee and pipe in hand.

Rory recalled one very amusing morning when they were all last there together. He had been watching Erick smoking his pipe, from the cottage, laughed when he had stood up and absentmindedly scratched his bottom, lifting his robe and flashing his naked buttocks, while continuing to contentedly draw on his pipe, oblivious to what he had done. Rhona, who had also witnessed the spectacle from the kitchen, had giggled and said,

"What`s he like? I can`t take him anywhere."

Rory giggled, thinking what a character his father had been, and how cathartic it must feel to be at an age when you no longer care what anyone thinks. He remembered how stroppy he had been at the airport when having to put all his pipe paraphernalia in the hold with the luggage.

Aware of how much he loved his pipe, Rory decided to fetch one from the shelf above the fireplace and try pipe smoking himself. He had already found a small bag of his tobacco on the bedroom windowsill and, with nothing else to use but his finger to depress the tobacco in the pipe, he set about lighting it.

There was obviously a knack to pipe smoking and initially, nothing happened, but having held the lighter over the tobacco for longer on his next try, it suddenly caught alight, and when he drew on it a blast of hot smoky air hit the back of his throat. This was unexpected, and sent him into a coughing fit, but, undeterred, he had a few more goes until he began to relax and quite enjoy it.

With his throat feeling dry, he retrieved the Poitin from the hiding place in the bathroom, poured a large glass, and carried it out and down to Erick`s favourite rock. With him he also carried the urn containing his and Rhona`s ashes, and the pipe, and began drinking sips of Poitin, drawing on Erick`s pipe, and sat for a while, contemplating. Gazing aimlessly around him, he started to feel very relaxed, the most relaxed he had felt for a while.

Everything was still and quiet, apart from birds tweeting in the trees in the dip down to his right. Above him, the sky was clear and blue, and sunlight glinted on the dew-covered greenery around him. Below, the lake was quietly shimmering in the sunshine, and beyond that, the Inish Isles were now more prominent on the horizon. A gentle breeze was blowing towards him carrying with it, the sound of a dog barking, and the gentle roar of a motorbike on the road to his right in the distance.

Sighing contentedly, he balanced his phone on a taller nearby rock, set the video timer and began recording. Smiling, he drew deeply on the pipe, raised the glass of Poitin, and shouted,

"Slainte, Erick and Rhona," at the top of his voice.

Lifting the urns one at a time, he slowly emptied them, allowing the ashes to scatter around the rock. It was strange because while doing that, he strongly felt like they were both there with him, and he pictured them both smiling at the spectacle. After he had finished, he sent the video to Padraig, who immediately replied with thumbs-up and smiley face emojis.

Feeling incredibly calm, Rory remained sitting on Erick`s rock for over an hour, gently puffing on the pipe, until he had finished all the Poitin. He recalled reading the poem Erick had written when he had first visited Cullenmara, it had been printed on the inside cover of the order of service, at his funeral, and how much he admired his father's eloquent use of words and his obvious love for the scenery around him. Now, with the sun rising above the clouds, and gently illuminating the scenery around him, he understood why Erick loved being there so much and sighed contentedly.

CHAPTER 98

Frank 1981

Pondering his ill-timed proposal on the journey back from Dorset, Frank felt very foolish. What had he been thinking? It had been so wrong of him to assume Evelyn would want to marry him just because he was William`s father, and when they had only been friends and nothing more. He had made a mortifying mistake and even though he had apologised profusely all week, he deeply regretted being so selfish and inconsiderate towards her and William.

It had, however, been lovely to see Evelyn looking so well, and been great to get to know William, who had gradually become less shy in his presence and who had appeared to enjoy talking to him by the end of the week. He and Evelyn were still important to him, and he vowed to stay connected with them from then on.

For the rest of his journey, his mind wandered back to Shauna. Evelyn was right, he had been very fond of her and still was, she had been the only woman he had ever felt such a strong connection to.

They had been through so much together, and she had been the one constant in his life, and unbeknown to her, had helped him through it, just as much as he had helped her.

Driving on he realised how much he missed her, and felt a physical emptiness in his chest, even thinking of her. They had been working together in such unusual circumstances, and his actions that night, had been unforgivable, and despite having to deal with so much hardship, stress, and horror at the Mother and Baby Home, she, compared to Evelyn, possessed an inner strength, not many women had, and completely fascinated him.

"There is something about her, that makes me feel different, and that we should be together," he said aloud to himself.

He returned to Dublin with a new-found vigour and even more committed to trying to find her, remained very unsettled once back home again. After having envisaged a life with Evelyn and his son, made him feel even more lonely but, his job gave him something to focus on, which certainly helped. It was over the weekends when he felt the most lost and depressed, and very often the only way he could cheer himself up was by thinking of Shauna. He never intended to, but often dreamt of her. In these vivid dreams, h they often saw each other again and became intimate, and he would awake, unable to remember much else, but was left with feelings of warmth and comfort afterwards, at the thought of being with her again.

One thing was certain, he now desperately needed to find her, but had no clue how to start.

CHAPTER 99

Frank 1982

Frank photocopied all the information he had collected and sent to the Gardi and kept it all in a small filing cabinet in his office. He had given too many years of his life to the Mother and Baby Home, and latterly, the Adoption Home, for it to all have been in vain, and so kept it in case he ever needed it. One rainy weekend, feeling bored, he retrieved it all from the filing cabinet and read all his notes again. It was strange to think how much he and Shauna had logged over the years. But at least now, the Gardi were analysing their findings, and could hopefully, prevent anything like that from happening again.

Opening Shauna`s notes, which contained the memorised names of mothers and baby names, he marvelled at the detail she had sometimes gone into. There was much information about Maureen and all that had happened to her, and a description of the baby they had saved, whom Shauna called David. Also with those notes, he found other women`s names and details of their babies, many of which Shauna had put little crosses by, which Frank took to mean they had died. She had also numbered each entry, and he wondered why she had done that.

Longing to discuss it all further with her, but needing her birth name to find her, he wondered how he could find that out. Ordinarily, once you have someone's surname, it would be a case of looking in the telephone directory, but without that, he was stuck.

He had been daydreaming about Shauna again one day when he suddenly realised what he could do, he could ask Micky. Although he and Micky had been good friends, they had not seen each other since the incident on the playing field. But knowing roughly where Mickey`s parents had retired to; he had an idea. Relieved to discover their number in the local directory, he was pleased to hear Micky`s mother Aileen`s distinctive voice when she answered the phone. She sounded extremely happy to hear from him after so long and agreed to meet with him the following day.

CHAPTER 100

Frank 1982

Frank rang the doorbell twice and waited patiently for some-one to answer. Soon he heard shuffling from behind the front door and it opened to reveal a woman with short grey hair, worn in a bob. After initially staring at her, unsure if he had gone to the right address because she looked vastly different from how he remembered, recognising him straight away, she exclaimed,

"My my, Frank, it`s good to see you, you haven`t changed a bit."

He knew that was not true but appreciated her kindness in saying it anyway.

She ushered him inside and along to the kitchen. The house was just as he remembered it as a child, and as Aileen bent down to retrieve something from the oven, the familiar smell of warm soda bread filled the air.

"Would you like some?" she asked.

She turned to look at him and he nodded, and she began to cut the soda bread up into chunks and spread butter all over it. As a doctor, Frank always tried to eat as healthily as possible, but the smell was so irresistible he had to have some and wash it down with a cup of strong sugary tea.

After they had finished eating, he asked,

"Aileen there is someone from around here, that I used to work with who I have lost contact with and want to find again. She was a friend of Micky`s. All I know is that her first name is Shauna, and she grew up near the playing field.”

Aileen sat with her hands in her lap and appeared to be thinking.

“There was a Shauna, she was in the year below Micky, she had long dark hair. Could it have been her?”

He shook his head.

“No, the Shauna I`m looking for was younger and was always blonde. Her parents died in a car accident a few years ago, she also had much younger twin sisters.”

Aileen suddenly became very animated and leaned forward excitedly.

“Oh, I know who you mean, so I do. The O`Shea girl. I remember the scandal about her, those poor twins, fostered by the O`Malley`s, so they were.”

When Frank asked about Micky, Aileen went noticeably quiet and looked forlorn.

“I can`t talk about him I`m afraid, apart from the fact that he let us down very badly and is now languishing in Dublin's jail. He got in with the wrong crowd, would he listen when we tried to talk to him? No!”

Being genuinely shocked hearing what had happened to his friend, Frank commiserated with Aileen before leaving, and she gave him a big hug. It felt strange being hugged, Evelyn his mother, rarely showed affection. It had been great to finally have an address for her.

On the drive back home, realising how easily he and Shauna could have ended up in jail themselves, made him even more determined, to track her down as soon as possible.

CHAPTER 101

Shauna 1982

Shauna had abandoned all hope of ever seeing her twin sisters or Frank, again and had the shock of her life, one morning when she answered the door when the doorbell rang. She had a woman staying with her who had recently given birth to triplets, and after two hours of continual crying, had only just got them off to sleep. Already worried it had awoken them, she had crept to the door and sheepishly peered out.

To her complete astonishment, facing her was a tall, spectacled man with thick longish hair, who she did not recognise at first, but seeing two identical young girls waiting patiently behind him, she grinned at them and suddenly shrieked,

"Oh, my goodness! I cannot believe it, is it really you Frank, and ... the twins?"

She could not believe it, not only him but also her younger twin sisters were standing outside her house. Unable to take her eyes off him, she studied him while still on the doorstep, his hair was longer than she remembered, and speckled with grey, but he was tanned and looked so much better than when she last saw him and told him,

"You look so much better than when I last saw you."

He smiled,

"So do you, you look lovely, Shauna.

She appeared to blush, and continued to stare openmouthed at him until he asked,

"Aren't you going to let us in then?"

She smiled, and realising she had been staring at him for some time, quickly apologised.

"I`m sorry, it`s just I had resigned myself to never seeing you, or the twins, again, Frank."

When the triplets she had been caring for started crying again, she called for their mother and quickly ushered her guests through the house and into the back garden, where it was quieter. After having pulled up some wooden chairs, they sat around a table in the sunshine.

She disappeared back inside to get fresh apple juice for them all, and realising her hands were visibly shaking, had to steady herself by taking some deep breaths, and returned when feeling more composed. She was not gone long, and Frank watched her walking towards them, the glasses chinking against each other on the tray she was carrying.

"Hey, let me take those," he said suddenly standing up, aware she was trembling.

She was wearing her blonde hair down now and he had never seen her like that. It suited her, softened her features, and accentuated the blueness of her eyes.

He placed the tray on the table and handed the drinks around, and she sat down and momentarily met his gaze, but feeling self-conscious, shyly turned her head to smile at the twins. This was all so much for her to take in. The twins had changed so much and were young girls now. Both appeared very shy but in the hot sun, gulped down the apple juice in a flourish, and she smiled, remembering their mother had often made some for them when they were all very young.

"I can`t believe this, Frank, how on earth did you find me and find the twins?"

Studying her more easily now she was sitting so close, Frank had butterflies in his stomach. She looked so beautiful, and his heart appeared to be turning cartwheels in his chest.

She looked back at him, awaiting his reply, and he paused for a few seconds to compose himself before responding,
  "I went to see an old neighbour of mine, wondering if they
  would know your surname. I`ve been trying to find you for
  a while, but my search was hopeless without that."
  He took a sip of apple juice before continuing,
  "Not only did they know your surname, but also knew
  the family who fostered these two!"
  "Oh Frank, I will always be indebted to you for doing this,"
  she exclaimed.
She leaned forward, took hold of both his hands, and held them tightly. The softness of her skin against his felt like an electric shock, and Frank had to stop himself from grabbing her and kissing her right there and then, which he knew would be inappropriate in front of the twins.

Beckoning the two girls over to her, Shauna hugged them both and when they looked a little alarmed, she realised how young they must have been when she last saw them, and that they probably did not remember her. Thinking this was heart-wrenching, and trying to put matters right, she explained,
  "I`m your sister, Shauna. I looked after you both when you
  were young. Unfortunately, I had to go away for a while,
  and after Mammy and Daddy died, I completely lost track
  of you."
It was only after she went inside a bit later and upstairs to get an old photograph album, that after showing them old photos, the twins began excitedly talking and did recognise her as their sister. From that moment on, both wanted to sit as close to her as possible, and she hugged them to her tightly.

Witnessing this, made Frank feel quite emotional, thinking how lost they must have felt after all they had endured. The twins and he stayed for another couple of hours, and until the sun started to go down and the air got colder. When having got to his feel up to leave and take them back home, Frank stopped, turned to Shauna, and said,

"I am so glad to have found you, Shauna, and I do hope we can see each other again very soon."

Overcome with emotion herself, she stepped forward, and as she had done so often in the past, hugged him tightly. They clung to each other and looked into each other's eyes, before pulling away, embarrassed. Shauna thanked Frank profusely for finding the twins and told him how indebted to him she was, again, before he left, and after having also hugged the girls again, vowed to stay in touch with them from then on.

After having quickly picked some flowers for them to take to their foster mother, Frank waited patiently. It was obvious that the girls did not want to let their sister go and clung tightly to her.

"Shall we arrange something now, so you got it to look forward to?" she suggested and they nodded.

"What about if I come to your house, and see where you live and meet your foster mammy, would you like that?" She scribbled her phone number on a scrap bit of paper and gave it to Frank,

"Can you get their foster mother to ring me? Only I want to ensure she`s happy with me seeing them."

Frank was relieved, he had been unsure how to ask for her number and very much wanted it.

After they had gone, Shauna`s heart was beating so fast. Frank looked so well and handsome, and she could not stop thinking about him.

While driving the twins back to their poster parents, Frank`s thoughts were all over the place. Although incredibly overjoyed to see Shauna again, seeing her he felt a strong compulsion to confess what had happened on the playing field, all those years ago. But doing that would be risking never seeing her again and, having only just found her, he could not bear that.

He called Shauna the following day, and although they saw each other a great deal over the following weeks and months, he could not bring himself to tell her what had happened.

Since that day, Shauna was on cloud nine, it had been wonderful seeing the twins again and to now have them back in her life, was incredible. She had met their foster mother a few times and liked her and she had no qualms about letting her see them as often as she wanted, which had been a huge relief. Suddenly it felt as if her life was turning around, all the harmful stuff was dissipating, and she and Frank looked forward to a long happy life together.

PART SIX

Chapters 102 - 135

CHAPTER 102

Evelyn September 1993

Evelyn was understandingly proud when William left university with a first-class degree in accounting and had then worked for a large firm of accountants in Bournemouth for three years, before being head-hunted by a big American Bank. Although she had serious reservations about William`s move to America at first, Evelyn was pleasantly surprised to see first-hand how well he was doing, when she finally managed to get over to see him with Jim.

William lived in a penthouse apartment in a very modern block, near where he worked. Large glass elevators ran up outside the building, and when given a tour, they found a swimming pool on the roof. She had clutched Jim`s hand nervously, as the lift sped up to the top floor in seconds, but the views from there and William`s terrace had been breath-taking. To her right she could see over skyscrapers, towards what looked like a forest and countryside, and to her left, was the sea.

Feeling very proud, she had sat on a comfortable sun lounger, stretched out in the sun and told him,

"Well William, I could certainly get used to this."

"You could move here if you wanted to, mum. The company looks after their staff, it would be no problem for you to move over too. The Americans are very into taking care of the olds."

"The olds, I suppose yes that`s what we are," she retorted

and added,

"You are even starting to sound American, now William."

Although they had only stayed a couple of weeks, Evelyn and Jim did seriously consider moving over to live with William, but soon dismissed it after returning to the calm and quiet of Swanage life.

"I don`t think I could cope with all those sirens going past all day long, and the sheer number of people," Evelyn admitted.

Both thoroughly enjoyed their holiday and soon after they returned, announced they had decided to get married the following Spring. Everything was planned meticulously, and they were to marry in a lovely old church in a beautiful part of the town. Only wanting a small, intimate affair, for just close family and friends, they planned to honeymoon in Italy afterwards, but William had other ideas. They did not take much persuading, and after William paid for a holiday in the Seychelles for their honeymoon, flying first class there and back, they had to give in and accept, but unfortunately never got to go.

Aware they had recently sold the flat and purchased an old cottage, that needed things done to it, William had booked a month`s stay before the wedding, in a small seaside hotel nearby. He was just leaving the "Nothing To Declare" exit into the Arrival Hall at Heathrow Airport, after his long flight over, when he was approached by Airport Police.

Aware he was on his way, and probably at the airport, hospital staff on Evelyn`s instruction, phoned the Airport Police to instruct him to go to the nearest help desk, where local police were waiting to escort him to Bournemouth Hospital after Jim was involved in a serious accident.

CHAPTER 103

William, Evelyn, and Jim Spring 1994

Jim had been replacing tiles and felt up on the roof of the building when he slipped and fell and landed face down on top of an outhouse at the back of the house. This had at least broken his fall, but he had fallen over sixty feet. Evelyn was washing up in the kitchen at the back of the house when having heard a loud thud, had rushed to the window to see what had happened. Unable to see anything from there, she had gone out of the back door, looked around and still not seeing him anywhere, called out to him.

Worried when he did not answer, she stepped back, intending to go inside and check he was there when she felt a drop of something wet land on her head. Looking up, she was horrified to see immediately above her, one of Jim`s hands dangling from the outbuilding roof, and blood was dripping down it. She screamed and shouted,

"Hang on in there Jim, I`m going to get help."

She disappeared inside to ring 999, but her hands were trembling so much, that even tapping the numbers into her phone was difficult. After explaining what had happened, she was told the ambulance would be there straight away and broke down in tears from the shock. Hearing loud crying, a neighbour became concerned and was there with her, when firefighters arrived to lift him off the roof and take him to a

waiting ambulance. He was still alive at that point, still breathing and had a pulse, but remained deeply unconscious.

Sobbing uncontrollably, she insisted on travelling in the
back of the ambulance and held his hand briefly until his vital
signs changed and he needed to be resuscitated by one of
the paramedics. Sitting silently wringing her hands, and feeling extremely worried, she watched everything the paramedics
were doing. They were administering all manner of drugs intravenously via a drip, while Jim, her beautiful beloved Jim, remained unresponsive.

To her relief, a monitor started rhythmically beeping and
could see waves pulsating on a little screen.

"We`ve got him back," said one paramedic to the other.

Evelyn let out a huge sigh of relief and the medic nearest
her, said,

"It was touch and go, but he`s strong, and is back with us
again. He has lost a lot of blood and remains in a critical
condition."

"Can I hold his hand again please?" she pleaded.

When allowed to, she stroked his hand and prayed with all
her might for the first time since she was at the Mother and
Baby Home.

Jim remained in a coma in the hospital for several months,
although Evelyn reported to staff that his eyelids flickered
sometimes, and he often murmured in his sleep, he remained
deeply unconscious. Used to the constant beeping of monitors
around her and the rhythmic rushing sound of the ventilator,
she had been spending hours every day by his side, hoping that
his condition would improve. But was becoming increasingly
worried as time went on, and despite quizzing the medical
staff about his condition, no one seemed able to give her a
satisfactory answer, other than,

"I`m afraid it's a waiting game now."

William extended his visit still further to be with her, but when work needed him, he had to return, and she spent many hours alone by Jim`s bedside, hoping for a miracle.

The staff there were great and always ensured she was plied with regular cups of tea and sandwiches, but it was tiring having to get the bus to and from the hospital each day, and this started to take its toll. After having fallen asleep in a chair at his bedside one day, she awoke to a loud rattling sound and was horrified to witness Jim having a type of seizure, that caused him to vomit all over the sheets.

Terrified, Evelyn rang the emergency call bell, a team of medics arrived, and she stood back out of their way, frightened by what she was witnessing. The staff, so absorbed in what they were doing, forgot she was there. She could tell they did their best to resuscitate him, but after working on Jim for over fifteen minutes, Evelyn finally heard the words she had been dreading,

"I`m calling it, time of death 8.14 pm."

With that, all the beeping monitors went quiet and there was silence, the medics stopped what they had been doing and left the room after straightening the bedsheets. Realising she was still in there and had seen everything, a nurse went to her aid with a cup of hot sweet tea, and seeing her, Evelyn broke down in tears.

"I`m so sorry," said the nurse,

"But we did everything we could to get him back, but his brain was starved of oxygen during the seizure, and there was nothing else we could do."

Beside herself with grief, Evelyn was grateful when the same nurse suggested she give her a lift home at the end of her shift. But being back in their new, basic, and very cold home was extremely upsetting. She gazed around at all the things Jim was going to do, buried her head in her hands and cried, all their shared dreams were now shattered, and she felt very alone indeed.

Surrounded also by numerous framed photos of the two of them, taken mainly on all the various holidays, desperate to blot out what she had witnessed in the hospital, Evelyn decided to concentrate on all the good times they had had together. But this proved very difficult over the ensuing months, he had been her soul mate and to lose him was devastating.

After eventually being able to write to tell Frank and Shauna what had happened, they flew over from Ireland, drove down to Swanage and accompanied her to the funeral, which was a huge comfort. Jim was very well-liked locally and because he worked as a retained firefighter before he retired, his usual crew whom Evelyn knew well, carried his coffin, and the local church was full to the brim with mourners.

Seeing how much the whole ordeal had affected his mother, and how vulnerable and alone she was feeling, William suggested she move over and live with him, in a wing of his new home. She hesitated at first, but after thinking it through, decided to go. There, although surrounded by all the luxuries she could ever need, she still felt completely lost without Jim and wondered if she would ever get over losing him.

CHAPTER 104

Rory April 2016

Rory felt better after scattering Erick`s ashes and began to settle into life in Ireland again. Keeping himself busy digging out the old potato patch, he also fished in the lake whenever he could, and eventually managed to take time off to see his old childhood friend Diarmuid, who was still living in his parent`s cottage in Snáithecoiréil, near the coral beach. It was strange being back there and although pleased to see his friend, he was sad to think of all that had gone on years earlier and had culminated in his girlfriend's death. He had long since tried to blot the whole episode out but being back there, brought memories back as if it had just happened.

Remembering what Rhona had taught him, he tried to concentrate on the positives of the here and now, and not dwell on the past. It was good to see that Diarmuid had not changed a bit and had been overjoyed to see his friend again, and the pair did not stop talking for over two hours.

Aware he could now see a whole lot more of his friend than he had been, Rory decided to return to the cottage before it got dark. The evenings were drawing in quickly, and with most of the Cullenmara roads having perilous hairpin bends and no edges, and nothing in the way of lighting, it was safest to return before darkness fell.

Back at the cottage, as usual, he gradually lit all the oil lamps, just as Erick had taught him; pumped some more water up from the lake, and after eating food he had collected from Bauch`s shop on his way back from Diarmuid`s, sat down to relax by the fire.

The cottage was lovely at this time of day, and under the flickering light of the oil lamps, he happily sat watching shadows dancing on the bare walls and listened to the soothing hiss of the gas lamps, before curling up in a chair to read. There was still a whole load of books in the spare bedroom, and he was enjoying re-reading the tales of Finn McCool, which had been one of his favourite books as a child.

Stopping to rest his eyes one evening, he left the fireside to stand in one of the windows and watch the moonlight shining on the rippling lake below, and the white-topped waves of the wild Atlantic Sea, crashing on rocks in the distance, all further reinforcement of why Erick loved the cottage so much. How he wished he and Rhona were still alive, and there with him now.

During the day to distract himself from brooding about it all, he busied himself doing a series of odd jobs around the place, cleaning out the fireplace, sorting through things, and very much looked forward to his evening reading by the fire. He was working his way through the books in the spare bedroom, and he was enjoying re-reading the tales of Finn McCool, which had been one of his favourite books as a child.

Sure, life there would be easier if there was electricity and proper hot and cold running water, but it would not be the same, and he liked the idea of carrying on the local traditions, just like his father had.

One evening after having drifted off mid-book, he awoke to the roar of an approaching motorbike. This was highly unusual and having grabbed his father`s homemade pottery candle holder, he opened the front door and ventured out into the cold. Of course, the flame blew out immediately when hit by the chilly air and he stood staring out into the blackness.

The motorcyclist had turned around in the boreen, and Rory, blinded by the brightness of the bike`s front headlight shining in his direction, worried that he had unwanted intruders, and unsure what to do, he just stood and watched. Whoever it was, had stopped just short of the gate, switched off their headlights, and could be heard cursing, as they tried to undo the latch.

Rory briefly stepped back inside, grabbed Erick`s large torch from the shelf by the door, and shone it at them.

"Whoever you are, please be warned I`m calling the Gardi."

He had no intention of doing that but hoped his bluff would scare them. It did not, and he watched the gate slowly open, and a figure dressed all in black, emerged and began walking down the path towards him.

"I`m sorry mate but are you, Erick Harper? Is this where
he lives?"

It was a very husky-sounding voice, with an Australian accent, and for a second Rory could not tell if it was a man or a woman. Waiting until the figure was immediately in front of him, by the light of the strong torch he saw a woman; she was only about five feet tall and dressed head to toe in black motorcycling leathers.

When she removed her helmet, a mane of bright red hair cascaded down over her shoulders, and they stared at each other. She was the first to speak, and asked,

"Aren't you going to invite me in, then? Only I have come
an exceptionally long way!"

CHAPTER 105

Janis April 2016

After she turned thirty Janis had decided to travel, and the first place she wanted to go to was England, to track down her biological father, Erick Harper. Taking a letter from her mother with her, after boarding the Virgin Atlantic flight from Perth to Heathrow, she relaxed in her seat, full of excitement. It was a great feeling to be doing something she had wanted for years. It was a long motorcycle ride through Ireland to the far west county of Cullenmara, and Janis was concerned when it started to get dark. Already tired, and having passed shops, all of which were closed, she had been feeling very hungry.

The further she rode, the more the terrain changed. She had not realised just how rugged and remote the area her father lived, would be. The area around her was becoming more and more like the surface of the moon and strewn with large granite boulders of all shapes and sizes, some of which looked quite eerie in the half-dark. At one point, on the rough Cullenmara roads, she had only just managed to right the heavy rented Harley Davidson motorbike, when it teetered close to the road edge on a sharp bend and prevented it from leaving the road completely.

She had continued unperturbed, thinking it must only be about another five miles now. Very soon, she was crossing two long road bridges in succession, and the road ahead became a bit straighter, but strangely more uneven, and riding the bike on it was like being on a rollercoaster. Seeing cottages on a hill in front of her in the distance, and in the dusk, their windows gently lit and welcoming, she hoped one of them was Erick`s.

Janis had decided that whatever happened, she would not let on exactly who she was until she had found her father, and had been surprised to see a much younger quite good-looking man, with blue eyes and a mane of dark hair, standing in the cottage doorway, and disappointed, worried she had gone to the wrong place, but it was too dark and too late to turn back now.

Seeing her, he ushered her quickly inside, sat her down, and gave her a coffee with Poitin in it to warm her up after she had appeared to be physically shivering. He had then explained he was caretaking the cottage because the family could not get over very easily to check on it.

He decided it best not to let on exactly who he was to this stranger in case she had sinister motives. But any concerns he initially had about her, soon vanished, after she drank her very alcoholic coffee, peeled off her thick motorcycle leathers, and revealed the very slim, muscular body, which had been hiding underneath. Although trying not to stare, as the woman sat back down, and crossed one leg over the other, under the flickering light of the oil lamps, he could not believe how beautiful she looked, and he nervously got to his feet and offered her food. All he had was leftover fish pie, which he retrieved from the fridge and heated on the Calor gas stove.

She seemed ravenous and after eating it all and wiping her plate with bread, asked,

"Don`t suppose I could have a bath, could I?"

"You can, but I`m afraid it will take a while," he replied. and explained,

"At this time of year, we need to boil the water in a big metal teapot that`s hanging from a hook over the fire, it`s heavy and will take several trips back and forth to fill it, but you will get a decent bath at the end of it."

She sat looking bemused, watching him going to and from the bathroom, wearing what looked like oversized oven gloves, to carry the big black kettle. Eventually, the bath was full enough and Rory sat back down at the dining table, exhausted, and poured himself another Poitin.

Janis, meanwhile, disappeared into the bathroom where, by the light of a flickering candle, she removed her clothes and got into the warm water.

"I don`t suppose you`ve got any more of that Poitin stuff, have you?" she shouted from the bathroom.

"I drink something similar back home, my uncle`s Aboriginal friends make it," she told him.

Rory poured another glass for himself and took one into her, expecting her to still be fully clothed, but she was lying stark naked in the bath, and he wished he had some foam bath to help preserve her modesty. But she did not seem to care. He blushed, gingerly stepped forward, and placed the glass on the far side of the bath, trying not to stare at her, but it was impossible, not to.

"Why don`t you bring your glass in and stay and talk to me?" she asked.

"Oh, I'm not sure I should do that," he said.

"Why, have you never seen a naked female body before?" she asked and gave him a quizzical smile.

Rory stuttered a little before eventually managing to say, "Of course, I have."

"Well then......?"

When he returned, she patted the side of the bath to indicate he should sit there, and Rory did what she asked. Feeling nervous, he gulped the Poitin back amazingly fast and soon began to feel quite drunk. She was gorgeous and transfixed by the multiple tattoos depicting what looked like countryside scenes and animals that covered her torso, he stared at her with his mouth open.

What happened next was very unexpected. She leant forward and whispered something to him that he was unable to hear, and when he moved even closer, she pulled him into the bath on top of her, still fully clothed. Laughing in surprise, Rory coughed and spluttered after having ingested some of the water, and in seconds her lips were on his and she was kissing him passionately.

When he awoke the next day, he vaguely remembered getting out of the bath, leaving a puddle on the flagstone floor, and walking nakedly back to the front room to retrieve the Poitin, but could not recall anything after that. He now found himself lying naked on top of a red sleeping bag on the floor, in front of the fire, and beside him, also naked but still fast asleep, lay Janis.

CHAPTER 106

Janis April 2016

Zena had told Janis all about her father and the cottage, mentioned how basic the amenities were there, and having grown up in a caravan in the outback which was also off-grid, Janis was unperturbed by the conditions at the cottage. Rory proved to be a very welcome surprise, and as the daughter of a hippy mother, believing in not hiding feelings, Janis had taken full advantage of him. She had fancied him from the moment she saw him, which was a bonus, and hoped he felt the same way about her.

She loved seeing the look on his face after she had called him into the bathroom. He had appeared shy, and she was a sucker for men like that. Coming around from her Poitin-induced sleep she blinked, rubbed her eyes, and realising Rory was lying beside her looking at her, she smiled. He is certainly very ruggedly handsome, she thought, and seeing her smiling, he smiled back sheepishly,

"I`m sorry, but I think I might have taken advantage of you, last night," he said.

"No man takes advantage of me unless I want them to," she said, winking.

"In fact. I think I might want to take advantage of you again, right now,"

After giving Rory a sexy look, she swung herself around, and they made love again, but in a much slower and less fraught way than they had done the previous evening. Afterwards, Rory cooked her a typical Irish breakfast and added black and white pudding and the usual traditional thin Irish sausages. Janis still appeared very hungry and after wolfing hers down quickly, sat back in her chair and let out a loud contented burp, which Rory found amusing. He had never met a woman quite like her, before.

CHAPTER 107

Later, over coffee, Janis explained that her mother had known Erick Harper very well, and had, for years, wondered what had happened to him. Not now in the best of health, she had promised her mother she would go off and find him.

"Do you know if there are any photos of him, please, only my mother hasn`t got any at all?" she asked.

Rory remembered seeing a large box marked "photos" in the top bedroom and having clambered up the ladder, soon found the box and carried it down. Janis, not wanting to let on that he was her father, tried to contain her excitement, at seeing photos of him.

It was strange, although her mother had described him, she had not expected to look so much like him. She had the same long nose and angular jawline, instead of brown hair, she had red, and although she had inherited her mother's bright green eyes, they were the same shape as her father`s.

"Could I have any of these to take back and show mum?" she asked.

Rory nodded,

"Don`t think it would hurt if you just took a few."

It was not easy seeing all those reminders of Erick again, but Rory could see by the earlier black-and-white photos, how much he looked like his dad, and felt proud about that. There were also photos of Erick and Rhona`s wedding and Janis appeared extremely interested to see them too. He explained how the pair had met and fallen in love, but deliberately missed the circumstances of his arrival on the scene.

Janis asked about the cottage in Newlyn, that her mother had described so clearly and Rory explained that Erick had moved from there, and over to a cottage he and Rhona converted, near the Trevaunce Beacon.

"I lodged there with them for some of that time, they had
lived there happily together for over twenty-seven years."

Feeling tears starting to well up, he suggested he make some more coffee and disappear into the kitchen, where he could splash his eyes. Wiping them dry, he sighed and realised he was not ready to talk about the accident, yet. But Janis asked the question he had been dreading when he returned to the front room.

"Where is Erick now then, is he back in England?"

Rory sat back down at the table opposite Janis, took a deep breath, and then told her,

"I know exactly where he is, he`s out there by that rock, his
favourite rock, I scattered his ashes there only last week."

Janis suddenly looked incredibly sad,

"Oh, mum will be upset to hear that," she said.

She went quiet and stared hard into her coffee cup, as if unsure what to say next.

"So how come you scattered them then? The ashes, I mean?"
she asked.

Rory told her,

"I`m his and Rhona`s son."

Hearing that, Janis suddenly looked very anxious. Her whole demeanour towards him changed, she hurriedly collected her things, wriggled herself back into her motorcycle leathers, and told him abruptly,

"Sorry, I`ve outstayed my welcome, and must go."

Rory was astounded and suddenly very confused.

"Do you have to go so suddenly?" he asked.

"I`m sorry, I shouldn`t have come here!" she said

and appeared no longer able to make eye contact.

He followed her outside where she burst into tears, and immediately felt silly. She was usually so strong, but there was something about Rory, and how caring he was, that melted her heart, and she was unused to that. She was much more of a "treat them mean, and keep them keen," type of girl. That was how a woman surrounded by men in the Australian outback, had to be. She tried to turn away from him, embarrassed, but he was immediately beside her and swung her around so she was facing him again.

"Please don't go, Janis, not like this!" he said trying to stare

into her eyes.

"I`ve never met anyone like you, before."

She stared back at him, leaned forward, and having given him a very enthusiastic kiss, walked purposefully out to her bike. Dumfounded, he watched her climb onto it, and when he hurriedly joined her by the gate, she told him firmly,

"We can`t ever do this again, do you understand? I must

go, Rory, we can`t ever do this again, please don`t...this is

wrong on *so* many different levels!"

He cupped her head in his hands and was about to kiss her, but she pushed him away.

"Why Janis, why are you behaving like this, why do you

have to leave so suddenly, and just as we are getting to

know each other, and getting on so well?" he asked.

He looked at her pleadingly, but she looked away, and as if suddenly having second thoughts, looked intently at him and admitted,

"I`m your biological sister, Rory!"

After having dropped that bombshell, she rode off down the boreen, leaving Rory standing by the gate with his mouth open.

CHAPTER 108

Rory April 2016

Meeting Janis had been extraordinary, it had been years since Rory had felt as reckless and carefree as he felt, that night spent with her at the cottage. He had been impressed by her looks, down-to-earth personality, and feisty nature, and missed her the moment she disappeared off on her motorbike. There had been a definite magnetism between them, and something he had never experienced with anyone else.

Understanding why she had to leave, Rory felt very ashamed about what they had done, but he had slept with her not knowing she was his sister. The sad truth was, that although what they had done was very wrong on so many levels, he could not get her out of his mind, and still longed to see her again, which made him feel very naughty.

Life after meeting Janis became particularly mundane, especially when the evenings drew in increasingly, and daylight hours dwindled. Having little money, apart from the small amount that Padraig paid him monthly, also did little to help Rory`s growing glumness. He struggled on through the cold and damp, helped by Brenna bringing him car-full`s of turf, she was always so cheery, no matter what the weather, and had a profound sense of humour.

The McDonough family, his nearest neighbours, and great friends of his father`s invited him over regularly for Sunday lunch, which at least got him out of the cottage, and he could catch up on all the local gossip. But although he enjoyed their company, Rory felt himself becoming increasingly depressed. Diarmuid noticed it first, after having driven down to see him several times.

"Are you feeling okay, Rory, only you don`t seem yourself now?" he asked his friend, concerned.

"I`m alright, well I was until Janis turned up."

"Jesus Rory, even out here in the middle of nowhere, you can still manage to find a woman!"

He teased his friend, but Rory didn`t smile.

"Oh, sorry mate, but who the feck is Janis?"

Rory got out the Poitin, and poured two glasses, before explaining,

"You are not going to believe this," he said.

He went on to tell Diarmuid what had happened in quite a lot of detail, and after he had finished, his friend looked shocked, and Rory wondered if telling him had been a mistake.

"Your sister, Rory! Well, I wasn`t expecting that. I thought that type of thing only went on over on the Inish Isles," he added, jokingly.

"Sorry, bad taste!"

Rory managed a half smile in response, and Diarmuid studied him.

"Feck Rory, you get yourself in some scrapes, don`t you?"

Rory felt better having at least been able to tell someone though.

"Wow, you couldn`t make it up, could you?" Diarmuid reiterated.

"But what can I do Diarmuid? She`s an amazing woman, I`ll never get the chance to meet someone like her again and I miss her," said Rory, now very animated.

Diarmuid shrugged his shoulders and laughed,

"Yeah, but was it all worth it, I mean was she good, was she good in the sack?" he asked cheekily, and Rory smiled.

CHAPTER 109

Frank and Shauna America 2012

Finally free of all their previous work constraints, Shauna, and Frank`s relationship, blossomed and the love between them grew and grew. After thirty years of living together, they decided to get married in a simple Registry Office ceremony and then would honeymoon in America, somewhere Frank said he had always wanted to go, and where they could meet up with Evelyn, too. Having left the cold Dublin winter behind them, and after a long and bumpy flight, Frank, and Shauna`s plane eventually touched down at the American airport. They collected their luggage, went through customs, and walked out of the Arrival`s building into bright warm sunshine.

"Ooh, what a lovely contrast to the weather back home," Shauna exclaimed straight away.

She found her sunglasses in her bag, and quickly put them on. As Evelyn had instructed, they wandered down to the far end of the taxi rank, where a blacked-out limousine, complete with its own black-capped, white-gloved chauffeur, was waiting for them. Seeing them, he immediately got out of the car, relieved them of their luggage which he stowed in the boot, and ushered them inside. Before driving off, he repositioned his rearview mirror, and looking directly at Shauna, said,

"Please help yourself to any drinks you fancy from the cabinet,"

Frank poured out two Bourbon whiskies,

"When in Rome," he said.

They sat back in their plush leather seats and smiled.

The journey took about half an hour. They soon left the industrial area around the airport well behind and sped smoothly past large Colonial-style houses with massive gardens, until they pulled up outside a drive with very ornate wrought iron electric gates. The driver keyed in a code, took the car up the drive, and stopped in front of the main entrance to the house. Suddenly Evelyn appeared, from inside. Seeing her, Frank did a double take, it was obvious how badly Jim`s sudden death a year earlier, had affected her. It had been the main reason for her move into the granny annexe next door.

Shauna stepped forward first,

"Oh Evelyn, it's been so long since we last saw each other at Jim`s funeral, it is wonderful to be here with you now."

The two women embraced, and Frank peered around them, hoping to get a quick glimpse of his son, but he was not there, and he was disappointed.

Suddenly, there was the sound of a helicopter flying overhead, and the three of them sought shelter in the hallway, as the force of air from its rotor blades got stronger. They watched it circle and land in the middle of the perfectly manicured front lawn. A small door opened in the cockpit and down stepped William. Frank gasped and hoped Shauna had not heard him. He must act normal, and as planned, William pretended to have only just met him. Frank walked forward to shake his outstretched hand, secretly immensely proud. He could not believe how much his son had changed. He was wearing an expensive designer suit, sported a stylish sweptback haircut, and his teeth were whiter than white.

"I`ve done alright, Dad," he said, out of earshot of the women.

"You certainly have, son," he said.

Frank walked over and introduced Shauna to William and Evelyn smiled at them both. Although not fully in agreement with it, she had decided to go along with Frank`s lie, for the time being. She knew William wanted to see his dad after such a long time, especially now that he had done so well, and hoped he would be proud of him.

It was obvious just how proud Frank was, especially after Shauna commented on what a nice man William was. He caught her looking at him fondly and felt very guilty but was not up to telling her the truth yet. When close enough, Frank hugged Evelyn and told her,

" It must still be difficult for you, even now."

She nodded,

"Yes, so much time has passed, and I still miss Jim terribly, but I`m just so glad we had all those years together. We were soul mates, and I still miss him terribly. William has been so good, inviting me out here to live with him, I was struggling back in England, and it has been good to now have him to share my memories with. Jim and William had become remarkably close over the years."

The first of the two weeks spent with his son flew by, and for Frank to have Shauna there too, Frank was the happiest he had ever been.

CHAPTER 110

Frank 2012

They were certainly getting a taste of the high life there, over-indulged in rich foods, and drank plenty of expensive wine and whisky. It was a whole other world than Shauna had ever experienced, but she fully embraced it and thoroughly enjoyed herself. One evening they had eaten early at an expensive restaurant, and then gone to see a show. But during the first half, Frank suddenly felt a bit strange. It was not uncommon for him to suffer heartburn after rich food, and finding some indigestion tablets in her bag, Shauna gave him two, hoping the discomfort would soon wear off. But he continued to feel extremely uncomfortable, and having loosened his collar, appeared very sweaty too. Shauna was keeping a close eye on him because he did not look right.

It was during the interval, and when Frank stood up to follow Shauna out into the foyer, that he gasped for air, clutched his chest, and collapsed. Seeing what had happened, William immediately knelt by his father`s side and began administering mouth-to-mouth. The theatre staff called for an ambulance and very soon two paramedics were on the scene to take over from William. He got to his feet and cleared an area around them so they could work. His stepfather`s complexion was ashen, his lips blue, and knowing that was bad, really hoped he would be all right.

Meanwhile, Shauna was being consoled by Evelyn, who was trying to say positive encouraging things, even though very worried. After the paramedics appeared to have stabilised Frank, he was rushed by ambulance to the nearest hospital Emergency Room, and shortly after, sent to the Operating Room.

All three had been waiting in the corridor for what seemed like hours, until finally, a white-coated Consultant approached and told them Frank was out of the theatre but needed to remain in Intensive Care overnight. Reluctant to leave the hospital, Shauna and Evelyn remained in the corridor pacing up and down, while William disappeared and returned with a thermos of tea and soft rugs, for them to make themselves as comfortable as possible in the waiting room. What they did not know was he had secretly pulled some strings and about an hour later, the three of them were taken along to the private wing, where they had ensuite bedrooms for the night, and could easily be contacted, if there was any change in Frank`s condition.

Shauna`s phone rang early the following morning, after quickly making her way along to Intensive Care, was relieved when told Frank was awake and asking for her. She was led into a dimly lit room by a nurse, where Frank was sitting propped up in a bed, attached to loudly bleeping cardiac monitors. He looked very grey, and his lips still had a bluish tinge. Although not looking at a well, he beckoned her to sit on the bed next to him,

"How are you my dear?" he asked.

This was so typical of Frank, thinking about everyone else but himself, even when he was so ill. She smiled, it was such a relief that he was alive. It had been difficult to imagine how things would pan out, especially when he had looked so ill the last time she saw him. But, as Evelyn had suggested, she had tried to remain positive.

"I`m much more worried about you, darling. What have
 they said?" she asked.
"Well, it`s not exactly good news, I`ve suffered a massive
coronary, but they`ve patched me up and put a stent in, but
the operation didn`t go as well as planned."
He explained it had something to do with his injection
fractions, and Shauna nodded despite not understanding what
he meant. Being a doctor himself, Frank often used medical
jargon when explaining things. He suddenly looked serious
and said,
"There was something you need to know Shauna, something I wish I could have told you sooner, but I`ve been
too scared I might lose you."
This was worrying, and Shauna wondered whatever it could
be, as Frank took hold her her hand, and began explaining,
"You know I`d never deliberately hurt you, don`t you? Only
I`ve been keeping a secret for many years, it is about some-
thing I did that I`m very ashamed of."
He sighed, his eyes fluttered, and suddenly all the cardiac
alarms went off, Shauna was panic-stricken, but he quickly
grabbed her hand and said clutching his chest,
"I can`t put this off any longer, Shauna, time is running
out. I`m William`s father, and you are his mother."
Suddenly the doors burst open, and in came two doctors
who pushed Shauna out of the way, immediately set about un-
plugging the monitors, and began moving Frank`s bed out of
the room, and down the corridor.
"He`s got to go back to the Operating Room urgently," said
one of them.
Shauna felt completely shell-shocked, not just because of
what Frank had just told her, but also because of his sudden
and very rapid decline.

CHAPTER 111

Shauna, 2013

Shauna was beside herself with worry, Frank was the love of her life, and the thought of losing him now, after having dropped such a bombshell, was unbearable. She paced the hospital corridors all night long trying to process what he had said, but it did not make any sense, and she assumed that Frank was confused. William and Evelyn were still in bed, unaware of recent developments, and she wondered if she should wake them. Considering what Frank had just told her, she should, but should she tell them what she knew? Did they already know? There had been no indication that they did. All these questions were running through her mind, as she wandered back to her room, and decided to wake William and leave Evelyn sleeping.

He came to the door looking very bleary-eyed, with his hair standing on end, and Shauna was aware of how much he looked like Frank did in the mornings. Even if Frank was his father, how did *she* fit into the picture? She could not work that out at all. Had it been true what everyone had said about Frank and Evelyn? Was Frank muddled while so ill? Could he have said her name instead of Evelyn`s? It was all disconcerting, during what was already an incredibly stressful time.

After briefly explaining Frank had been whisked back into the Operating Room, she waited while William threw on clothes and soon joined her, in the corridor outside. They initially sat together in silence, but unable to stop herself, Shauna told him,

"Frank said something strange, just before they took him back into the theatre."

"Why, what did he say, exactly Shauna?" William asked.

There was no going back now, so Shauna just blurted it all out,

"That he is your father, and I`m your mother. I know, it`s ludicrous isn`t it?"

William went quiet as if stuck for words, and then having composed himself, said,

"I`m so sorry you found out this way. For years I`d thought Evelyn was my real mother, and she was. But when I was about ten, Frank visited us in Dorset, and Evelyn told me he was my father. I didn`t take the news very well at first, but over the years, especially when she told me the full story, I understood why he behaved like he had. I also understood why she had done what she did, it had been a tricky situation."

"So, where do I fit into all of this then?" Shauna asked.

"I`m not the best person to be telling you this, I didn`t find out until Jim died, last year. I think Mum, Evelyn was concerned something might happen to her too, and I would otherwise, never know the truth."

Shauna wriggled uncomfortably in her seat, worried about what William was going to say.

"Shauna, Evelyn told me all about you, and what you went through on the playing field, that night. The night you were raped."

"But how did she know about that?" I only ever told my mother...and Frank...."

Shauna stared into space for a few seconds and asked,
"How on earth did Evelyn know about that?"
"Frank must have told her, I guess," said William sheepishly.

"I do remember telling Frank but don't understand what
that`s got to do with anything."
William turned to face her and in a serious tone, explained,
"It was Frank, Shauna, who drunkenly raped you that night.
I know it`s a shock, but he has done everything in his power
to help you ever since, and at the time, ensured I did not get
adopted."
Shauna was finding all this exceedingly difficult to take in.
It was only later that it dawned on her, that Frank had lied
when he had said her baby died. She felt sick to her stomach,
and when her legs went from beneath her, William helped her
onto a chair.
She put her head in her hands in anguish.
"Oh my god, I don`t believe it. How could he? How could he
have lied to me like that, and not told me what happened?
He even said that you were born with congenital deformities,
you can imagine what pictures I conjured up in my mind.
I blamed myself for your death and have carried that around
inside me ever since."
"I`ve asked him about that on several occasions, but he`s
always maintained, it was for the best," said William.
With that, she turned around and virtually ran along the
corridor, and down the stairs, and only stopped when she
had reached the sidewalk outside. It felt like she could not
breathe, and her heart was pounding from the shock. She tried
taking deep breaths, but that did not help. Spying a bar across
the road, she stepped onto the marked crosswalk outside the
hospital and after waiting for the traffic to stop, crossed to
the central reservation, and seeing the other side was clear,
continued until she reached the bar. To go to a bar alone at
night in America, was so far out of her comfort zone, but
she desperately needed a drink. Sitting on one of the stools
near the bartender, she ordered a double whisky and soda and
he watched, as she drank it down in one, and automatically

poured her another, which she drank slower and began to feel more relaxed.

How could he? How could Frank lie to her all these years? she pondered it all while continuing to sip her drink. Why had he been at the playing fields in the first place? She could recall bits of that night very clearly, like it happened only yesterday, and remembered the alcohol smell on his breath. Although they both drank quite a bit while in America, this was unusual, Frank had always only drank occasionally, never went too far, and always acted responsibly. But he was very young back then, and she presumed out of his depth.

She was about to chastise herself again for allowing herself to be in that position all those years ago but then thought about William, her handsome, charming, and phenomenally successful son. If Frank had not intervened, he would most certainly been taken from her and could have ended up God knows where. But it was because he took matters into his own hands, that he was here alive and well in America, waiting for her back at the hospital, and she suddenly began to feel a bit better about the situation.

CHAPTER 112

Shauna returned to the hospital to find William pacing up and down in the foyer, looking very worried. He joined her, and she followed him back upstairs.

"Oh God, has something else happened to Frank?" she asked, concerned.

"No Shauna, I haven`t heard anything, it was you I was worried about."

She stared hard at William, leaned forward, hugged him tightly and tears of joy trickled down her cheeks.

"I cannot believe it; you are my boy and are very much alive!"

They were interrupted by Frank, being brought out of the Operating Room on his bed. Shauna took one look at him and burst into tears, seeing he was still deeply unconscious, and William gripped her hand tightly, trying not to cry himself. They followed him back along to Intensive Care, where she pleaded to be able to spend five minutes with him. Tears were streaming down her face when she leaned forward, took hold of one of his hands, and told him,

"Do not leave me, Frank, please do not leave me. It is going to be difficult for me to come to terms with what you`ve done, and I`m going to need time to process it, but I can`t bear the thought of losing you, my darling."

CHAPTER 113

Shauna 2013

Frank was not the same for a while after his heart attack and Shauna decided it best to never refer to the incident on the playing field again. It hurt too much to even think of it, let alone confront Frank when his life was still only just dangling by a thread. She had learned about the power of forgiveness at the Convent years earlier and did not believe it healthy to hold onto negative feelings for long. Frank had a reason for doing what he had done and had thought it best. But now she had found her very much alive and lovely son, at the grand old age of sixty, she was just beside herself with joy.

But it was still difficult to comprehend, especially after they had been together so long and had married. The fact that Frank had never said anything at all still hurt, but reflecting on it, she was pleased to have Frank in her life when she could have so easily lost him for good. She had also gained so much, now knowing that her son William was alive and well, and her relationship with him continued to blossom throughout Frank`s convalescence.

Frank`s poor health had completely taken over their usual routines, and life had become a constant series of medical checks, medications, healthy eating, and doctor`s appointments. They had to remain in America for another three months until it was safe for Frank to fly back. It was like he had aged overnight. He could only walk slowly and frequently got out of breath. His speech had slowed, along with his brain, but Shauna still loved him and was determined to look after him as well as she could.

After they returned to Ireland, William rang his father every other day and would always have a chat with Shauna beforehand. Sometimes they Skyped each other for hours, which allowed Shauna some much-needed respite from caring for him, which she appreciated.

She had been feeling tired recently and a bit out of sorts, and after also suffering abdominal discomfort, she eventually went to the doctor. Following routine blood tests and a scan, the doctor explained that he had found a suspicious growth in her stomach. This would need to be biopsied to be sure, but he was about ninety per cent sure it was cancer. Although initially shocked by the diagnosis, Shauna accepted the news and resigned herself to making the most of whatever time she had left.

The Doctor was concerned and explained,

"It`s probably fully operable, and there may be a need for some follow-up treatment, post-op, but I`m confident we can get all of it."

"I couldn`t possibly do that, I`ve got Frank to look after," she replied.

"I'm sure if you explained it to him, he would understand, you must tell him, you can`t handle all this alone."

Shauna nodded, but then explained,

"I can`t, it would kill him, he`s been through too much, it would set him back."

The doctor was surprised by her reaction, and she explained,

"I`ve been through a great deal, and Frank has always been there for me so many times. I would be doing him and God a disservice if I abandoned him now. I would rather live the rest of my life on my terms, and if that means not telling him and carrying on, then so be it."

Frank never knew about Shauna`s diagnosis, she just continued as normal and managed to cover up her symptoms and keep Frank in the dark, aware the worry of knowing would surely kill him. But as time went by, she found herself thinking increasingly about the babies that had died, as the Inquiry into the Mother and Baby Home continued and felt bad still having so much additional information in her head, that was never given to the Gardi. The urge to do something was bugging her and she could not let things lie especially now, with time running out.

The mass grave discovered at the back of the Mother and Baby Home was still years later, one of the main topics of gossip when she went into town. It was so sad to think of all those unnamed babies, buried under the very ground she had walked over so frequently.

She often opened the large box file containing all the documentation and studied it, racking her brain for anything else she could remember, no matter how minute the detail was. Looking through her notes, she decided to list all the babies she could remember, give the ones whose names she could not remember, names, and add a description of their mother, to a smaller notebook.

Since she had decided to take matters into her own hands, this information would be even more important for those poor mothers who never knew what became of their babies. When the land that was previously the playing field came up for sale, Shauna bought a large piece of it using her savings. She employed a local labourer to enclose the area with a traditional stone wall, planted a sapling in memory of each baby that died and attached a brass plaque with their corresponding number.

It took her an exceedingly long time to get all of them in the ground, but she persevered. Although she often felt exhausted after all her efforts and was stressed worrying about and looking after Frank, she was more determined than ever to make the memorial garden as beautiful as possible. She dug out flower beds around the trees and planted masses of brightly coloured local wildflowers near the roots. She was delighted when they all bloomed after only a few weeks and was incredibly pleased with the result.

But that was only phase one of her plan, and she had not finished yet.

CHAPTER 114

William 2014

William decided to stay in Dublin until he had sorted out his mother's funeral, cleared the house, and put it on the market. It felt wrong, riffling through all her belongings like a common thief, but it needed doing, and clearing the house one room at a time, he became more aware of the sort of person Shauna was. She certainly liked hoarding things, including herbs and spices, which he was horrified to discover, had expired over twenty years earlier. There were bottle tops, foil trays, and plastic bags stowed in kitchen cupboards, plus a whole load of rubbish for him to take to the local tip and recycling centre. Getting rid of it all felt cathartic, and it felt like with it, went a whole load of stress, which left him feeling much better.

Having long since given up his room at the Bed and Breakfast, he had cleared Shauna's bedroom first, changed the sheets on the bed, and would remain happily ensconced there until he had finished it all. To his surprise, even after what he had initially witnessed, he grew to like the house. It was a very peaceful, tranquil place to live, and as the days began to draw out, he often sat out in the back garden, contentedly drinking a glass of red wine or two, feeling himself relax. Living a much simpler life than what he had become accustomed to in America, was much better than he thought it might be, and mulling it all over, he realised how little he missed all the trappings of his luxurious lifestyle.

He counted himself very blessed and would be forever grateful for how it all had turned out. If Frank had not intervened, his life would have been quite different. Although sacrificing relationships and family for his work, now owning his own company, he could pause and take time out, anytime he wanted. He had left behind a good team who rarely contacted him.

He remembered how pleased Shauna was to meet him all those years ago, when still completely unaware of who he was. It had taken his father`s sudden heart attack, for him to confess all to her, and she had taken the news that William was her son, the son she thought had died, so remarkably well. He presumed it was her training at the convent and admired how gracefully she had accepted it.

They had been worried about how long Frank had to live, but he had lived longer than the medics anticipated, which he knew was due to Shauna`s forgiveness and kind, gentle manner. His father was tough, and after a few years of slowing right down, had even been back to playing golf and walking just like he used to, until his sudden death from another heart attack, less than a year ago.

This had been a huge shock and William reckoned it was the related stress that exacerbated Shauna`s illness, and he had been unsurprised to hear she had cancer. Shauna had confided in him the time, and worried it might be detrimental to his father`s health, had made him swear not to tell Frank, which he had found difficult. But Shauna managed to keep it secret, fearing the news would, "Finish him off," as she put it, and died only six months after Frank.

The pair had been together for over forty years. William could not imagine being with someone for so long. But hats off to her, she certainly loved his father and always did her best to help him.

Immediately after she lost Frank, Shauna confided in William increasingly about life at the Mother and Baby Home, and the Catholic Adoption Home, and although he had read about it from the findings of the Inquiry in the press, to hear it first hand, had been particularly disturbing, and he often recalled their conversations in his mind, thinking how incredibly lucky they had been to find each other in such dire circumstances.

CHAPTER 115

William 2014

One particularly sunny day, William took his early morning cup of tea outside, unfolded a garden chair, and was sitting deliberating what to do with all the furniture, when he noticed the ground beneath him appeared soggy and wet. He traced the leak back to a drain hidden under the long grass. On closer examination, he discovered the roots of a nearby tree had somehow managed to grow into it and completely blocked it. Puzzling about what to do, he reckoned he needed to cut the root, and after fetching the saw he found in the shed the previous week, he set about cutting it. The saw was very blunt but eventually, the root gave way.

Underneath, to his surprise, he found a rusty metal box the size of a shoe box, which he thought was very strange. The box appeared wedged in place, and after unsuccessfully trying to lift it out with his hands, he resorted to using a crowbar, that he had also found in the shed. When the box suddenly came free, he fell backwards still clutching it tightly, and lay in the wet grass laughing, thinking how strange this was, and hoping Shauna was looking down and laughing too.

By the time he composed himself and got up again, his jeans were wet through, but unconcerned about those and more excited about his find, he took the box inside the house. It was quite muddy and after cleaning it, he gently levered the lid off, taking the rusty hinges with it, and peered curiously inside.

CHAPTER 116

William 2014

To his surprise, the box contained a notebook, and on the cover, he saw Shauna had written in shaky handwriting:

"For William."

He immediately opened it and turned to the first page, where he found clear instructions.

"I knew you would find this eventually. I am sorry to put all this responsibility on your shoulders, but please read this notebook through, and then give it to the local council and Gardi. All this information I have stored in my head for years, and it is such a relief to get it out on paper. I feel very guilty for not coming forward with this added information sooner, but in my now poor health, I could not risk prison, for my part in it all. Your father and I both did our best to stop it, and to care for those poor wretched mothers who lost their babies."

William took a deep breath and thumbed through the book.

His mother had numbered each entry and added information that might help mothers who had lost their babies to identify what had happened to them and locate them if they had been adopted, or if they had ended up buried in the mass grave at the back of the Mother and Baby Home.

Suddenly what Shauna had said on her deathbed about, "Babies in the Wood" and getting to the "Root of the problem," all began to make sense.

Aware she did not have long to live, she had died trusting that William would find the notebook she had hidden. Seeing the numbering in the book, it was clear to him she was referring to the trees she had planted, and of course, each tree represented a child she knew had died. Realising this, he became overwhelmed with pride and admiration about what Shauna had done.

She had courageously taken matters into her own hands, despite the risk and her actions now meant the babies lost to adoption, could be reunited with their biological parents. She had also ensured those mothers whose babies had died, also had somewhere fitting to go to remember them.

He did as she requested and handed the notebook over to the Gardi. They were non-plussed at first, but when DNA confirmed the names she mentioned, were the babies later found in the mass grave, they began to take it much more seriously. Now it was all out in the open, William set about planning her funeral. She had only wanted a simple service, but once someone leaked the information to the press, it turned into something else entirely. He was surprised to receive a phone call from someone at the local council, asking if he would like to hold Shauna`s funeral in the area`s main cathedral.

His immediate reaction was,

"Oh, ah, that`s a nice thought, but I don`t think that many people will come, and anyway, it was her request to have a short simple service."

The council official then explained,

"I don`t think you realise the extent of the publicity there has been since her notebook was leaked and the news got out about her memorial garden?"

William admitted he had not read any local papers for a while and used them instead to wrap precious ornaments and photos, for transportation back with him to America. He told the official he would call back later, started unpacking his boxes, and retrieved several pages of the most recent local newspaper which he smoothed out on the kitchen table.

He started reading, and one headline said,

"Local woman labelled a saint."

Another headline was,

"Thousands expected to pay their respects to an amazing local woman."

William now understood the need for his mother`s funeral to be in the city`s main Catholic Cathedral, as opposed to the tiny local Catholic church, and soon became swept along with the council`s plans for the big day.

CHAPTER 117

William 2014

There was a throng of press and television crews outside the Catholic cathedral on the day of Shauna`s funeral, and William was glad to get into the calm sereneness of the main building, where Father Pat heartily shook his hand. The priest had reserved him a space in the pew at the front, and he had sat smiling proudly, listening to an address from the mayor, followed by Father Pat`s account of how hard Shauna had worked despite being so ill.

Although used to addressing his employees in America, he was feeling a little nervous when he needed to give the Eulogy, but it was very well-received, by the several hundred mourners, many of whom had queued through the night to get a seat.

The atmosphere in the cathedral was incredible. When everyone got to their feet to sing the Magnificat, the combination of the cathedral organ, and so many people singing loudly in unison, was indescribable and very moving.

William had cried often during the service but left feeling elated. Countless people shook his hand afterwards and told him how proud they were of his mother, and later he returned to the house feeling proud to have been Shauna`s son.

Shauna`s gardens were immediately opened to the public, as per her wishes and even the Irish Prime Minister came to cut the ribbon and shake William`s hand during an official opening ceremony. It was all very surreal, and after the crowds had dissipated, he sat alone on a bench and gazed around him at the now well-established trees and shrubs festooned with an abundance of brightly coloured flowers and bright greenery, sighed, and felt the most relaxed he had ever felt in his life before.

CHAPTER 118

Janis April 2016

Janis left Cullenmara and Rory behind and sped off back up to Dublin. As she rode, the ramifications of what they had both done, hit home hard. She was still in shock about it and at the back of her mind, was worried she could be pregnant. Unsure what to do and not wanting to return to Australia prematurely, she contacted Erica, one of her mother's oldest friends. She was a nurse, and she had always liked her and felt sure she would be able to help. She also wanted to discover more about her father and to visit all the places he had lived.

When the time came to give it back, Janis was sad to leave her rented motorbike behind, and despite what had happened at the cottage, had very much enjoyed motorcycling across Ireland. As her plane touched down at Bristol Airport, she hoped to be able to rent another bike from there, but unfortunately, because she had not booked one in advance, another bike would not be available for a week. After deciding to try to rent one from Treyrow, she caught a coach and collected it from near the station and rode away from the city and off towards Haystow, where she joined the coast road and loved riding its bends and turns.

It was not long before she started to feel hungry and having seen the sign, stopped off at Hell`s Mouth Café, where she tried a traditional Cornish Cream tea. Her mother had often mentioned how lovely they were, and she thoroughly enjoyed it, washed down with a pot of Earl Grey tea, something else she had never tried. After venturing across the road to see what "Hell`s Mouth" was all about, she stood marvelled at the rough ruggedness of the north Cornwall coast and stared down at the seals lying on the beach beneath her.

The next bit of the ride was dramatic, and the views were fabulous as the road steadily climbed upwards. From here a far-reaching panoramic view of the entire coastline spread out in front of her. She could see a white lighthouse in the near distance, that road signs indicated was "Treavy Lighthouse," and beyond that, and across the sea was what she reckoned must be Seachapel, another place that her mother had mentioned fondly.

She motorcycled on and after a quarter of an hour arrived at the little row of cottages, situated across the road from the Care Home, where Erica had told her she lived in the end house. She knocked on the door and waited, and when she answered, Erica appeared incredibly pleased to see her. She admitted her mother Zena, had rung her, worried because it was Janis`s first proper holiday on her own.

Janis felt very tired after days of travelling, and after an early night awoke to the sun streaming around her bedroom window blind. She got up excitedly, went to the window, and pulled up the blind. She had not properly taken it in the evening before, but almost immediately to her right, across the road was a fabulous beach.

It was still early, and having taken a towel from the bathroom, she let herself quietly out of the cottage and ran across the road. She was soon on the soft white sand and the sea looked so inviting, that while there was no one around, she took off her clothes and dived in naked. To her horror, instead of being warm and inviting, the sea was cold, and she immediately ran back out and put her clothes back on as soon as possible. By the time she had arrived back at the cottage, she was shivering profusely.

Erica was now up and sitting in the kitchen and having seen her from the kitchen window, was laughing.

"I bet that was cold, you`re not in Australia now you know," she said.

"Come on, come, and stand by the Aga, you`ll soon warm up, it's the warmest place in the house."

CHAPTER 119

Time went on and with Diamuid`s help, Rory gradually felt better and relaxed into Irish life. He often thought of Janis, what they had done, and wondered where she had gone. He was pleased when he got a call from Padraig, inviting him to his wedding, which they had decided to have down in Cornwall the following month, this gave him something to look forward to. Everything was arranged, he would get a taxi from Bristol Airport to Bristol Temple Meads, where he would get the Trezance train, and Heidi would meet him at the station, and drive him over to his old caravan, and she had told him that he could stay as long as he wanted.

When the time came, the journey went well, but being back in the caravan was difficult. The memories of that last night, when he had fought with Roger, and his disastrous relationship with Angela, all came flooding back like they had only just happened.

But he was glad to be away from the cottage for a while and looked forward to seeing Padraig, Lou, the rest of the family, and Heidi again. The wedding would be at Truro Registry Office, followed by a blessing at the same place Rhona and Erick had theirs, the little Fisherman`s Chapel above Seachapel. Both were not until the end of the week, and he was pleased to have time to relax in Cornwall first.

CHAPTER 120

Heidi June 2016

Heidi was excited when she had a call from Rory telling her he would be back for a couple of weeks and would stay in the caravan again. She had missed him and thought he remained happily ensconced with Angela on his brother`s farm. Her heart did a little flip when she saw him pulling up in the Jeep. She had spent more time than usual on her hair and was wearing a top, that everyone at work had said complimented her skin tone.

He climbed out of the Jeep, and seeing her, commented, "Wow Heidi, have you done something different with your hair? You are looking very well."

He stepped forward and hugged her tightly, and she was close enough to smell his aftershave and feel the newly shaved softness of his cheek against hers. They stood like that for a few seconds until he awkwardly pulled away.

Wondering if she had done the wrong thing hugging him so tightly, she hurried him inside and put the kettle on, wanting to know all that had happened. When she heard that his relationship with Angela had ended so abruptly, she felt deeply sorry for Rory, but secretly relieved. There was something about Angela, that she had felt unsure about, and in his grief-filled state, had worried he had made a big mistake going off with her, and now she realised she had been right.

She was flabbergasted when he explained he had been living in Cullenmara in the cottage for the past three months, but at least now she knew he had not been in contact because the phone signal was poor there. She had been feeling very hurt and worried that they had lost touch.

Over the next couple of days, they went walking together, and although it was obvious that they got along like a house on fire, she sensed Rory was not on the same page as her, as far as liking her was concerned. But, knowing all that he had been through, she decided it best to wait and not rush things, hoping that one day, he may feel the same way about her, as she did about him. They had returned to the Fishing Boat Inn in Treggenhow, where although slightly tearful, they had reminisced and told funny stories about Rhona and Erick.

When it came time for Heidi to return to work, Rory was initially at a loss about what to do and had chilled in the caravan and watched way too much television, making up for the time spent in the cottage without one. She had been great as usual and had kindly left casseroles and lasagne for him to eat, after returning home from work. On one occasion, he grabbed hold of her hand, when she passed the food to him and said,

"You are such a good friend to me Heidi, I do appreciate everything you do for me."

Although she smiled back at him, she returned to the house and burst into tears as soon as she shut the door, upset that he seemed to only regard her as a friend when she wanted so much more.

CHAPTER 121

Heidi June 2016

Heidi was excited when she had a call from Rory telling her he would be back for a couple of weeks and would stay in the caravan again. She had missed him and thought he remained happily ensconced with Angela on his brother`s farm. Her heart did a little flip when she saw him pulling up in the Jeep. She had spent more time than usual on her hair and was wearing a top, that everyone at work had said complimented her skin tone.

He climbed out of the Jeep, and seeing her, commented, "Wow Heidi, have you done something different with your hair? You are looking very well."

He stepped forward and hugged her tightly, and she was close enough to smell his aftershave and feel the newly shaved softness of his cheek against hers. They stood like that for a few seconds until he awkwardly pulled away.

Wondering if she had done the wrong thing hugging him so tightly, she hurried him inside and put the kettle on, wanting to know all that had happened. When she heard that his relationship with Angela had ended so abruptly, she felt deeply sorry for Rory, but secretly relieved. There was something about Angela, that she had felt unsure about, and in his grief-filled state, had worried he had made a big mistake going off with her, and now she realised she had been right.

She was flabbergasted when he explained he had been living in Cullenmara in the cottage for the past three months, but at least now she knew he had not been in contact because the phone signal was poor there. She had been feeling very hurt and worried that they had lost touch.

Over the next couple of days, they went walking together, and although it was obvious that they got along like a house on fire, she sensed Rory was not on the same page as her, as far as liking her was concerned. But, knowing all that he had been through, she decided it best to wait and not rush things, hoping that one day, he may feel the same way about her, as she did about him. They had returned to the Fishing Boat Inn in Treggenhow, where although slightly tearful, they had reminisced and told funny stories about Rhona and Erick.

When it came time for Heidi to return to work, Rory was initially at a loss about what to do and had chilled in the caravan and watched way too much television, making up for the time spent in the cottage without one. She had been great as usual and had kindly left casseroles and lasagne for him to eat, after returning home from work. On one occasion, he grabbed hold of her hand, when she passed the food to him and said,

"You are such a good friend to me Heidi, I do appreciate everything you do for me."

Although she smiled back at him, she returned to the house and burst into tears as soon as she shut the door, upset that he seemed to only regard her as a friend when she wanted so much more.

CHAPTER 122

Rory June 2016

Rory enjoyed spending a couple of days in Heidi`s company, chilling in the caravan after she returned to work, and on the fourth day, went to visit Rhona`s grave and while so close, decided to see Erica at the Care Home. She had told him if he were ever back in Cornwall, he could go and stay with her. She appeared surprised to see him, and he thought nervous, which was unusual.

Erica never thought Rory would take her up on her offer, and after hurriedly making him a cup of tea, she was needed elsewhere, and he waited in her office. She was busy, and he felt bad for turning up unannounced. She reappeared about half an hour later looking less flustered, after having gone over to warn Janis of his arrival and tell her he was expecting to stay. Erica kept Rory chatting long enough to allow Janis enough time to move her things to the campsite over the road, and she suggested he go back with her to her cottage after her shift finished.

Rory loved her little cottage when he saw it and was even more thrilled to see the lovely views of the beach and lighthouse from the guest bedroom, where she put him for the night. He awoke early the following day and decided to walk along the beach. It was lovely and peaceful there, and he stood listening to the rhythmic sound of the undulating waves, lapping the seashore, trying to be mindful, just like Rhona had taught him.

The sun was rising, and he walked towards the farthest end of the beach, and after turning and starting to walk back again, he saw what looked like a Harley Davidson motorbike, parked up beside a large tent.

"It can`t be," he said aloud.

The tent was closed, and he could not ascertain if anyone was in it. Thinking he was being foolish, he continued walking. When he had got about halfway back along the beach, he saw a mane of red hair in the distance, and excited that it could be Janis, instinctively waved. But instead of waving back, she turned tail and began running awkwardly in the other direction. He watched her clutching her belly as she ran, and it dawned on him that she could be pregnant.

Wanting desperately to talk to her he shouted after her, ran down the beach, and across the road where he watched surprised when she disappeared into Erica`s house. Seeing Rory again, with her hormones raging, Janis had been in a blind panic. Her first instinct was to flee across the road and back into the safety of Erica`s house, where she quickly locked the front door. But Rory called through the letterbox and hammered loudly on the door.

Not wanting to see him, she sneaked out of the back door, and after collecting her tent and Harley from the campsite, sped past Rory at considerable speed, and did not look back.

Rory was upset to see her speeding off like that. The thought of becoming a father again was thrilling, but because of their circumstances, was also scary, and he needed to know for sure if she was pregnant.

CHAPTER 123

Rory June 2016

Rory was crestfallen to have not had the chance to speak to Janis, and Erica returned home after her shift to find him in her kitchen, drinking her cooking sherry, and looked deeply sorry for himself and seeing her, immediately apologised,

"I`m sorry Erica, but I needed a drink."

Erica felt uncomfortable, having kept quiet about Janis having already been staying with her for months, and thought it best to just come clean about it all.

"You know I told you that I knew Rhona years ago, Well, Zena my best friend back then had been in a relationship with Erick for over 4 years, and suddenly left, without telling anyone where she was going. We had lost touch until she suddenly reappeared a couple of years back when her father was ill. We arranged to meet, and she explained how she was now living in Western Australia, with a lovely man called Mitch, and her daughter Janis. I was a bit taken aback, she had never struck me as particularly maternal, but she had quit drinking and appeared incredibly happy, and I was pleased for her."

Erica sighed, and continued,

"I remember her being upset when she could not track Erick down, she was only on a flying visit and had to go back. It had been lovely to see her, and I had missed her, so when she phoned saying she was too ill to visit, but her daughter

Janis would be coming over, I was extremely happy to say she could stay with me if she wanted. Only after Janis arrived, did I realise she was Erick`s daughter."

Hearing all that, Rory told Erica everything that had happened, and that he believed Janis was carrying his baby. Erica was shocked, having not known who the father was, and now understood why he was so upset. He was completely inconsolable for the evening. Erica was in an awkward position and glad she had no idea where Janis had gone because it would have been difficult lying to him otherwise. Deciding he would rather be alone, he thanked her for letting him stay, and she drove him back to the caravan.

Seeing him back sooner than planned, Heidi was concerned but he did not seem to want to talk about what was bothering him. Padraig and Lou must have had a sixth sense that all was not well with him too, when they decided to stop off and see him, on their way down to Seachapel for their wedding preparations that same evening.

They both rapped loudly on the caravan door before getting any answer and when he eventually came to the door, he looked terrible. His clothes were very dishevelled, his face unshaven, and he smelt very strongly of alcohol, and seeing them both he burst into tears.

"It's so good to see you, you know, thanks, guys,"
he said, sniffing loudly, and wiping his nose on his sleeve.

Insisting on hugging them both tightly, he told them how much he loved them, and feeling embarrassed, vowed he would never drink again. He wanted to tell them why he was so upset and expose his guilty secret but decided that would be a bad move. He was unsure how they would take the idea of him having slept with his half-sister and that he had got her pregnant. They did not stay long and left to go off to their hotel, after cooking him food, in the hope it would soak up the alcohol.

The following morning, although hungover, Rory decided he should go and check on his Camluggan flat but first, had to give the tenants the required twenty-four hours' notice. They sounded surprised, having never met him before, but agreed to the inspection. When he drove up the next day, he was pleasantly surprised by how homely the place looked. The tenants were a genuinely nice young couple, who liked living there and had tried to look after the place, so he decided to continue to rent it out for the time being.

Just as he was going to leave one of the tenants stopped him.

"I think this must be for you," he said, handing him the small, padded envelope, marked, "Urgent."

No one had used that address for him in years, and Rory idly flung the letter into his rucksack. It was not until back in Heidi`s caravan later, that he remembered it, got it out, and opened it. He had heard about the Investigation into the Mother and Baby Unit on The News and had certainly not expected to be any part of it. But this letter indicated that the investigators wanted extra information because their records had shown his adoption, around the same time as numerous babies had been illegally sent to America. The letter also requested that he send strands of his hair, for DNA testing.

He had sent the parcel the following day, never expecting what would happen next.

CHAPTER 124

Padraig and Lou`s Wedding, July 2016

It was good for Rory to have something to take his mind off the DNA result, and on the day of Padraig and Lou`s wedding, as best man, he had to admit that Lou looked amazing in her low-cut, figure-hugging dress, so different from how she usually looked in her green farming overalls. Padraig was initially quite tongue-tied seeing her walking elegantly towards him down the aisle and was relieved when he managed to say his vows correctly, despite being so nervous. All this was completely out of his comfort zone and used to spending most of his days working alone, suddenly being thrust into the limelight and being the centre of attention was very daunting. It was a great relief when the whole ordeal was over, and he could finally kiss his bride.

Everyone laughed when Lou threw her bouquet backwards over her head after they emerged from the Registry Office and Rory, not expecting it to come his way, accidentally caught it. Embarrassed, he immediately threw it at Belinda with such force, that she scowled at him when she caught it.

Rory made a great best man; his funny speech went down well with all the guests. Lou had been worried he would turn up drunk and ruin everything and was very relieved when he did seem to have heeded what they suggested and stopped drinking. She watched him closely all day and, was proud when he had not drunk a single drop of alcohol. Rory was feeling

incredibly nervous in the run-up to his speech, he never particularly liked being the centre of attention at the best of times,
but being completely sober too, made it all extra stressful.

But remembering what Rhona told him about calming his
nervous system down with deep belly breaths, he briefly went
outside beforehand, and walked up and down, breathing air
into his belly, counting to five, holding his breath for five, and
then breathing out again slowly for a count of seven. After
returning he had gone straight to the top table, and feeling
extraordinarily calm, had enjoyed giving his speech.

Padraig and Lou had their wedding blessed the next day, in
the little church up on the island in St Ives, just like Rhona
and Erick had done thirty years earlier. The blessing was only
for close friends and family and was very private, and intimate, and with the wind howling around the old stone chapel,
it was also very atmospheric. While standing there watching
them, and witnessing how much in love they were, Rory`s
mind was wandering back to Janis and was suddenly overcome
with sadness. It was horrible to think that after having such a
good connection between them, they may never be able to be
together.

But remembering what Erick had said about never giving
up hope, he tried to relax and focus on the happy couple and
making the most of his time with his brothers and sisters.

CHAPTER 125

Rory July 2016

Rory was feeling on top of the world, not only after being surrounded by friends and family again at the wedding, after having been alone in Cullenmara, but he was also looking forward to receiving DNA confirmation of his parentage, and finally proving that Belinda was wrong about him. His good mood continued, and while Padraig and Lou were off on honeymoon on the Scilly Isles, he decided to try to get himself fitter again.

It had been a while since he had last walked the coast path, and now feeling a whole load more positive, he decided he could cope with doing the Tregenhow to Nansmorrow Cove walk, just as Rhona and Erick had done so often when they were alive. After parking up in Treggenhow, he walked up tiny footpaths towards fields, where he found the wider tracks that took him across the top of the cliffs and gave him far-reaching panoramic views of the sea and coastline, stretching out in front of him. It was a little cloudy, but warm as he strolled along happily along the path, that suddenly bore right, taking him down the side of a cowshed on a farm. Emerging from the other side on an overgrown, stony footpath, that was a little difficult to walk down due to channels of water flowing downwards, run-off from the fields, he felt his feet slipping on the wet rocks, and was worried he might fall. But, soon finding himself on top of a hill looking down over Nansmorrow

Cove, after standing for a while taking in the view, when he continued, the path got steeper but was less wet, and when he reached the bottom near a couple of old cottages, he could see large blue rolling waves, splashing over the stone harbour sides and hear the roar of the sea much louder.

On the last bit of the walk down into the Cove, he was astonished to see a Harley Davidson motorbike, just like the one Janis was riding when he last saw her, and a tent pitched on a flat tufty grass just above the rocky water's edge. What was even more unbelievable, was that this was the exact spot where Rhona had been sitting and looking out to sea, when Erick had tapped her on the shoulder, after they had been apart for over twelve years. It was uncanny, and liking coincidences, just like Erick, he was a little spooked but excited.

The thought that this might be Janis`s bike and tent was unexpected, and he stood for a while looking at the sea before eventually summoning up the courage to go around the front of the tent and call her name. To his dismay, he heard nothing from inside and felt very deflated. But, hearing a sudden loud gasp from behind him, he turned sharply around and came face to face with Janis.

"I guess you`re looking for me," she said in her husky Australian accent. Her belly was protruding more than ever now, and he could not help but stare at it for a few moments, imagining his baby lying curled up in there, before replying.

"Well, I wasn`t looking for you specifically, I was just enjoying a walk, I used to walk with my parents,"

"I know, Erica told me it was where Rhona and Erick met again after twelve years apart," she said.

She remained where she was, as if afraid to get any closer.

"I`ve been worried about you," he admitted.

"There was no need to worry about me, I`m a survivor," she replied.

She brushed past him to put the toilet roll she was carrying, back into her tent.

"Can we talk please, Janis?" he asked.

She nodded, and they wandered over to the little café on the other side of the cove, where over coffee, Rory explained more about his childhood, Cullenmara and his life after he left and moved to Cornwall. He told Janis how he had met Rhona and mentioned how good she had been to him. Janis asked lots more questions about her father, and he told her as much as he could about him.

"You are genuinely like him, Janis. He was comfortable talking to anyone, a bit rebellious and alternative, and not afraid to do things differently from everyone else. He always had a lovely sense of fun, and he and Rhona would often giggle away together sometimes, over the silliest of things. He loved Stephan Grappelli and Yehudi Menuhin and liked Simon and Garfunkel and other different pop songs, jazz, and classical music. Your dad was a real character. A very genuinely warm man, enthusiastic about world causes, socialism, and, well, lots of things, usually all at once."
She smiled,
"Mum said I was like him, and I`m glad I am."
When she smiled again, Rory could not help but smile back.

She was looking very well, and seeing her again up close, she looked even more beautiful than he remembered, and his heart nearly missed a beat.

He took some deep breaths to calm himself.

"Are you ok Rory only you seem a bit out of breath?"
she said.

He nodded and they finished their coffees and walked back to her tent together.

Rory enjoyed chatting with Janis again, he had wanted to be angry with her for running off, but all she had done was look at him with her beautiful green eyes, and any anger he was still holding on to, had melted away and he forgave her instantly. At least we have left each other on good terms now, he thought, as he drove back to the caravan after finishing his walk.

CHAPTER 126

Rory July 2016

It was Rory`s last week in Cornwall, and when she saw him, Heidi noticed he had more of a spring in his step, and the old cheeky sparkle was back in his blue eyes again, which was good to see. Rory felt much better having finally seen Janis again and had enjoyed exploring the area more. He wandered around Seachapel and the Island and swam in the sea at Tresea Cove, just as he had done with Rhona and Erick, years earlier. The highlight of his week was when she phoned to arrange to see him again before his planned return to Cullenmara. She suggested they meet at the Fishing Boat Inn at seven in the evening, and Rory spent much of the day feeling quite unsettled and excited about his "date."

Heidi knocked on his door around midday and handed him a very official-looking letter, sent to the main house by mistake. Realising immediately that it was the DNA result, Rory hurriedly opened it but took a deep breath before reading it. Ordinarily, when this stressed and excited, he would have needed to get himself a drink, but having been sober now for weeks, he reckoned he could manage whatever news it contained.

Since the sample went to the laboratory, he had been unable to contemplate the idea that Erick and Rhona could not be his parents, and had tried not to think about it, but he was now going to get his answer. He carefully opened the folded letter and began to read.

CHAPTER 127

Belinda May 2015

Since graduating from University, Belinda worked for different law firms as an investigator, and having heard about the public Inquiry into the Mother and Baby Unit and the Catholic Adoption Home, she followed its initial findings with interest. She decided to apply to be one of their investigators and was incredibly pleased when she was among those chosen for the task. Trained investigators were welcome from outside Ireland; it was a good career move. The whole Inquiry attracted a huge amount of publicity, and Belinda relished the opportunity to be one of the people instrumental in helping uncover exactly what had gone on.

She remained laid back about it all at first, but over time was becoming increasingly shocked about what had happened as more details became discovered. Hearing first-hand all the testimonials of all the children and hearing how badly treated the adults living at the Home, were, was harrowing. Most were scarred for life, after their time there, and she felt for the unmarried mothers, many well under the age of consent. After what they had gone through, to have their babies taken away with no explanation, and later told they had died, was a travesty.

She was in her seventh month as an investigator, when she received a large envelope containing over a thousand tiny slips of paper in the post, all supposed to have been legally registered birth and death certificates. Each one needed logging and cross-referencing against a large database, and it was her job to clarify if the information they contained was real or fake.

It was laborious work, and she often spent days sitting in front of her computer at home, trawling through all the information, cross-checking every single bit of evidence. When she finally reached the end of the pile, she found a Birth Certificate dated 28 May 1975. Turning it over, it stated that the parents listed were Rhona Marshall and Erick Harper. She read on and saw that the boy`s Christian name, listed as "Billy," further confirming it was Rory`s. It was strange seeing his name and her parent`s names in black and white, but it did now mean that she could officially investigate him, and in her official capacity, would also hopefully be able to locate him. When examining the birth certificate again later, she realised there were staple marks, as if something had been attached to it.

It took a while, but after she had painstakingly sifted through all the paperwork again, she found a note counter-signed by someone called Sister Shauna, indicating Rory had remained in Ireland. She had originally tried to track Rory down in 2014 and to legally force him to provide DNA, after discovering the strands of hair she had obtained at the cottage before it was rented out, were inadmissible in court because it was obtained without his consent, but she was thrilled to finally be able to track him down and find out if he truly was her brother or not.

Her obsession with Rory had got out of hand, and she had not only lost Toby since her father died but had also lost contact with Padraig and Orla over it, and she regretted her behaviour now. She had now calmed down considerably since she had started to process the circumstances of her father`s sudden death, and properly grieve for his loss from her life. Since becoming involved with the Inquiry, and now feeling much less anger towards him, Belinda wondered if Rory had been one of the babies given a forged birth certificate, as happened to so many at that time.

Although she had always sensed he was not her actual biological brother, this birth certificate confirmed Billy was indeed Erick and Rhona`s child, so maybe she had been wrong about him all along. This was a worry. The only way this information could checked was through DNA, so she was back at square one, which was incredibly frustrating. But was aware that of course, this time was different, not only had she been officially instructed to send kits to everyone in the UK who had possibly been adopted in Ireland, but in her new position, she had much better access to electoral rolls and other records, and so should be able to track him down much more easily.

Her counterparts all over the World were also checking their countries for adoptees. Unaware of Padraig`s arrangement with Rory to look after the Cullenmara cottage, she posted Rory`s kit out to the last address listed on the electoral roll, his flat in Camluggan and held her breath, hoping he would follow the instructions, and send it back promptly, and waited anxiously for his swab results, from the laboratory.

CHAPTER 128

Rory July 2016

The letter was from an official from the inquiry, and in it, they explained that his DNA result confirmed Erick Harper and Rhona Marsh were *not* his biological parents. Rory steadied himself, completely dumbfounded, and re-read it again. This cannot be right. This must be a mistake, he thought. Feeling suddenly very clammy, breathless, and as if he were suffocating, he collapsed into the nearest chair and instinctively reached up into a cupboard above his head, where he knew a small flask of whisky was.

Trembling, he momentarily stared at it, quickly opened it, and took a large swig.

"This can`t be true, it can`t!" he exclaimed aloud.

He could not understand this at all. Feeling suddenly sick to his stomach, he rushed over to the sink just in time to throw up all the whisky. After guiltily brushing his teeth several times to rid himself of the taste and smell, he decided, that rather than try to process this alone, he needed to talk to Heidi, she was always particularly good at putting things into perspective.

By the time he had got to her cottage, he was having another panic attack. She was worried when she saw his ashen face.

"Whatever`s happened Rory?" She asked.

Seeing he was struggling to breathe, she helped him into a chair, and after scrabbling around in her kitchen drawers found

a brown paper bag, scrunched the top together, and handed
it to him.

"Rory, it`s alright, hold this to your lips and breathe into
it, that`s right, don`t worry, it's just a panic attack, it will
pass."

When his breathing slowed, and he was calmer he showed
her the letter.

She was astonished at the news, and told him,

"I`m just as shocked as you are, Rory. This must be such a
blow, but knowing the truth is important. It`s a lot to take
in but try to look back at your time with Rhona and Erick,
positively. It was a bonus meeting them and you should be
grateful they died thinking you were their son and loved you
just as if you were, and that`s really what mattered most.
Many people only have one set of parents, but you had
Lizzie and Jonjo and your grandmother, Máiréad, Erick, and
Rhona, who all loved you very much."

"I hadn`t thought about it like that, Heidi," he admitted,
and left her house, feeling so much calmer.

CHAPTER 129

Janis and Rory July 2016

Rory was feeling better by the time he met Janis later. It had been a long time since he had last been on a date and he was wearing his favourite mid-blue shirt that matched his eyes, his best jeans, and even a little aftershave. Janis appeared pleased to see him, gave him a polite kiss on the cheek, and commented,

"You scrub up well and smell nice too."

This is a perfect start, he thought. She had said this straight away before she even sat down. Seeing him blush, she smiled again, and he immediately relaxed. Janis looked amazing, she had been in the sun and was more tanned than when he last saw her. She was wearing a simple knee-length maternity dress made from a shimmery turquoise material, and on her feet were delicate strappy sandals with turquoise-coloured gem-stones embedded in them.

"You look amazing Janis, pregnancy suits you," he said.

After a pint of Guinness, and feeling even more relaxed, he could not help but blurt out the news about his parentage. If she was shocked, she did not appear so. It was only when he had said the words aloud that he realised that instead of being incredibly sad, unwelcome news, it was, the best news either of them could have ever wished to receive.

Janis had smiled knowingly and taken hold of his hand across the table. Rory could not stop himself from gazing into her beautiful green eyes, and she gave him a long lingering look back. He was in seventh heaven and realised then, that this meeting was completely unlike the others.

"I reckon that news deserves a toast," she said.

She clinked her alcohol-free lager against his Guinness glass and laughed. Not only did this mean what they had done was not wrong, but also their baby would be fine.

CHAPTER 130

Rory and Heidi

Rory returned to the caravan, excited about what all this meant for him and Janis, and seeing he was back, Heidi popped over to invite him to hers for dinner, aware that it might be her last chance to chat with him before he returned to Cullenmara. He appeared in good spirits, but she was sad that he did not comment on the recently purchased dress, she had put on especially for the occasion. She had even lit candles on the table and soft music was playing in the background, much to his amusement.

The food she cooked was lovely and he told her so, and after they finished eating, she suggested they go outside, it was a full moon and a very balmy evening. She hoped to be able to tell him how she felt about him. But before she had the chance, Rory had sat back in his chair and began to explain what had happened between him and Janis, and after having been so hopeful, she felt deflated.

"You ok Heidi? he asked, seeing her looking sad.

"I`m fine Rory, probably just a little tired, that`s all,"
she said quietly.

She sat staring at the ground, feeling very foolish as he told her the whole story, including the good news about the DNA test result, which meant they could now be a proper family.

"You`ll love Janis, Heidi, I`ve never met anyone like her.
She is not afraid of anything! Nothing phases her at all.

I know she`ll make a wonderful mother for our child."

Rory looked so happy that Heidi wished him all the best, asked him to stay connected, and told him she hoped he would have a safe journey back the next day. It was not that she did not mean everything she said but was unable to believe she was saying it when she had hoped to convince him to stay, with her. But unbeknown to her, Rory, whom she had been thinking of constantly over the past three months, had fallen in love with someone else.

It was heartbreaking, and she went back inside the house after he had left and cried her eyes out again.

CHAPTER 131

Belinda late 2016

Belinda continued working on the Inquiry and after discovering that Erick and Rhona were not Rory`s parents, felt bad about how she had treated him, especially when realising he had genuinely thought they were and had not been lying. She was impressed by the amount of information provided by two former employees of the Mother and Baby Home, and latterly, the Adoption Home, Doctor Frank Clancy, and Sister Shauna O`Shea. They had both worked tirelessly to obtain evidence and get the truth into the public domain.

She struggled to imagine what those poor mothers went through; most having had their babies removed the instant they gave birth and told they had died. The evidence the couple provided confirmed that most of those women had been given forged death certificates, hiding the fact that their babies were still very much alive and had been sent over to America, in return for generous charity donations.

Her part of the Inquiry was now reaching its end and she would soon be back working for her usual Legal Firm, in Sydenham, where she had settled after she and Toby split up. But, before she returned. However, after being summoned to present all her findings from the Inquiry before Judges in several court cases in Dublin, she arrived at the hotel near the courthouse, feeling apprehensive.

The role of expert witness was the pinnacle of her career and she felt enormously proud that all her hard work had paid off, especially when the court cases attracted so much publicity.

She had arrived at the Courthouse early the following morning and been returning to her seat from the washrooms when she collided with a very well-dressed, slim, dark-haired man with glasses, who she could tell by his accent, was American.

"Dang, I`m sorry!" he had said awkwardly.

He retrieved a clean handkerchief from his breast pocket, knelt, and wiped the coffee off her court shoe as best as he could. Belinda, slightly embarrassed by his actions and unable to move, had stood looking down at him. She liked the cut of his thick hair, admired his immaculate suit, and wondered what his part in it all, was.

When he had suggested he buy her another coffee, she had followed him back over the road to the coffee shop, where they sat outside at a table in the sunshine.

Curious about him, she asked,

"What brings you here, then? Are you part of any of the Trials?"

"Me, no, I`m just an interested party, that`s all," he said.

She eyed him and he added,

"My parents worked in the Mother and Baby Home and the Catholic Adoption Home. I was one of the babies that would have been taken to America, had it not been for my father`s best friend, Evelyn, who agreed to foster me instead."

"Where does your American accent come from then?" she asked.

He smiled,

"Yeah, I know it's ironic, that I should end up in America, with my own Accountancy Firm."

After he said that, they heard the court bell announcing the start of the next session, and both hurried back over the road again and along to the assigned court, where they sat in full view of the proceedings, in the public viewing gallery.

Sister Mary took the stand first, and after swearing on the Holy Bible, proceeded to confidently give a fabricated version of everyday life at the Mother and Baby Home.

William, as she now knew him, leaned forward, and whispered,

"That`s all complete bullshit, of course."

She nodded and explained that she had seen all the evidence to the contrary.

"She was one of the worst," he said.

"I know. Well, she`s going to be squirming when I`m called to give evidence," she said, giving him a cheeky wink.

Although a little surprised by her forwardness, William quite liked it.

Later, back at the Hotel, it suddenly dawned on her who William was, and that Frank and Shauna must have been his parents, and she was very much hoping to get to know him better.

CHAPTER 132

Belinda late 2016

Belinda spent all the following day in the courtroom with William, and although disappointed not to testify, she thoroughly enjoyed his company, and they arranged to sit together again on day two. She was first to take the stand after the court was back in session the following day. It was daunting being there, with the court artist scribbling away on his iPad, and a huge audience watching from the public gallery and worldwide, via a streaming service.

The Barrister leading the Inquiry stepped forward and probed Belinda with questions about her findings for hours until the court adjourned again. When she returned to her seat in the Public Gallery, William looked genuinely immensely proud of her. They watched as the next expert witness took the stand, one of several that day, and by the time the court adjourned much later, Belinda was feeling exhausted.

Having declined William`s offer of dining out that evening, she returned to the hotel, where she sieved through all her findings again, worried she may have left out something crucial. It had been a relief to retreat to the hotel, and although aware she would be needed the following day, and probably other days too, the evidence she had given that day had been the most difficult to explain, and so it felt good to have got it out of the way.

She relaxed, had a snooze on her bed, and awoke later after it was dark. The hotel room was stuffy and in need of air, she opened the French windows and was immediately greeted by the sound of traffic and police sirens emanating up from the busy Dublin streets that were sprawling out below.

Venturing out onto the terrace with a glass of wine, the cool early evening air was refreshing, and she leaned against the terrace railings and peered down at the people milling around the softly lit pedestrianised area, below her to her left. She was about to go back inside when she felt her phone vibrating in her pocket.

She retrieved it, and seeing it was William, answered the call.

"You`re up late," he said.

"Fancy some company?"

She had momentarily hesitated, but quickly changed her mind, and within minutes he knocked on her door. She opened it, gazed deeply into his hazel eyes, hurriedly grabbed hold of the lapels of his coat, and pulled him inside.

CHAPTER 133

William and Belinda late 2016

William was not usually so bold, but seeing Belinda standing on the terrace alone, he had felt a strong compulsion to be with her. He sensed Belinda had been very wary of him. She had met his type before, good-looking, ultra-confident, and often very shallow. But as she got to know him, her opinion changed. He was, far more down to earth than his appearance indicated, and was also kind-hearted, funny, and turned out to be hilarious in bed. Toby had been so serious, and sometimes incredibly boring, by comparison. William constantly made her laugh, and having had so many different life experiences, was also fascinating to talk to.

The Public Inquiry continued for months, and although he had to return to America part way through, William returned for the final week and sat next to Belinda in the Public Gallery again. The findings were as expected, and there were huge sighs of relief from all the unmarried mothers and others who worked at the Homes when they heard they would receive compensation.

In addition to the imprisonment of the nuns, both Linton and Jefferson`s trials were in a closed court, after they were tracked to a remote island in Indonesia, where they had fled. The presiding Judge had no hesitation in pronouncing them guilty of endangering the lives of hundreds of young women, children, and babies; several counts of rape, and profiting from the illegal sale of babies. They were both incarcerated in the most notoriously dangerous prison, in Dublin, for the rest of their lives.

On the final day of the Inquiry, to Belinda`s surprise, William approached the bench and after clearing his throat loudly, addressed the court and public gallery,

"My father, Dr Frank Clancy worked at the Mother and Baby Home and The Catholic Adoption Home for over twenty years and my mother was one of the pregnant unmarried girls forced to move there in 1970, aged sixteen. For young girls like my mother, once there, the Mother and Baby Home was somewhere impossible to leave. The often-grieving mothers exploited by the nuns for cheap labour and subjected to terrible cruelty. The conditions they had to endure on a day-to-day basis were horrendous. The pregnant women were all malnourished, and most carried infections due to poor cleanliness, which they often passed on to their babies. Expectant young mothers died, even before giving birth, due to the unsanitary conditions, and many were forced to continue working right up until their labour pains started, and consequently, were so exhausted that many died in childbirth. In such instances, my father had to either remove their babies surgically or leave them to die inside their mothers. The underage women who did manage to give birth would then have their babies cruelly taken from them and given to wealthy American couples, in return for large donations. Both my mother and father risked a lot, continuously collecting and collating very damning evidence over the eight years they worked together, which they sent to the authorities. They made it their mission to try to help the pregnant women and make them as comfortable as possible while in the Delivery Room. After she took her vows, my mother had the horrid job of collecting babies for adoption overseas, from the wider community. This was very harrowing but over four years, she managed to singlehandedly intercept over seventy babies, preventing them from going to the Adoption Home, stopping them from being sent away, and placing them instead, with good local families, in the hope they would be easier to find by their true birth mothers. In the months before she died in 2014, my mother created a memorial garden, despite being in the latter stages of advanced stomach cancer. She wrote down everything she could remember about each of the thirty babies and their mothers, in a notebook, which proved extremely useful to the Inquiry and enabled mothers to tell if their babies had died, to track and find their lost babies and reunite with them. During their time at the Mother and Baby Home, my parents personally witnessed the deaths of over seventy babies. Despite being so ill, after hearing about the bones found in an area at the back of the Home, my mother bought land and created a memorial garden. She planted over seventy trees and surrounded them with beautiful flowers and shrubs. Each one she gave a name and number so that every grieving mother would have somewhere to go to remember their babies, a fitting living memorial of their short lives. My parents also documented accounts of incidences of rape of incredibly young mothers, and nuns, conducted by the Home`s owners, Declan, and  Jefferson. My father, after having infiltrated the management of the Home,  and gained Jefferson and Declan`s trust then had access to all their records. This was when he discovered forged birth certificates and, forged death certificates of babies that, despite what their mothers thought were very much alive and had been sent to America. All this information was particularly crucial to this Inquiry going ahead, and I`m so immensely proud of them both.”

William`s voice faltered when he said that, and when he returned to his seat, was overwhelmed when the crowd who had been silently listening, stood up around him and clapped for a long time.

CHAPTER 134

Rory`s Mother in late 2016

Sitting with all the others right at the back of the court-house, was Rory`s birth mother. She had been listening intently to William`s speech and had been incredibly surprised to hear about the forged death certificates. She had long believed her baby boy had died, and it was incredible to think this might not now be the case, and that she had a fully grown-up adult boy, somewhere. At her age, this was quite a shock, and after shakily getting up from her seat, she slowly descended the wooden stairs and skirted around the crowds and press, gathered in the courtroom foyer.

After exiting the main doors, she had started walking carefully down the stone steps outside, when a nice-looking man with a mass of deep brown hair, collided with her. Pleased to be out of the stuffy courtroom and in the fresh air again, she smiled at him and thanked him as he politely stood to one side to let her pass.

By that time, it was early evening and coldness was descending fast, and she tucked her grey curly hair under her hat, pulled the collar of her Mac up around her neck, and hailed a taxi to take her to the station, it was too far to walk from there.

While sitting in the taxi as it sped off through the crowded streets, she thought back to when she had given birth and the sadness she felt, discovering her baby was gone. But by the time the taxi pulled up outside the railway station, she had decided that she had to find her son, no matter what it took.

CHAPTER 135

Rory, late 2016

Rory returned to Ireland still reeling from the shock of discovering Erick and Rhona were not his biological parents. He often studied what he thought was his legal birth certificate, remembering how shocked and excited he was when he discovered it and a letter from his grandma, in the bottom of her jewellery box, and learning that Rhona and Erick were his parents. It had been such a strange coincidence, especially when he had lived with them for over two years and only met them by pure chance. It felt as if it was all meant to be.

The DNA result had certainly been confusing, and all he wanted was an end to all this renewed uncertainty about his parenthood as soon as possible. It was very unsettling not knowing who his biological parents were, and after giving his predicament a great deal of thought, he concluded the best person to help him was Belinda.

He had followed the Inquiry into the Mother and Baby Home and the Catholic Adoption Home in Dublin and was aware she was an expert in the field. But could he count on her to help him now, after all those years she had spent hating him?

He arrived at the courthouse in Dublin just as the Inquiry finished, hoping to see her, he had pushed his way through the throng of Press outside, and then briefly collided with a grey-haired elderly woman wearing a rain mac, who had been walking carefully down the stone steps, and immediately apologised. She thanked him and smiled as he moved to one side to let her through. Her very striking blue eyes reminded him of Rhona, and stood momentarily watching her descend the bottom steps. She was quite wobbly on her feet, and he was worried she might fall. Seemingly in a hurry, after hailing a taxi from the rank on the road, she soon disappeared in the Dublin traffic.

Rory sighed and headed up the steps and into the foyer of the main courthouse, where he saw Belinda talking to a dark-haired, very smartly dressed man. He waited, trying to pluck up the courage to approach her.

Other Books By the Same Author
SAFE PLACE
(Book 1 in the enchanting trilogy)

An intriguing family saga/ love story spanning over forty years begins when an unlikely friendship forms between a delivery driver (Rory) and an older woman (Rhona). She reminds him of his grandma and helps him deal with his past.

The reader travels led back through Rhona`s life: her strange abusive husband, unexpected affair with a married man (Erick) and escape to a remote cottage in the West of Ireland where she gives birth but must give the baby away.

Unable to stay there, she flees to Cornwall thinking she may never see Erick or her baby again. She meets and falls in love with a handsome Welshman, but after suffering a double tragedy, her life spirals out of control. On the advice of a friend, she goes off to a Keralan Retreat.

Meanwhile, Erick`s life has also started to unravel. His dreams of living self-sufficiently with his family in Ireland now shattered, he struggles on his own, often thinking of Rhona and the baby they had to give away.

Ge eventually returns to England and unexpectedly sees Rhona with her new man, and they look very much in love. Trying to forget her he embarks on a relationship with a wild, unpredictable much younger woman, but later, finds himself alone again.

Rory lodges with Rhona after an illness and confesses something shocking about his past.

Following several strange twists of fate, the three main characters' lives become entwined, and Rory discovers an astonishing family secret that alters the course of their lives forever.

Available print on demand from all good bookshops and online.

Other Books By the same Author

SAFE PLACE

An intriguing family saga/ love story spanning over forty years begins when an unlikely friendship is formed between a delivery driver (Rory) and an older woman(Rhona). She reminds him of his grandma and helps him come to terms with his past.

The reader is transported back through Rhona`s life: her strange abusive husband, unexpected affair with a married man (Erick) and escape to a remote cottage in the West of Ireland where she gives birth, but must give the baby away.

Unable to stay there, she flees to Cornwall thinking she may never see Erick or her baby again. She meets and falls in love with a handsome Welshman, but after suffering a double tragedy, her life spirals out of control. On the advice of a friend, she goes off to a Keralan Retreat.

Meanwhile, Erick`s life has also started to unravel. His dreams of living self-sufficiently with his family in Ireland are now shattered, he struggles on his own, often thinking of Rhona and the baby they had to give away.

Ge eventually returns to England and unexpectedly sees Rhona with her new man and they look very much in love. Trying to forget her he embarks on a relationship with a wild, unpredictable much younger woman, but later, finds himself alone again.

Rory lodges with Rhona after an illness, and confesses something shocking about his past.

Following several strange twists of fate, the three main characters' lives become entwined and Rory discovers an astonishing family secret that alters the course of their lives forever.

Available print on demand from
all good bookshops and online.